SOUL SEARCHING
WITH THE BRASS BAND

A NOVEL
BY
VICKI RENFRO

Vicki Renfro

Soul Searching with the Brass Band

ISBN: 978 0 9890612 3 0
Printed in the United States of America

This book is dedicated to the healers of the world
who keep mankind breathing.

Vicki Renfro

ACKNOWLEDGMENTS

I would like to thank the Spirit Guides who watch over me.
Thank you for your sometimes less than subtle shoves
that have placed me upon this path.

AUTHOR'S NOTE

The battle between the light and dark is well underway, and what hangs in the balance is a more peaceful planet. It is happening around every one of us at this very moment—right now, this instant—and is influenced by every action we take. Every belief system in the world points to this being the time of the Earth's transition either into peace or darkness. Call it what you please—the Age of Aquarius, the end of the Mayan calendar, or the Twilight of the Kali Yuga. But understand that you are an intricate part of the outcome, whether you chose to be involved consciously or unconsciously.

If you watch closely, you can see the fluidity of the dance each and every day. Sometimes the compassion of mankind is overwhelming, and we see sacrifices being made to uplift others, only to be swallowed up a moment later by the unimaginable horrors one human can inflict on another living being. So, how is this battle being waged?

For a moment, consider that your outer world is merely a reflection of the conflicts being fought within, and that your mind sees *only* those things around you that support your preconceived notions. If this is how reality is shaped, the answer is simple. The change will happen as people, one by one, decide to seek a path of compassion and understanding.

Turn off the evening news and strive to practice mindfulness. Learn to recognize negative thoughts, bless them, and let them go. Do what brings you joy. Dream again, and become aware of just how important *you* really are on this journey toward enlightenment.

Although the book you are about to read is a work of fiction, the forces that propel its characters are very much alive in the real world, and sometimes we can only comprehend what is happening through the telling of a story.

Vicki Renfro

CHAPTER ONE

September 21 AD 38

I am the final rider to abandon the battlefield, with no other choice but to leave our dead and dying behind. I feel as if I am suffocating, being dragged under by the screams of the fallen and the stench of blood that's held aloft by the unrelenting humidity. Gillian, the sole survivor of the untainted Druid bloodline, sits precariously atop the rump of my mare, mounted backward to face the Roman soldiers who are in pursuit, his heels digging into her hindquarters in order to stay astride her. The tiny, enchanted Gillian is my best hope. Our escape depends totally on him using his ancient Druid magic to weave a fog bank within which we can hide.

My mare's hooves hit solid rock as we slide down a sheer hillside toward the turbulent river below. I fear the enemy can hear our decent even over the racket of their own armor. We hit the waist-deep water with such force that I reach out behind me to grab Gillian by his shirt. It is the only thing that keeps my magical friend from disappearing into the swift current.

Emerging from the water on the opposite shore, my mare's hooves land upon the sodden leaves of the forest bed. At last our progress becomes silent, and I feel my heartbeat slow as the world changes. The fog thickens. We become invisible as we soundlessly disappear into the haze.

September 21, 2011

I woke with perspiration soaking my hair and knew without opening my eyes that the light of the full moon would be streaming through my bedroom window. I'd grown used to these out-of-body midnight journeys, and used to the ghostly white moonlight that filled my apartment when I returned. Rolling on my side and opening my eyes slowly, I looked at the pillow next to me for reassurance. I needed to see Will still lying beside me, alive and unharmed.

A year ago, when I began having these dreams about my Druid incarnation, I would fight to remember every detail. Now I would give almost anything to not relive the deaths of my friends in vivid Technicolor at each full moon, when the pull of the lunar tide takes my soul back to the time of the standing stones.

I quietly slipped out of bed and into the living room to phone my best friend, Ruth, who lived below us with her boyfriend, George. She had learned to anticipate my calls when the full moon dominated the night sky.

"We're still here, Hillary. Everything is okay," Ruth assured me. Her voice was calm as she predicted each of my questions. "Go back to sleep now, sweetie."

I hung up and hit speed dial, waiting impatiently for Gilbert to answer. Frantically, I spun the new gold wedding band on my finger. It shimmered in the moonlight, the feel of it still unfamiliar to me.

When Gilbert answered I asked him, "Can you make fog?"

"Well, yes! The physics department has a machine and—"

"No, I mean *you* ... can *you* make fog?"

"What was our dream about tonight, Hils? If McCollum wants me to begin developing the capacity—"

"You were riding on the rear end of my mare and weaving a fog bank with your old Druid magic," I told him, willing his brain to conjure images as sharp and real as the ones I had swirling around in my head.

"No Hils, I'm here in my bed and my toes are still not webbed, although I'm sure my hair will soon be totally white if I don't get my beauty rest. Go back to bed. Write everything down, if you need to. We'll talk in the morning, but for now go back to bed."

It was unlike me to stay caught between two worlds like I was tonight, not knowing for sure which details belonged in which lifetime. But it was the equinox, and at the instant the night and day became exactly equal, my consciousness was released, and I once again roamed the past.

Mindlessly, I stood at our front window, gazing half hypnotized at the dance between the breeze and the trees that lined the street outside. The shadows appeared to move independently from their hosts, but in reality they were just a reflection of the trees' physical forms. It reminded me of the images I experienced from the past, and how they mirrored so much of my present life. Things were packaged differently in this life, but the people and the journey were very much a reflection of my past life.

I was surprised to feel Will's arms wrap around me in a gentle embrace. I hadn't heard him get out of bed or walk across the living room floor. I relaxed into him without turning.

"Come back to me, Hillary," he whispered softly into my sleep-tousled hair. "It's 2011. You are a student at Kansas State University, and we have found each other again."

When I turned to look into his bottomless blue eyes, I had no doubt about which life I preferred. He picked me up as if I were weightless. I rested my head on his shoulder, breathing in the scent of him as he carried me back to the comfort of our rumpled, warm bed.

Last night's bloody battle was one of many I had relived during my nightly travels back to the time of my Druid warrior incarnation. These travels had begun a year ago, when I was a freshman in college, pulling me back at each full moon to my primitive existence in a place where food was sparse and the damp air cut through my tattered cloak, making me think I would never be warm again. I spent those nights sleepless and alone on the hard ground of a homeland I fiercely defended, returning at dawn to my comfortable apartment, bed piled high with pillows and the central heat maintaining a pleasant temperature. There in my bed, I would replay the details of that faraway lifetime over and over again in my mind, trying to put my memories in chronological order.

During the past year I had spent innumerable hours fretting over how I was to fulfill the role I was playing in this lifetime if I remained no more than plain old Hillary Rubner-Emerald. If McCollum's insights into the future were accurate—and I believed that to be the case—I was destined to become the same mighty warrior I had been in my Druid life, when I lived as Hilsbeth.

McCollum was either blessed or cursed, depending on the way you looked at it, for he lived with total recall of the ancient plan we'd put into motion two thousand years ago. He had explained many times to me that I was to be a major player in the Earth's transition into a higher dimension. And believe me when I say there is still plenty that I don't understand.

For the past year, I had thought of little else but how to regain those Druid powers. I had come to the conclusion that I needed to return to that very first battle scene that I had experienced while asleep in my freshman dorm room a year ago. At that time I foolishly brushed it off as just another dream, not realizing its significance. I couldn't have guessed that those same Druids would be so intricately woven into the pattern of this life.

Through the process of reorganizing the timeline of all my nightly visions from two centuries ago, I was beginning to realize what had happened to Hilsbeth—me—during that grim time. I felt the crashing sorrow that had shattered her as she watched Liam—her heart, her lover—die when he took an arrow that had been meant for her. Hilsbeth's Druid soul was torn between living or dying, and utter despair propelled half of that soul on a futile journey to follow Liam into the light, leaving the remaining part earthbound, locked in a bloody struggle to save her people from annihilation. That split had weakened me in this incarnation, and I surmised that if I could consciously return to that place in time again and save Liam's life, that would correct everything, allowing my abilities as that "Mystical Druid Warrior" to move forward with me into this life. Or at least I desperately prayed they would.

So now I found myself, each night as I closed my eyes to sleep, hoping once again to find myself at the forest's edge, feeling my mare's skin twitch with nervous tension beneath me as I waited silently to lead my militia into battle against the great Roman general, Marcus Flavius. That was when I would change my future by stopping the arrow that had taken my beloved Liam's life.

September 21, 2011, morning following the equinox
I woke feeling exhausted, and looked over at the clock on my nightstand. It was long past the time my alarm should have gone off. I smiled to myself as it dawned on me that I had gotten a few extra hours of sleep thanks to my husband's thoughtfulness. I eased my legs over the edge of the bed, finding the movement painful and my joints stiff. I furrowed my brow in an effort to figure out why. Then the ghost of the previous night's events passed before my eyes, and I glimpsed the fierce battle that I had fought as Hilsbeth. I rotated my shoulders and lifted my right arm, the one that brandished my long sword. This type of weapon had an exceptionally long hilt, requiring two hands to maneuver the weight, but I had the smith balance mine in a fashion that allowed me to use it as I pleased. I moaned with pain and found myself eager to let last night's journey fade back into the past from whence it had come.

Gaining my legs, I limped to the bedroom door. Upon opening it, I faced a small group of expectant faces. Will, George, Ruth, and Gilbert were sitting in our living room, while Mom, Dad, Dr. Edwards, and Father John appeared on a flat screen that Gilbert had kindly mounted on the largest wall of our small apartment. This modern technology allowed the far-flung members of the Brass Band, which was what our reincarnated group of Druids called ourselves, to interact together.

"Hi everyone," I groaned as I hobbled my way over to the well-worn corduroy wingchair that had become my place of honor.

My stiff, wobbly physical state after returning from a past- life excursion was now such a regular occurrence that the emotions in the room ranged from humor to sympathy. Will, being his perfect self, placed a cup of strong, hot coffee in my hands.

"The equinox looks like it took a toll," Gilbert commented, with a huge yawn that reminded me that I had disrupted his sleep with my phone call the night before.

I shifted in my chair until I found the least painful position, and I gave a lame and embarrassed wave toward the large screen. "Hi all. Give me a minute here." I took a swig of coffee and closed my eyes, regretfully trying to dredge up the details of my night's adventure.

I took my time to play it all the way through in my mind, from beginning to end. I traveled back until I could feel the humidity weigh on my skin and inhaled the scent of the damp forest, tinged with the smell of my own sour sweat. Then I began to speak.

"We were losing ground, being pushed from the open field into the trees. The Roman cohort advanced in heavy pursuit, trampling the bodies that lay in their path." I stopped to take a deep breath, trying to block out the screams and the putrid smell of the deceased and still dying. The crash of swords rang in my ears, and I felt another thunderous reverberation run up my arm as my sword made contact with a Roman chest plate. "I only saw Dr. Edwards … Lee," I corrected, "above us on the ridge. I think McCollum had already been wounded, but not mortally."

The group let me abbreviate and expound on the story as needed. They listened closely, but for the most part they had heard about this particular battle before. Once I had determined the parts that I'd conveyed previously, I began to skip things, only filling them in on the newest details.

Gilbert was moving to the front edge of his chair, trying unsuccessfully to hide his goofy smile. He was waiting for me to tell of our escape, but I let my voice trail off from exhaustion, filling in the end of the account with "blah, blah, blah."

Gilbert was incensed! "Wait just a minute!" he exclaimed. "You've left out the best part!"

"What's that?" Ruth asked, assuming that if the story had changed, I would have mentioned it to her during our midnight call.

"The part about me," Gilbert declared. "It's new! Hillary, tell them what you asked me last night!"

I closed my eyes, and it came back to me. I saw the small figure of Gillian, facing backward, legs straining to hold tight to my mare's hindquarters as we shot headlong into the undergrowth. And since Gilbert so very seldom got to be the hero, I took my time to embellish the story. I watched Gilbert's face light up as I explained that his ancient magic, his ability to draw power directly from nature itself, had saved the lives of hundreds of Druids and enabled my army to hide in plain sight, concealed within Gillian's enchanted fog.

CHAPTER TWO

My life had vastly changed since the evening last spring when our group of Druid incarnations had decided to name ourselves the Brass Band. I was oddly comforted by the fact that our nine souls traveled through time together and would as long as we took physical forms. This didn't make us particularly unique or special. I now knew that everyone traveled through time in groups, but I was particularly delighted with mine.

A year ago I had been a shy, lonely freshman, straight off the farm and so innocent that I believed my big adventure in life would be attending a major university. But that idea was soon dispelled. On that infamous day of the Spring Fling I thought I was attending a large party, but found myself at an intimate party for four. It soon became apparent that destiny was in charge, because on that day I met my best friend, Ruth, along with a couple of genuine blue-eyed mystics.

I was mesmerized by the one named Will Emerald, and caught off guard when my pounding heart and inexperience with the opposite sex merged into a feeling of nausea. In hindsight I have to laugh, because in truth it was my proximity to Will and his astonishing life force that created that sensation inside me. Today I experience it as soft electric current, but that night it felt like I had eaten an expired can of tuna.

That same evening was the first time I met McCollum, an intense man who stood well over six feet tall and held the knowledge of the cosmos in another set of those deep blue eyes. Will and George had stood at attention when he interrupted our intimate party, which he obviously had not sanctioned. McCollum insisted Ruth and I leave, and it was a number of months before I laid eyes on him again.

On the occasion of our next meeting McCollum explained the plan we had made two thousand years ago to reunite during the time of the Twilight of the Kali Yuga. I suppose a more evolved soul would have understood what McCollum was saying when he talked about *The Enlightenment of the Planet*, but in those early days his words sounded like things of fairytales and fantasy.

McCollum was the first of our group to reincarnate back onto this planet, and he was the most advanced soul among us. With his third eye open, he had both insight into the future and memory of the past, and he used that knowledge to assemble a group of young mystics. Will and George were two of those boys, and they were living in his ashram-like household when Ruth and I met them at that very small party. And although McCollum was initially unsure if I was the great Druid warrior from his past, he recognized Ruth's big booming energy instantly, and knew that Ruth would stand beside no other soul than that of Hilsbeth.

Next came Gilbert, the quirky quantum physicist whose friendship I cherished. His spiritual insight helped me form a foundation for the path I unexpectedly found myself on.

I was amazed to discover that the two Druid Dreamers whom I'd entrusted with the protection of our encampment had incarnated to become my parents. They combined their energy in an effort to pull my broken soul back into a physical body. But like most beings born onto this plane of existence, their veils fell firmly into place at the moment of their births, leaving them with no conscious memory of their mission beyond a nurturing love for their daughter.

Dr. Lee Edwards, a charismatic professor who had become my friend when we'd met in a magical section of the university library, soon fell comfortably back into his position as McCollum's confidant, much as he had two thousand years earlier when he'd ventured into our camp as an alchemist. Lastly came Father John, an ex-priest whom I had never seen in any of my midnight journeys. But because McCollum welcomed him enthusiastically, we accepted him as one of our own.

I'd also discovered the difference between infatuation and love. It happened the night Will took me into his arms, and I knew our connection stemmed from something considerably deeper than our mere physical attraction to each other. We were two halves of the same soul, which had separated into male and female, yin and yang, when we'd first taken lives beyond the etheric realms. We were soul mates.

So when the school year drew to a close I found my loyalties split. I was pulled back to my folks' farm by obligation, but my heart broke a little bit each day that I was away from Will. For as long as I could remember I'd spent my summers weeding Mom's garden, tending the chickens, and operating whatever equipment I was mature enough to handle, and I knew my help was necessary to keep the family farm going.

My parents saw what I was going through, even though I tried to hide it. They were wise enough to understand that my life had separated from our family unit, even if I was physically still there. So one evening, with a conspiratorial smile between them, they suggested that I move home ... to the home I had made with Will.

It took a full month for me to tie up the loose ends well enough that I felt comfortable leaving the place where I had grown up. I spent most evenings walking the perimeter of the fields, remembering the small things that I wanted to etch into my memory. Closing my eyes, I could still fell the thrill of the first time I'd perched on Dad's lap to steer the combine, and I wondered how time could pass so quickly. Sometimes after sunset, Mom and I would sit on the front porch swing listening to the crickets' chirping and the rumble of the train in the distance, smiling when it sounded its horn as it entered the outskirts of town. I needed to be both mentally and physically prepared for this separation, because I knew that I would never return again for more than just a casual visit. I also felt a keen responsibility to stay until Mom and Dad could find a suitable farmhand to take over my chores … permanently.

During my final the days on the farm I was accompanied everywhere I went by Giuseppe, Mom's pet crow who was affectionately known to everyone merely as Gus. He spent hour after patient hour perched on fence posts watching me weed Mom's vegetable garden and listening to my tales of Druid heartbreak, Roman battles, and my deepest fears about the part I was to play in the times to come.

As the days went by, Gus learned to hop from tree to tree to stay near me while I did my chores, and it wasn't long before I noticed him following my car into town. He easily kept pace with me as he gracefully sailed above the waving wheat fields, cawing loudly to let me know he was nearby. When I parked, he always sat steadfastly like a sentinel, guarding my vehicle as if he had been sent to protect me.

The first time I returned to the parking lot, I winced with embarrassment when I saw the unlucky car parked beneath Gus's roost. It was covered with big purple blobs of crow poop, a result of Gus's appetite for wild berries, and I cringed at the realization that the car belonged to the vice-principal of the high school. My mortification turned to amusement, and I silently vowed to park more strategically as I left a couple of bucks under the windshield wiper so Gus's victim could run it through a carwash.

I slipped into my driver's seat and watched Gus take flight as I pulled into traffic.

On the day I drove away from the farm, I knew my childhood was completely behind me. I spent my time on the road daydreaming about that simple life, and it became crystal clear that each day on that farm had prepared me for my future. All the events that had once seemed so totally random had woven a fabric in which I could now see a perfect pattern.

CHAPTER
THREE

June 21, AD 28

Tonight I will participate in my first sacred Druid ritual. My mother eagerly helps me dress in my new ceremonial robes because this, the eve of my thirteenth birthday, is to be my passage from childhood into my place in the Druid hierarchy. I straighten to my full height, unaffected by the whispers behind me about my blossoming female shape, and walk outside just as the moon reaches its zenith.

As I stand looking up at the June moon—known to be inspiring for lovers—I feel a hand slip into mine. My heart leaps as I delight in the feelings of first love. I hold his hand tightly, hardly breathing as I watch the elders light the fire that is to ignite my soul.

The scent of lavender fills the air as wreaths are sacrificed to the flames. Inhaling deeply, I am intoxicated by the promise that tonight's ritual will reveal my future. With the help of the old crones, I will glimpse the abilities that lie hidden within me.

Shyly, I move alone to my position by the fire. I sit cross-legged, and a headdress of feathers is placed upon my head and a braid of flowers around my shoulders. My eyelids close, feeling heavy from the pungent camphor smoke wafting around me. My head begins to swim with unfamiliar images that take me to where the great stones stand.

I see the figure of a splendid warrior standing erect before the altar stone. Square shoulders reflect the strength that lies beneath the surface, and the stance of the body indicates the power within. Dressed in a leather tunic accented by an indigo blue undergarment, the image is breathtaking, but my eyes are drawn to the workmanship of the blade that hangs at her side. She gracefully turns at my approach, and I find her intense scrutiny of me intimidating until she finally offers a greeting smile. Magnificent and powerful, she wears a chest plate and weaponry far more sophisticated than that which is made in our small village foundry. I gaze into a set of shockingly blue eyes, and I realize I am confronting myself as a grown woman. I see little resemblance to the child I will leave behind tonight.

Waking from my trance alone and alarmed, I am frightened of the future that has been shown to me, but I force myself to smile for those who may be watching. Locating Liam across the smoldering remains of the fire, I look into his eyes and find myself overflowing with intense emotions, not fully understanding their meaning. He tilts his head, eyes twinkling with irrepressible mischief, and at that moment we both know our destinies will to be entwined forever more. I find myself anticipating what tomorrow will bring, but still filled with the innocent feeling of youth. I willingly put off the events of tonight for one more day of childhood.

July 28, 2011

Three months ago in the privacy of McCollum's chambers, Will and I were married, reigniting once again the love we felt in our Druid lives as Hilsbeth and Liam. With the other seven members of the Brass Band as witnesses, the simplicity of the ceremony was absolute perfection! Mom and Ruth cried, George joked, Gilbert philosophized, and we all celebrated with great joy.

That day, Will had moved all his belongings upstairs to my apartment, which thrilled my roommate Ruth, who moved her things downstairs to Will's old apartment, where her boyfriend, George, lived.

October 1, 2011

Hearing a knock at the door, I rushed toward it yelling, "Just a minute!"

Upon opening the door, I saw Ruth standing there with her fifty-pound designer handbag slung over her shoulder. "It's our day!" she said, smiling at me. Now that we were no longer roommates, we both looked forward to our private time together.

"Let me grab my backpack," I said, leaving her standing at the door. Our plan was to pick up a latte, find a place to sit in the sun, and just catch up. We descended the stairs and fell into step, beginning where we had left off the last time we were together.

"Is George with the boys today?" I asked, taking a seat as we reached our favorite bench in front of the campus library. *The boys* had become our nickname for the group of young mystics McCollum had gathered into his household for training. They, like Will and George, had never truly fit into the outside world because they had entered this lifetime at least partially conscious—unlike Ruth and me; our awakening was just beginning.

"Yep, McCollum needed some heavy lifting done today and George was his man."

It was quickly approaching a year since Will and George had moved out of McCollum's household. They, of course, were the oldest and had decided to leave once they had reached manhood, but they would always be sorely missed.

We had just settled in when I spotted a familiar silhouette exiting the science building across the way; Gilbert's build and gait were unmistakable. He waved and began to jog toward us.

"Hey, Hils, Ruth. Lucky I found you, because I have a proposition for you."

"Really?" Ruth said suspiciously. "Are we going to like it?"

"I hope so, because I think it's a great idea."

"We'll be the judge," Ruth teased, tapping into her drama major for extra effect. "Go ahead, Gilbert, just lay it on us."

Gilbert tried to squeeze between us on the bench, but when neither of us budged, he relented and squatted in front of us. "Lately, Father John and I have become pen pals," he said with a goofy grin. "Well … at first I wrote to him because I was curious about who he was, but one thing led to another, and eventually the subject of physics came up."

"The subject just came up," Ruth goaded.

"Well, yeah. He really took an interest, so I invited him to sit in on the class I'm teaching this semester, and that's where you come in, Ruth."

"Really?" Ruth repeated, giving him the evil eye.

"You and George have a spare room, and Father John needs a place to stay a couple nights a week, so I was thinking that's a pretty good match."

Ruth just stared at Gilbert for a long time before she finally gave him a break and said she'd discuss it with George. "Once George agrees, should we call you?"

"Sooner the better. Father John's never taken a college course before, and he's extremely excited about it." When Gilbert moved to make himself more comfortable, we both said in unison, "Girl time! Go away, Gilbert."

Since our girl time had become somewhat notorious, Gilbert's feelings weren't hurt. He stood, bowed, and walked back in the direction from whence he'd come.

Ruth and I smiled at each other and audibly exhaled as we leaned back and closed our eyes. Taking in the sounds of the birds and the breeze blowing through the trees, I relaxed and placed my hand on hers.

We were back at my apartment having some iced tea when Ruth's cell phone rang. Even though the caller ID said the number was George's, the voice on the other end was Gilbert's. "I know your gab session usually ends around six, but you and Hillary need to come downstairs for dinner before this food gets cold. It promises to be a gourmet meal because George is cooking, and by the smell of it, I think we're having Italian. Okay, see you in a few." He hung up before Ruth could respond.

"I guess Gilbert's in a real hurry to find out if Father John can bunk with us," Ruth said, still staring at the phone in her hand. "He's downstairs with George. You should give Will a call to see if he'll be home in time to join us."

"If it's dinner with his best friend George," I said, "he'll make a point to be here ..." I heard footsteps on the landing ... "right about now!" When the door opened, I saw my husband's handsome and very exhausted face.

"Come in and rest those weary bones, " Ruth said, taking him by the hand. "You've got about five minutes before we're expected downstairs for dinner."

Will met my eyes with a silent plea for an early evening. I just shook my head and shrugged. "Gilbert set this thing up. We need to go down for just a little while." Resignation fell over his face. Ruth and I each took an arm and walked him back out the door and down the steps to the lower apartment.

"Did I hear my last dinner guests arriving?" George asked, as he set an enormous platter of chicken picante on the table. "So, Gilbert, I suppose you didn't set up this meeting just because you like my cooking."

"I do like your cooking, but that's not the whole reason I'm here," Gilbert admitted. He waited until we were all seated and served before continuing. Gilbert shifted in his chair, looking uncomfortable. He was banking on the good food making everyone more amenable.

"No time like the present," Gilbert finally declared, taking a drink of water to clear his throat. "I'm teaching a physics 101 class this semester, my very first solo teaching gig."

"That's great," George roared, raising his water glass. "To Gilbert's success!"

"Well," Gilbert continued, bolstered by George's toast, "It's a freshman-level course, and when I mentioned it to Father John, he was pretty jazzed. I think that's when I might have mentioned that it was possible to audit my class. Evidentially, attending a university is on his bucket list, and I guess, I have the unique opportunity to make that dream come true."

As George raised his glass again, Gilbert waved it off. "This is where you come in, George."

"Me?"

"Well, you and Ruth."

George looked baffled, and Ruth looked like she'd just swallowed a bug.

"I thought Father John could use your spare room a few nights a week. My studio apartment just isn't big enough for two."

"Or clean enough." Ruth added.

"How about it George? Gilbert pleaded. "It would be a perfect opportunity to get to know him better."

"It's an interesting proposition," George agreed.

"He won't be a problem. He tends to be very solitary and quiet."

I couldn't help but add, "He's the only *Brass Band* member that's never appeared in any of my Druid dreams."

"I've always found that to be a little curious myself," Will said, right before a huge yawn. "Say yes, George, and if it doesn't work out, he can stay in our spare room. We can use the time to figure out his connection to us, because I really don't have the slightest idea."

Standing, I pulled Will to his feet. "It's all fascinating, and I can't wait to hear what you guys decide, but for now, I'm going to get my man into bed." And we waved goodbye as the door closed behind us.

October 12, 2011

Father John soon became our newest neighbor. He arrived the evening before his first class, and we all joined him for a cup of tea before turning in. I instantly recognized why my parents were so drawn to him. He was like a deep pond with only an occasional ripple that moved across the surface, leaving you to wonder what lay beneath that vast calm.

Ruth noticed that her new roommate traveled light, bringing with him only a few black outfits and well-loved books. "Must be leftover from his days as a priest," we surmised as we gossiped in the kitchen. Arranging the cookies on a plate to serve with the tea, we both agreed this guy was going to be easy to like.

"What do ya say? Who's available to walk Father John to his first university-level course tomorrow?" Gilbert asked proudly. He had come tonight to make sure Father John was settled in, but truth be told, he had become a fixture around our house as of late.

Father John smiled and looked at the two ladies. "I don't have a GED, ACT, or GPA, and no good reason for being so drawn to take this physics course." He laughed softly. "But I want to be a part of Gilbert's class and celebrate the achievement. And even though I am capable of finding his classroom on my own, I would be honored to be escorted by either of you beautiful young ladies."

Will and George leaned back in their chairs to watch Ruth's reaction and mine. We both jumped at the chance to walk across campus with this man whom McCollum had once referred to as a well-worn book cover. Being there to watch him step into his first college class seemed very important—shorn gray hair, studded earring and all.

Just before sunrise and still half asleep, Will and I shuffled to the apartment to join Ruth, George, and Father John for morning meditation. The scent of incense enveloped me as we opened their front door, and caused my soul to begin to detach from my body. The pull to expand beyond the perimeter of my physical form had become so great that merely preparing for meditation caused it to begin to happen.

I sat on my cushion in my normal spot. Closing my eyes, I felt Gilbert joining us as he sat on his meditation pillow in his small apartment. I knew he wanted to celebrate the auspicious occasion of Father John's first day of college. I could feel my own spirit growing with excitement as I disengaged from my body, and instinctively I knew this was going to be an exceptional day.

As my meditation drew to an end, I began my silent integration to bring peace into my life. I opened my eyes and leaned back against the hearth in the soft candlelight, to wait for everyone else to return from the ethers.

And there he was, sitting at the edge of our circle, holding our brass bowl, the artifact that was the center of our spiritual practices and our namesake. I watched as Father John lifted it to his heart chakra, third eye, and crown. Then he brought it slowly to his lips and gently kissed it. Holding his eyes tightly shut to dam a flood of emotions, he bowed his head.

The bowl began to emit a low, resonant sound, as if it were awakening from a long sleep. I saw everyone's eyes slowly open, but no one moved a muscle. We didn't want to disturb the ceremony being performed before us. It was as intimate and lovely as watching a quiet moment between a mother and her newborn baby.

Father John opened his tear-filled eyes. Holding the brass bowl to his heart, he whispered, "I spent many an evening in your parents' living room, Hillary, using my imagination to see this bowl in my mind's eye, so I could perform the meditation they had taught me. It caused my consciousness to expand far beyond what I had ever experienced before. I was at peace, and felt more at home than I had felt in years."

I moved to sit by John because I was curious; I wondered if the meditation was the link that bound us together. "What made you feel at home, John? Was it the company of my parents or the meditation itself?"

He slowly raised his eyes until they met mine. "Neither. It's the bowl! I know this holy object as well as I know my own hands." He lowered it to the pillow on which it always rested. The subtle ringing of the bowl that had permeated the room when Father John held it disappeared. "I came here to attend Gilbert's class, but I realize now that I have also been drawn to spend time with this magical vessel, which I now know is a very old friend of mine."

I knew he spoke the truth because the union between the two of them was a very tangible thing.

CHAPTER FOUR

October 13, 2011

Following morning showers, an egg on toast, and a big cup of hot coffee, Ruth and I were ready to escort John to his first class, Physics 101. It didn't matter that he was only auditing the class, or it was already nearing mid-semester. Today was the beginning of something new, and you could see it written in the enormous smile on Father John's craggy face.

I picked up his leather satchel, which he had obviously carried for years, and even though the edges were frayed and worn, it had been freshly oiled and held his textbook, notebook, and pens. Lifting it so he could slip one arm through the shoulder strap, I looked impatiently at Ruth's bedroom door. "Hurry up, Ruth. Time to go."

She opened the door with something obviously hidden behind her back. "No kid should be sent off to class without the essentials," she said. She smiled and held out a small, flat package wrapped in a vibrant flowered paper. "Come on John, open it."

Slowly he reached for it and began to tug at the tape.

"No, not like that," Ruth instructed. "Like this!" she said, ripping the paper free.

John stood stunned as he looked at the laptop in his hands. "I can't possibly," he stammered, trying to hand it back to Ruth.

She swiftly hid her hands behind her back. "It's no big deal, John.

My parents are loaded. I get a new one every year, so I've decided this one is yours."

John was visibly touched. "No one has ever—"

"Well, they should have," Ruth interrupted before things got too sentimental. "Come on now, let's get you to class before you're tardy." Ruth opened the flap on his leather bag and slipped the laptop into it.

We dropped Father John off at the first set of auditorium doors and then moved to the second set to watch him. The room was huge, and filled to the brim with undergrads because it was a required course for half the student body.

"I feel like his mom," Ruth commented, as we watched John excuse his way to a seat in the center of a long row. "Or maybe a helicopter. Isn't that what you call parents who hover?" I elbowed her when I saw Gilbert take the podium. He had an impressive air of confidence, and seemed to be keeping his fidgeting to a minimum. Touched to see the culmination of Gilbert's efforts, I watched John unload the contents of his backpack onto his flip-up desktop, and saw him smile as he ran his hand tenderly across the top of his new computer.

"That was really a nice thing you did," I said, not looking over at Ruth.

"Oh, it was nothing," Ruth insisted, still watching the class get settled. "I figured he's here alone, and in case he's actually alone in this world, I wanted him to know that we're his family now."

"When I turned to look at her, she was already walking away. I ran to catch up with her and put my arm around her shoulder. "You're a good person, Ruth."

Ruth hurried off to her first class, and I headed toward the Student Union to burn an hour before my first class. The morning was clear, and with the warmth of the sun on my face, I found myself falling short of my destination and sat on the first bench I came to.

Within moments I heard the familiar call of a dear friend. Surprised, I opened my eyes and followed the sound to a lower limb on a nearby tree, and was overjoyed when I saw Gus perched there. Gus had been raised on my parents' farm, but after the hours I had spent spilling my insecurities and aspirations to him last summer, he often made the flight to visit me at school.

"Hi, Gus," I said, holding out my arm. I watched the mighty crow open up his three-foot wingspan and drift down, wrapping his talons gently around my arm. This action often caused cars to brake and people to gasp, because it was so reminiscent of the birds attacking in the movie of the same name.

"How'd you find me, big fella," I was tempted to ask … but then I recalled having a distinct feeling of being watched for the past few days, and realized it had probably been Gus all along.

The sweet moment between us was shattered when I heard an unwelcome voice behind me. "Hi, Gus" the voice said, as no other than Jackson Black walked around the end of the bench and sat down beside me. My skin crawled and the hair on my arms stood on end as I slid away from him.

"This is a private conversation," I responded. "Go away!"

"Gus and I are old friends. Come on Gus, let's prove to Hillary that I also understand you. Tell me your real name."

The creep definitely had my attention now, as he leaned closer to my crow. "Oh, you say your true name is Giuseppe. And what other secrets are your friends trying to keep from me?"

My heart lurched as Gus screeched and flew to the tree above us. I stood and backed away, startled that anyone could possibly know that detail. "I've got class," I said, turning to rush away.

He grabbed my arm, and I felt his hand tighten around it. "You can't get away from me that easily."

As I turned to jerk myself free, my wild friend dropped with a flurry of wings and screams, and his claws drew blood from Black's forehead. The grip on my arm released, and I ran through the gathering crowd to lose myself among the campus buildings. I hit the front doors of the library with the force of a crazed animal and entered the front lobby. Running toward the stacks, I looked behind me for the first time. To my relief, I was alone, so I headed to the place where I always felt safe.

Tapping my fingers on the shelving to discharge the static electricity as I entered the glass-floored room, I began to breathe more evenly. Exhausted, I looked at the chairs around the reference table, but instead found myself sliding down the wall onto the floor where the bookcases could conceal me. I then I placed hands over my face and sobbed.

I had cried myself almost to sleep when I felt *that* feeling again. I was being watched. Looking around, I saw no one, but upon standing I heard a soft chirp, and I looked up at the topmost shelf of the bookcase.

"Buddy," I said, tearing up again, "Did Gus send you in here to find me?" I felt my chest tighten, knowing the courage it took for this small sparrow to reenter the library after almost losing his life in this very room. Dad had found the tiny creature a year ago, laying in the corner, lost and exhausted, when he was unable to find his way out of the building he had accidentally entered.

"Yes, Gus sent us both," I heard from the doorway. "He has his way of making himself understood." Will crossed the room and took my hand as he wiped away a stray tear. "The details were filled in by passers by on campus. I guess a bird attack is quite a novelty," he said softly, teasing me. "Come on," he said pulling me into his arms. "Father

John's waiting for us in the lobby. He saw the aftermath of the battle, and he said Gus really knows how to defend a lady's honor."

"Let's go home, Buddy," I said, holding out my hand. Buddy obliged by landing on my palm and rolling into a soft, feathered ball, which I gently placed in Will's jacket pocket.

CHAPTER FIVE

October 20, 2011

"All knowledge is available to those who have the ability to hear it," McCollum explained upon our next meeting. "A person's virtue is not necessarily what determines that; only their ability to reach The River of Knowledge. The fact that the sorcerer Jackson Black knew Gus's given name does NOT mean you were forsaken by your beloved friend, but only that he had found it in the place were all information exists."

"I'm not sure that makes me feel better," I replied. "I thought The River of Knowledge was our advantage over the dark side!"

"No, Dear One," McCollum replied. "Our advantage is that we love."

Ruth, in her usual blunt manner, said, "Really … that's our biggest advantage over evil?"

Smiling, McCollum continued. "Yes, love is what ultimately gives us our power. The heart is more than an organ that pumps our blood."

"I think I'm going to need more of an explanation," Ruth insisted, and crossed her hands in her lap.

I knew Ruth's body language well enough to know we weren't going anywhere until she got an answer. I took a moment to make myself more comfortable and looked to McCollum for the wisdom that would set us free.

He also saw Ruth's determination, and closed his eyes to arrange his thoughts in an order that could enable a novice to understand the magnitude of love.

"The heart chakra is positioned at the center point of your energetic body," McCollum began. "Three chakras above and three below. The three chakras below deal more with the world of matter and survival." His hands moved deftly from the base chakra to the naval and solar plexus. "The three chakras above the heart deal with the world of spirit and divine self. They are the throat, third eye, and the crown. Each chakra holds within it the light and the dark, the yin and the yang, and the heart chakra is the balance."

McCollum's hands flowed upward though the system, but as they reached the location of the crown at the top of the head, they opened to insinuate that this chakra encompassed everything. "The opening of this chakra is the goal."

"It sounds simple," Ruth said, as her hands mirrored the gestures McCollum had made.

"Oh, but my dear Ruth, it is not. It takes enormous dedication and precise practices to raise your consciousness up through the chakric system. Mankind began his struggle to move upward millennia ago. Some have succeeded, as Jesus and Buddha did, but many more still struggle with the lower aspects of basic survival. The list is long, and encompasses everything from relationship ills such as jealousy, betrayal, and lack of self-esteem all the way to things as insidious as the need to exploit or control others. This is not a quick or easy journey, and most are waylaid many times along the way, but when the heart chakra finally begins to open, it is pure magic."

"I see myself in each of those negative things, McCollum," I admitted, struggling with my own self-esteem. "What does that say about me and my path?"

"It says that you are human, Hillary. We dance every day when we choose between understanding and anger, or when we choose creativity rather than crisis, or self respect over falling victim to shame.

Most times it is a thin line that we walk, but these ordinary choices we make are what propel us toward consciousness.

"It is said that a man is bound by his karma, the things he carries from one life to another, and what fate has in store for him. But as the heart chakra starts to open, you begin to deal with your higher self and have the clarity of thought to make decisions that you have never known existed.

"Eventually you will find self-forgiveness in the act of forgiving others, allowing the opening of the chakra of self-knowledge at your throat, divine wisdom at the third eye, and so on to the last chakra at your crown." With mischief in his eyes and arms spread wide, he continued, "And when that chakra opens, you become enlightened, and you are truly free! In that state, evil has no power because you have become all things, and the darkness, which once was so terrifying, now simply exists as an insignificant part within you."

I closed my eyes to take it all in, when Gilbert interrupted my thoughts. "I understand the big picture, but what do we do about evil in the meantime?"

"We love, forgive, and if necessary, defend ourselves and the ones we love by turning the tide of darkness back upon itself."

When we were dismissed from McCollum's quarters, he asked me to remain behind for a moment.

"Hillary, I want you to know that Gus is the embodiment of your spirit animal and has been sent to assist you." He chuckled, "I know it would be easier to understand if Gus were a big fierce dog, but a crow is associated with insight and magic. As your totem, this powerful bird can support you in your transformation and connect you with life's mysteries."

"Who sent him?"

"Dear One, he was sent by the higher aspect of you."

October 31, 2011

I was so tired that I was barely able to stay awake during my classes. In fact, I'd been truly exhausted for days, and dreading the full moon, which would come up at dusk tonight. Tonight's blood moon would bring with it the thinning of the barrier between the worlds of the living and dead, and I feared what that might bring. At bedtime Will wrapped his arms tightly around me, whispering in my ear that he wouldn't let go of me until the sun rose. I then slipped away slowly into a fitful sleep.

October 31, AD 38

I have never walked the ground in the aftermath of a battle, once the wretchedness of killing was done. Always in advance or retreat, my army has always left relatives or scavengers to clean up behind us. I scarcely know who has lived or died until we are able to make camp, sometimes days after the battle's end.

But this time is different, for I find myself walking among my dead, and so I have a chance to bid them a final farewell. I make myself look at the mutilated bodies as my mind tries to justify this brutality, and I wonder if any of us will ever find peace.

At first I think that it is the sun shimmering through the mist that makes the strange glow that lies on the ground, and I become alarmed when I see it begin to move. I dismiss the sword that hangs at my side, for what good would it be against this invisible force? So I watch ... and I listen.

I hear the sound of voices in light conversation, and then I fall to my knees, undone by the magnificence of it all. The spirits of the fallen begin to rise, and I recognize these forms as my brethren. They stand, one then another, shimmering in their light bodies, as their physical forms lie decaying beneath them. I kneel before them, my forehead touching the ground, and give thanks that I am able to bear witness to such a moment.

"Stand with us one last time, My Lady, for we must soon be on our

way."

I rise to my feet, my chest heaving with emotion as the men line up before me. As they approach, they drop to one knee to honor me as their leader. I place my hand lightly on each head, even though their ghostly bodies hold no substance. The opportunity to honor the passing of my comrades, who fought with immense courage against unfathomable odds, calms my soul.

A roar pierces the silence, and I move instinctively to protect my men from this unfamiliar noise. In one motion, I draw my sword and turn in the direction of the sound to see a figure striding toward me. The strange female is clad in unorthodox clothing. Her leather battle wear is immaculate, and fits her like a second skin, nothing like the primitive clothing we wear.

As my soldiers move into battle formation, I reassure them that this person is a friend, though I am not sure that I speak the truth.

As she approaches, I realize that she also comes to me in death, only cloaked in her light body.

"He killed me, ya know," she says as I meet her eyes.

"Who?" I ask, feeling a strange pull to return to my body.

"He did, but his greatest trophy is going to be your husband, Will."

An immediate melee begins between my two worlds as the roar becomes deafening. I see the flash of metal as my comrades draw their swords in my defense, while at the same time I feel Will's arms tighten around me in fierce protection.

"Who killed you? Who wants to harm Will?" I yell, as one world collides with the other.

Shhhh, Hillary. It's okay. Come back to me now." Will's soothing voice was coxing me back into the body that lay next to him.

I jerked upright as I slammed back into my body, and the sudden transition caused me to gasp as I took in a deep breath. "Will! Will, are you here?" Panic wrapped around my heart as a fleeting thought ran though my mind, "She called you Will … not Liam!"

"I've got you Hillary," Will said, holding me tight. "You're safe. I won't let anything happen to you."

I relaxed into his embrace and let the dream go.

November 1, 2011

When I woke hours later, I slipped out of bed and rushed to the bathroom to puke. Confused by the strange lady in my dream, who had come from a different time, my whole psyche was off balance. Closing the toilet lid, I sat and rested my head against the sink, trying to make sense of it.

"Hillary, are you okay?" a loving voice inquired from the other side of the closed door.

"I'm good," I said, standing to gargle some mouthwash.

"The sun is rising. The Brass Band will be gathering in our living room soon." I could hear the sympathy in Will's voice. "You'll feel better once you get through this and have a chance to meditate. We can spend the rest of the day doing whatever you like, whatever will bring you totally back to this world and me."

I knew he was right, so I splashed water on my face, opened the door, and walked into Will's open arms.

This was Father John's first full-moon aftermath discussion with me, and because he found it absolutely fascinating, it helped lighten my mood.

"As everyone knows, last night was All Hallows' Eve, the night when the veils are the thinnest between the living and dead." I stopped talking and felt myself shiver. I was terrified to close my eyes and shroud myself in the memories—I was afraid I might puke again—but finally I just did what I had to do and continued recalling the details.

"The air held a damp chill, the kind that takes your breath, and there was a fog within the forest that made it feel impassable. The ground was covered with the morning dew, and the remnants of our army lay dead and dismembered at my feet. I walked among them, remembering each of them in my mind. I recalled their bravery, the families they had left behind, and how they had given everything to defend what we loved." I opened my eyes and felt the rigidness in my body ease a bit. "That was when their light bodies began to rise. I actually saw them as they began their journey to the beyond."

There was a bit of a gasp from Father John.

"They were literally transparent," I said. "They were bragging and laughing as talked about the splendor of their last stand against the Roman hordes."

"That would be an accurate description of the men who fought by my side," George reaffirmed.

I explained how I had placed my hand upon each of them, and without exception they held no blame. "It was a profound moment," I said, as I paused to choose the correct words, "because I can see clearly now how death is merely a move between worlds."

The room was silent until Ruth quietly asked, "Did you see any of us in our light bodies?"

"I looked for you, all of you," I said, gazing around the room, "but something strange happened." I closed my eyes, and with effort, remembered the details. I once again heard the roar, which from this time frame I easily recognized as the revving throttle of a motorcycle. Baffled by the bleed-through of a modern time into my Druid lifetime, I told the story of the strange lady in motorcycle leathers.

When my full-moon stories came to a close, Ruth brought out the coffee and Vern's doughnuts, which were usually my favorite breakfast treat—but this morning I was very tired and still a little sick. "I'm going back to bed," I announced, as I opened the bedroom door. No one argued.

I slept like the dead until the growling of my stomach was stronger than my need to escape into that void of nothingness. I dragged myself upright, ran my fingers through my hair, and stood to face the rest of the day. Will had left me a note on the counter informing me that he and George had gone to visit McCollum. I figured that meant Ruth might be downstairs with some gourmet leftovers, so I found my slippers and headed to her apartment.

Thinking she would be alone, I was surprised to find her at the kitchen table with Gilbert and Father John. "Hey," I said, embarrassed that I hadn't bothered to get dressed.

"Hey, yourself," Gilbert replied, standing to pull another chair up to the table. "Feeling better?"

"Lots," I said, as Ruth aimed me toward my seat, which now had a cup of coffee and a doughnut sitting on the table in front of it, and then gave me a little push of encouragement.

Gilbert picked up the conversation where he had left off. "We've been talking about the strange thing that's been happening in my classroom. At first I thought it was my imagination, because it appeared randomly at the edges of my peripheral vision. You know … maybe I'm going crazy."

I had to laugh, but Ruth beat me to the punch, saying, "We already know that."

Gilbert just laughed along with us and continued. "Next, I figured it must be an eye problem, and when I contacted an optometrist and told him my symptoms, he rushed me right in for an appointment. They seriously thought that I had torn my retina, but tests showed that I was okay. In fact, my vision is perfect, 20/20. The frustrating thing is that its always to one side or the other, never in my direct line of vision, so I am having a hard time getting a handle on what is going on. I've thought about florescent tubes burning out, but the janitorial service says the lights are fine. I've wondered if it is has something to do with cell phones or laptops or … right now, your guess is as good as mine." He sounded exasperated. "Last week I decided to try to keep track of it, but it's so distracting that I'm afraid I'll forget where I am in my lecture and make a fool of myself." Holding up his hands to keep Ruth or me from making a wisecrack, he finished with, "Not what I want getting back to the head of my department."

I finished stuffing the last of my doughnut in my mouth and washed it down with a big gulp of coffee. "I think I've missed the point of your story, Gilbert," I confessed.

He placed several papers in the center of the table. They were rough drawings of his classroom auditorium, laid out in order by date. I stood and leaned across the table for a better view. I rested my elbows on the table and my chin in my hands.

"You see here," he said, pointing at a series of red X's. "I've marked the places where I've seen the flashes of light." He looked up at me to make sure that I had caught on. "But lately they seem to be moving into a more concentrated pattern, but look how the location changes."

We all looked at the drawings and agreed with him, not knowing what advice to offer. It was Father John who stepped forward.

"How can we help?" he asked.

"I was thinking that next week Ruth and Hillary could walk you to class again, and they could sit to the side of my podium. All you'd have to do is scan the auditorium to see if I am losing my mind or if there is actually something going on here!"

"Sounds fun, I've got time. How about you, Hillary?"

"Why not?" I agreed. All of a sudden I was famished, and the doughnut just wasn't going to be enough.

CHAPTER SIX

Gus was on high alert when the three of us headed toward campus Monday morning. I didn't expect anything out of the ordinary to happen, but Gus hadn't calmed down since his encounter with Jackson Black.

Father John was his normal happy-go-lucky self, but a little amped up because he just loved going to class. We walked him as far as the auditorium door, and then Ruth and I went downstairs to meet Gilbert.

"Over here," a familiar voice called. We turned to see Gilbert, bright with anticipation. "Okay ladies, let's prove I'm not insane," he said, showing us to our seats next to his podium. "Just scan the students and see if you spot any flashes during class." He smirked. "Maybe it's the ghosts of battles past."

When I turned to sit down and got my first look at the hundreds of students who were streaming into the huge auditorium, I gained new respect for Gilbert. I didn't find anything inviting about standing in front of such an enormous group of people, and was impressed that Gilbert had the capability to convince this mass of humanity to sit down and listen because he had something important to say.

Gilbert stepped onto the stage, and when he began his lecture, I discovered that he was pretty entertaining. His eyes danced, and the jokes came easily. His audience was hooked, and they were soaking knowledge in easily. As he tried to control his twitching hands, his feet took over with a little dance. I smiled to myself … and then I saw the first flash in my peripheral vision.

Ruth grabbed my hand and looked at me to see whether I too had seen the flash... I nodded yes, and then there was another. I pulled one of Gilbert's auditorium drawings from my notebook and began making X's in the general vicinity of where I had seen the odd light. By the end of class I must have made a dozen marks on my paper.

Gilbert came off the stage exhausted. I knew it must have been hard for him to keep his train of thought with the light show going on around him.

By 10:00 a.m., Gilbert, John, Ruth, and I were sitting in the Student Union with our papers on the table in front of us. "Lets consolidate both of your papers with the ones I did last week to see if there is a pattern," Gilbert suggested.

"Here, do this," Father John said as he picked up the stack and strode toward the front windows. Pulling a chair up to the glass, he placed the papers against it, two at a time. Using it as a modified light table, he was able to transfer all of our X's to one master sheet within minutes. "Here you go, son," he said, handing everything to Gilbert.

We all studied the consolidated sheet over his shoulder.

"Nothing," Gilbert commented, "except for the fact that three of us saw it. Father John, did you see anything from your vantage point?"

"No, not really. Next week I'll move to the other side of the auditorium to see if I can spot what all of you are seeing." And with that, I had to rush off to my next class.

I knew I was not alone as I walked home after work. I couldn't hear Gus, but I could see his dark shadow moving from tree to tree. The afternoons were becoming quite crisp, and the sun was already setting. So I picked up speed, thinking of our nice warm apartment.

The door opened as I reached the top step, and my eyes locked on Will's smiling face. "I've made dinner," he said. "Come in and get warm." He took my hand to pull me the last few feet into the apartment and then into his arms. "Tell me about your day."

"Well, Ruth and I both saw what Gilbert was talking about, but I still have no clue what it is. Have you had a chance to ask McCollum what he thinks it might be?"

"No, but McCollum and I did talk about the lady who was in your dream last night. I thought he might know who she was."

Will saw my apprehension and tried to put me at ease. He admitted that McCollum knew nothing in particular about the lady in leather. "He might have a few ideas that we can start with, but no, he didn't tell me what they were. He wants the Brass Band to come to the house next week to talk about this as a group. I'll get the details and let you know, but for now, sit! Your food is getting cold."

I turned to see Will lighting a candle.

"Have I missed a special occasion?" I asked, as I sat in the chair he pulled out for me.

"The special occasion is me getting home early enough to cook for you. The candles are because I much prefer looking at you in a soft glow rather than in artificial light. It reminds me of the evening meals we ate by firelight a few thousand years ago."

He'd never talked about of having memories of our Druid life together, and I was eager to know more. He must have sensed my curiosity, because he began to answer my questions before I asked them.

"It's more of a feeling than a clear picture," he said, smiling. "I look at you now, in this soft candlelight, and I get a sense of a more primitive time. Sometimes your laughter takes me back to a time when we were young and I can smell soggy horsehide. Other times it's me I smell." He laughed. "Or the fresh-cooked rabbit over the fire. I see the streaks of mud on your beautiful face that came from the pounding hooves of our horses. Those were the days long before we had even heard the word *Roman*." Holding up his hand to quiet me, he went on. "Then there are times I look at you and flash on a grown woman who has taken her place among the Druid warriors, fighting her way to a place of honor among their ranks. During those years your face grew thinner, and I seldom saw you smile, but you were just as beautiful. The streaks on your face then were blood, and the fire was only lit when light was needed to plan the coming battles."

I gazed into Will's blue eyes and as the candle flickered, I was taken back to the campfire, too.

"The veils are still thin, aren't they?" he asked.

Taking a deep breath, I had to agree. I could smell the smoke and hear the murmured words of the battle to come. "Thin," I answered, and the spell was broken. The fire once again became the candle between us, and Will became a man of the twenty-first century.

"My heart has always belonged to you and you alone, Hillary, no matter the lifetime."

When I entered the lower apartment for our morning practices, George, Will, Father John, and Gilbert were already deeply immersed in The River of Knowledge. Ruth was the only one with her feet firmly in this world. As our eyes met, she patted the pillow beside her, so I scooted in next to her. She gave my knee a squeeze before she closed her eyes.

"Timing's a little off lately," Ruth said, as I opened my eyes to a room that was empty except for the two of us.

"Yes, I seem to be late for everything."

"Will said you're spending extra time in the bathroom ... and believe me girl, I know by the looks of you that you're not spending that time primping!"

I wanted to laugh, but felt like crying instead. "I'm not sure what's wrong with me! Ever since school started, I've felt tired and a little sick. The full moon cycles seem to be taking a toll on me!"

Ruth looked at me as if she had a different idea. "I think we ought to go to the store to pick up a test and see if you come up *plus or minus*."

It hung in the air between us, until it finally dawned on me that Ruth was talking about a pregnancy test. "Oh, no! That's definitely not it! We've been very careful."

"Maybe you have, but if birth control pills can be altered by something as simple as using them with thyroid medicine, imagine how you might be altering the pill's effectiveness. I mean, really ... you spend a lot of time moving from body to light body, and from 2011 to 37 AD. Your energetic body is always in flux."

"Okay, I'll do it," I said, resigned. "But only to satisfy your curiosity, Ruth." I really felt like go back to bed, but agreed to go to the store with her.

"You bet!" she said, standing and tossing her meditation pillows into the corner and placing the brass bowl back on the mantle. "I love the way the bowl sings now that Father John's here."

We bought the test, and in spite of Ruth's insistence that I find a restroom and take it immediately, I put it in my backpack and headed toward campus. "Did George tell you what day we'll be meeting with

McCollum?"

Ruth let the subject change without an argument. "Yes, I believe it will be at the waning moon. I figure he wants it to be easy on you."

When we entered the Student Union, I was baffled by what I saw. "Hey, look! There's Gilbert with Will and George. It's not that often we see them on campus." Then I remembered that they had attended his class.

Again, Gilbert's papers were fanned out across the table. "How's the research coming?" Ruth inquired, as she slid one of the plastic cafeteria chairs up to the table.

"We were short an observer this morning," Gilbert responded without looking away from the papers. "Father John headed back to the farm to help your Dad with a few things so they'd be free to attend McCollum's meeting. Besides, I think it's time the Brass Band were all together with the *bowl* again. Its singing has to be significant."

"How come the flashes appear on the left sometimes, and other times they seem to be on the right?" Will asked.

"Who knows," Gilbert answered with annoyance. "I'm finding it more difficult to concentrate, and that's not a good thing for my untenured status. I need to impress the faculty with my brilliance, not my stupidity."

"Don't worry, Gilbert!" George said. "We'll figure it out even if it takes getting McCollum down here to have a look. Maybe you should concentrate on teaching and let us take over the rest."

"Let me see your papers from today!" I demanded, excited to see what George and Will's pattern looked like.

"Here," George said, tossing a blank sheet of paper toward me.

"I don't understand. Didn't you and Will see anything?" I looked up into their faces.

"Not a thing," George admitted. "We can't figure out if we scared whatever it was away or just couldn't detect it."

"The auditorium lights were up a tad brighter today," Gilbert offered as an excuse. "I'm sure it couldn't have been you and George."

"Well, the only way to tell is to send the ladies in again. How about it girls?" George bellowed in his inside voice.

"Yeah, I guess I could fit it in next week," I said, checking with Ruth as she pulled up her schedule on her phone.

"Next week on Thursday is good for me, too, and if your parents are here, we can have them sit with Father John."

I stopped to rest on the bench outside the library and to think about Will and the pregnancy test in my backpack. I was deep in thought when I heard Gus caw and glanced at my phone for the time. More than twenty minutes had passed. I thanked Gus for bringing me back to my senses in time for work.

Pushing through the library doors, I hurried up the stairs to Ann Marie's desk. She had everyone's work assignments arranged in folders, and I was thrilled to find that mine was filled with a stack of requests from Dr. Edwards.

I found my way to the glass-floored room where books on Dr. Edwards' requests were always located, hoping I could find an answer for myself. I ran my hand along the shelves, gathering Dr. Edwards' research material, waiting for that energetic pull that meant that I had discovered the book that contained my solution. My fingers were drawn to a thin book with a gold-embossed binding that said, *The Prophet*. I closed my eyes and let it fall open.

And a woman who held a babe against her bosom said, "Speak to us of Children."

And he said, "Your children are not your children. They are the sons and daughters of Life's longing for itself. They come through you but not for you. And though they are with you, yet they belong not to you.

"You may give them your love but not your thoughts. For they have their own thoughts. For their souls dwell in the house of

tomorrow, which you cannot visit, not even in your dreams.

"You may strive to be like them, but seek not to make them like you, for life goes not backward nor tarries with yesterday.

"You are the bow from which your children as living arrows are sent forth.

"The archer sees the mark upon the path of the infinite, and He bends you with His might that His arrows may go swift and far.

"Let your bending in the archer's hand be for gladness: For even as He loves the arrow that flies, so He loves also the bow that is stable."

I felt peaceful as I walked home, determined to talk to Will about the test that was in the bottom of my backpack, knowing that whether Will and I were to have a baby or not, everything was as it should be. Winter was approaching, but the smells of fall still lingered as I walked through the last of the colorful fallen leaves. I found myself absorbed in the silence as the sun began to fall behind the enormous elms that edged the neighborhood.

I was yanked from my tranquility by the roar of a motorcycle. Panic gripped me as I remembered her words. *"He killed me, but his greatest trophy is going to be your husband, Will!"*

Running as fast as I could, I saw Gus leading the way around trees and over dried lawns. Without pausing to look back for the source of my terror, I took my front stairs two at a time and grabbed the door handle, turning it to find it still locked. Frantic, I shook the knob. It opened from the inside and I ran headlong into Will.

"Slow down, Hillary," Will said, brushing my hair back from my face. "Tell me what happened."

"It could have been her," I said. "Or him." But as I calmed down, I realized it was probably neither.

"Who?" Will asked.

"I heard a motorcycle … I heard her say that *your death would be his greatest trophy,* and I ran … to find you? To hide? To gather an army? I don't know what I was doing," I finally had to admit. "But she called you *Will.* I know this isn't part of the past."

"Believe me, Hillary, when I say that I don't take your dreams lightly. McCollum and I have discussed this, and he has instructed me to go nowhere without George by my side. Until we figure all of this out—the lady, the flashes of light, even the singing bowl—George, Gus, and I are taking extra precautions. Even the boys are on alert, and McCollum has sent word to your parents and Dr. Edwards that they should report anything out of the ordinary."

"Something is happening, isn't it?"

"Something is always happening," Will replied, smiling. "It's just never been as clear to you." I held him tight and let his words penetrate my being. "You're beginning to consciously see how all of it fits together. When you can see the past and how it fits with the present, it makes it easier to predict the future. But we can't let ourselves become preoccupied with it, because the future is what we have come to change!"

CHAPTER
SEVEN

November 12, 2011

It was the following afternoon when one of my favorite things happened. I walked into the glass-floored room at the library to find an imposing figure standing with his back toward me, a book open in his hands.

"What are you researching today?" I asked moving closer.

Dr. Lee Edwards looked down to meet my smile with one of his own. "Actually, I'm searching historical texts for legends about a mysterious brass bowl. Intellectually, I believe they must exist. Even if a group of holy men were able to keep the information about a manifesting bowl secret, I find it difficult to believe that a bowl that literally sings wouldn't have been talked about. Judging from what Father John has told me, the bowl sings with such abandon that it has moved your meditations to higher level."

"Of course Father John would feel that way, I replied. "I think it's singing for him and it resonates so deep within him that he and the bowl are almost one. The bowl came to McCollum, but I'm sure it belongs to Father John."

"Well, it will be interesting talking to John about the bowl because I haven't had any luck tracking it's history," Lee said, snapping his book shut. "Do you already have a date for tonight, or can I take you out for dinner?"

There was a time when an offer like that would have made me blush and my knees go weak. "How about giving me a ride home and having dinner with us?" I asked, not knowing exactly who *us* would be. Lee might be in for anything from a quiet evening with Will and me to an explosion of discussion with whichever *Band* members showed up.

"That sounds wonderful," he said.

"Just one more thing," I said, turning toward the bookshelves. I closed my eyes, walked until I felt a slight pull, and reached for a book on the shelf. Blowing it off, I turned to see an amused Dr. Edwards. "I'm looking for a few answers, and this is how I pick my research material."

With a chuckle, Lee took my arm and we walked down the stairs.

Gilbert joined us for dinner, which ended up being a fun-filled evening of storytelling and investigation. The most interesting news of all was that two of McCollum's oldest boys were on the verge of leaving to join a group in Australia. Will was enthusiastic about the move because his group and the Aussies had been crossing paths on their *out of body experiences* for quite some time now. The group down under was advancing at least as fast as McCollum's, and it was thought that they would make good allies.

When the talk turned to Gilbert and his auditorium scorecards, Lee was all in. Dr. Edwards would keep his own tally for the first portion of Gilbert's next class and then take over as Gilbert's guest speaker for the second half, freeing Gilbert for the first time to look around for himself. Having six sheets from one class would be our most rigorous experiment to date.

Once it was time for bed and we had all retired to our own quarters, I had my first chance to look at the book I had pulled off of the library shelf. I closed my eyes and let it fall open to see what wisdom it had to offer:

> *It is better to conquer yourself than*
> *to win a thousand battles. Then the victory*
> *is yours. It cannot be taken from you, not*
> *by angels or by demons, heaven, or hell.*
> *—Buddha*

It was no surprise that our meeting with McCollum fell on the same day as Gilbert's next class, and even though Mom and Dad wouldn't arrive until evening, they would still be included in the discussion about our latest data.

Will and George decided to sit near Father John, while Ruth and I took our same places by the stage. Gilbert took his place behind the podium, with Dr. Edwards seated by his side. By now our worksheets were a more sophisticated drawing of the room, and each of us was prepared with our clipboards in hand.

"One, two, three," I counted as the lights dimmed and Gilbert walked to the podium. When the flashes began to happen I tried to write the time by each X I marked on my paper, but they were coming fast and furious—four, five, and the count went on.

When Gilbert took the seat next to me, I could tell that he was exhausted from his time at the podium. On the other hand, Dr. Edwards seemed to come alive when he began to talk. He spoke very little about physics, instead choosing to lecture on the effect our mind has upon what we call the physical world.

In my peripheral vision I saw Gilbert's hand flying across his paper. The guy had memorized all the flashes from the first half of the class, and was recording them as fast as he could.

"No wonder he's tired," Ruth whispered into my ear. "The guy's mind never rests!"

We met at the Student Union, and to my enormous surprise Mom and Dad were sitting at my favorite table having lunch. Their smiles welcomed us, and we hugged before taking our seats around the table.

"Okay, let's see this research," Dad asked enthusiastically. "Fresh eyes might make a difference."

"Well, the consistency is remarkable," Dr. Edwards commented. "All of the papers look alike."

Dad scrutinized the information, studying the sheets in silence before finally speaking. "The only information that is missing is all of *your* locations in the auditorium. I'd like to see the positions of these light flashes in relation to each of you." He looked up at the group.

Gilbert laughed, smacking himself on the forehead. "How could I not have thought of that?" he said as he gathered the papers to mark our locations. "This will be our data point for today. Is it too much to ask for everyone to switch locations in the room the next time we do this?"

We were all so deep into this mystery by now that we were disappointed to have to wait four days for Gilbert's next class.

"No one can sit in the same place or with the same person. Let's shuffle the deck and see if thing change next time," Will confirmed.

As the sun fell below the horizon, we found ourselves sitting in McCollum's company. It was the first gathering in McCollum's quarters that Father John had attended, and he had insisted on bringing the brass bowl with him, feeling it would be inappropriate to leave such a valuable member of our group at home.

A fire burned in the huge fireplace that adorned the ornately furnished room. The chairs and pillows were arranged in their normal positions with one addition, a pillow for Father John. I watched as he crossed his feet and limberly dropped to the cushion as if he were half his age. After becoming comfortable, he removed the brass bowl from his satchel and placed it lovingly in front of him.

McCollum smiled broadly and then engaged us one at a time. "Gilbert, I hear you have embarked upon a very interesting project! Are you approaching a conclusion?"

"No, sir, but we have a plan. Do you think—"

"I think, my dear Gilbert, that you have the fortitude and insight to solve this conundrum without my input," McCollum answered. "After all, you belong to the oldest Druid bloodline, and their power of observation was remarkable. This should be no great feat for you, and I will be very excited to see where this leads you." Gilbert was left speechless.

Turning next to Father John, McCollum suddenly sat back in his chair with delight. Out of curiosity, the rest of us turned as well. Father John sat with his head bowed, eyes closed, with a look of total bliss upon his face, as he held his now-singing bowl. It began very quietly, but as it got louder and louder, McCollum couldn't contain his pleasure and began to laugh uncontrollably. His laughter immediately became contagious. Slowly, Father John returned to us and opened his eyes with a flurry of blinks. It was endearing to see a fully-grown man blush with embarrassment at being the center of attention.

"I had that bowl in my possessions for years," McCollum said to Father John, "and I never knew it was capable of expressing such joy. Not once did it raise its voice in song for me! Will has told me about your relationship with the brass bowl, but actually seeing it warms my heart."

Father John bowed his head in response, and without thought raised the bowl to his heart … and the bowl moaned with pleasure.

"I also look forward to watching where you and your bowl lead us," McCollum said with pride, and his eyes rested a moment longer on Father John.

Next he turned to me and stared. He was so transfixed that it made me feel uncomfortable. When he was finally able to speak, McCollum said bluntly, "Dear One, your aura has changed. The energy you are radiating is so different that I wonder what the explanation might be?"

Ruth bent forward, so she could see me clearly from where she sat on the other side of George. She was obviously implying *I told you so*, but held her tongue.

I thought of the test I had neglected to take because I'd been too swept up in my anxiety about the lady in leather. I turned to Will, wanting him to be the first to know, and with my heart in my hands began. "I think McCollum has confirmed what I have not yet confirmed for myself."

I had to stop, fining myself short of breath. "Will … how do you feel about … I know this wasn't the plan—"

"Oh, spill it!" Ruth blurted.

And with everyone in the room now looking at me, I squeezed my eyes shut so I could muster all my courage, and said, "Will, you're going to be a father." The room went so silent that I was afraid to open my eyes, but eventually I had no other choice. As I gazed into my husband's baby blues, I watched a tear roll down his cheek and knew it was for joy.

"Wow!" was all that came from his lips. "Wow!"

"That would be the explanation," McCollum said, breaking the silence. "I can see it now—the two energies are overlapped, intertwined because there is another soul who has come to join us."

"I'm not sure how it happened," I said, and heard Ruth laugh.

"It is the flow of things. You could have done nothing to stop it," was McCollum's answer. "It is meant to be. Let me be the first to offer my congratulations."

CHAPTER
EIGHT

December 1, 2011

Needless to say, Mom and Dad were ecstatic about my pregnancy, and after my first doctor's appointment, it was confirmed that I was about two months along. I was happy the baby was due in early summer because it would give me time to consider my options for continuing school. I wanted dearly to finish my degree.

Going to college kept me sane. It was the normality I required to balance my life with McCollum. My mind could contemplate a mathematical equation and find a concrete answer, which gave me a place to rest and pretend that the world was still at least partially what I used to believe it to be. Sometimes, when I stopped to think about the dual life I was living between Hillary and Hilsbeth, I began to feel a little insane. So I did what I could to put one foot in front of the other, and prayed that when I arrived at *that point in time,* I would have become the person McCollum believed I could be.

In quiet moments I daydreamed about the baby I carried, and wondered what part he or she would play in the grand scheme of the Brass Band. Other times, I fantasized about having a normal life with a white picket fence and all that went along with it. But Will was the piece of the puzzle I couldn't get into place, the thing that didn't fit into my housewife fantasy. He would never have a normal nine to five job or a 401K, or carry a briefcase. Will was a time traveler, a mystic, The

Teacher; and he swam in The River of Knowledge like a fish. So the pendulum swung and I strived simply to *BE*.

December 13, 2011

As the last days of the fall semester dwindled, so did our chances of solving Gilbert's mystery. We had two more classes to discover the source of the odd phenomenon, and we had all hands on deck, including Mom and Dad. We mapped out our seating, each moving to an opposite location than the ones we'd used before, and with diagrams of the auditorium in hand we were in place when the bell rang for class. Gilbert dimmed the lights, and while all the students remained oblivious to the light show we were watching, the Brass Band began recording flashes of light.

"I'll make dinner if everyone can meet at around 5:00 p.m.," Mom offered when we gathered by Gilbert's podium at the end of class. "Then we can compare notes and talk at our leisure."

Of course we all agreed, because who didn't love Mom's cooking. There was far too much data to look at now, and we all needed to get on with our individual days. I had classes, and I knew Will had meditation planned with the boys. Knowing I'd see him after he finished with his students, I hugged him good-bye and hurried off to class.

I was enjoying my walk to class, just letting my thoughts roll around in my head. It was an unusually sunshiny day for winter, and I loved seeing the trees barren of leaves. The intricate structure of the limbs reminded me of a skeleton, and I marveled at how they could go totally dormant only to return to life in the spring. *Not that different from us,* I mused. Our bodies turn to bones after the winter of our lives, and we are born once again into the spring of life as a newborn babies.

I was halfway across campus when I heard someone say, "You cling to goodness like a tick to a dog," and I was overwhelmed by a feeling of dread. "But the tick eventually becomes bloated and falls off its host, just as you will fall away from your spiritual delusions. And then you will come crawling to me."

"Get lost, Jackson, before my birds descend upon your head," I spat viciously. His new boldness terrified me, but my instincts told me I couldn't appear weak.

"Gus, isn't with you today, but yet you are not alone. What should I make of that?" he said, looking me up and down, settling his gaze upon my womb. I felt my stomach turn. "I'm twice the man your husband will ever be, because unlike him and his young boys, I like girls!"

Sickened, I turned and crashed through the library doors rather than continuing to my class, and hurried to the area designated for employees only, closing it tightly behind me. I moved past the banks of computers and entered the lounge, turning to watch the door behind me to make sure that Black hadn't followed me. I grabbed a bottle of water from the refrigerator and dropped into a chair that faced the door. I drank it all, mindlessly, willing myself to calm down.

I was reassured by the passing of time, but I still didn't feel safe going back outside. So I figured that if I couldn't attend class, I could at least work. Eventually I found myself headed toward the glass-floored room, more for comfort than out of necessity. I have discovered an unexpected benefit to transcendental meditation—psychic abilities. I'm not sure whether people who meditate develop these abilities because they become more sensitive to what is happening around them or because they begin tapping into that place where everything exists, but either way mine were telling me that Dad and Dr. Edwards were near. As I approached the room, all those nasty feelings Black had brought up in me began to dissipate.

"Hey, Kiddo," Dad said, looking up from his books. He had his usual stack in front of him.

"Hey, yourself," I said. I walked over to give him a hug, and when I held on to him just a little too long, he knew something was wrong. Holding me at arm's length, he looked into my eyes and said, "Tell your old Dad what's wrong."

"Jackson Black again," I said, letting my dammed up of frustration loose. "He follows me sometimes, and it makes me feel vulnerable and afraid … and that makes me mad."

Dr. Edwards got up from the table to stand beside Dad. "I don't mean to sound insensitive," he said, "but do you think he might have an ulterior motive?"

"I hope," Dad said, as he watched me pace the room. "I'd like it to be anything besides him stalking my daughter!"

Dr. Edwards continued. "I've been thinking that Black might be testing the water to see how many will come to Hillary's aid. He has no other way of learning how many Druids that have chosen to reincarnate with her."

"I don't think he's that smart," Dad said, making eye contact with me, "but maybe subconsciously he recognized you as Hilsbeth, and if he wants to know how many will come to your defense, I think maybe it's time we showed him."

"I think this is something we need to talk to McCollum about," I countered, not wanting to let things get out of hand. "I don't want to drag any of you into this."

"Okay," Dad said, resigned. "Let's stay calm and let that precious little soul inside you sleep. But until we figure this out, we'll make sure you're never alone." I felt him squeeze my hand, and I knew he would go to the ends of the Earth to make absolutely sure I was safe.

Dad and Dr. Edwards waited until I had finished my work and drove me home. Mom had been cooking all afternoon, and with a half hour to spare, Dad and I donned oven mitts to help her move the food to the lower apartment for our five o'clock meeting. Ruth and George's apartment was filled with the aroma of rosemary as we finished with the final preparations, and everyone took their usual seats around the large kitchen table.

Dinner was delicious as always, and discovering what everyone had been up to was wonderful, but this evening was about Gilbert. So Ruth and George cleared the table, Mom and Dad served the coffee, and Gilbert spread the morning's tally sheets out in front of him. Ruth and I were eager to see if everyone's marks matched, or better yet, if they revealed evidence that would solve our mystery. So when our impatience got the best of us, Gilbert obliged us by overlaying our three sheets and holding them up to the overhead light. We examined the pattern and saw that our marks matched exactly.

One by one, as the others joined us, we compiled all the information onto one master sheet.

"I'll be." Father John whispered. "I'm dead center!"

"Well, that's the answer! Now, what's the question?" Gilbert wondered out loud.

"I've been giving these so-called lights a bit of thought," Will said, "and I think they are actually the students' auras and we're just seeing an energy spike of some sort. There must be something that's causing it."

Father John leaned back to think. "Do you suppose it's something about the subject matter, or do you think it's more of a relationship between the people in the auditorium?"

"I think it has to do with you, my friend," Will stated flatly. "The day you missed class, George and I didn't see a thing. That tells me that it's you."

"I've got a wild idea!" Ruth announced, her eyes lit with excitement. "The thing what we've got to do next is segregate these sparkling people from the rest of the students in class, and I think it's safe to assume we should use Father John as the bait."

I saw Will and George look at each other. "My lady's brilliant," George hooted, winking at Ruth. "We have to get the okay from McCollum, but that won't be hard. We'll just need to catch him tonight before evening practices."

"I'll drive you," Dad suggested. "And then I'll meet you two at the library." He pointed at Dr. Edwards and Father John.

I just settled deeper into my comfy corduroy chair, kicking my legs up over one of the overstuffed arms. I was totally befuddled, not understanding anything that was transpiring.

"Anyone up for a latte?" Mom asked with a shrug. "I'll buy."

We took our normal table near the back of the coffee shop, and when I offered to take everyone's orders, Mom laughed.

"We'll help you," she insisted, along with Ruth. They must not have thought me capable of juggling four hot drinks. "We'll only be a minute, Gilbert."

I had to admit that carrying two cups of coffee was probably my limit. So, with all my attention focused on not spilling the hot beverages, I almost ran into Ruth when she pulled up short in front of me.

"What are you doing, Ruth? You almost got a hot bath ..." I trailed off as I saw what she was looking at. There at our table sat an ivory-skinned beauty with huge mahogany eyes. "She was so petite she made Gilbert look tall and ruggedly masculine by comparison.

Ruth slid silently into a chair at the nearest table and gawked. Her coffee cup slid slowly from her fingers and I heard the little click when it hit the table. I sat next to her, with Mom standing behind us. We were all charmed by the sweetness we were observing between the young lady and Gilbert.

"Who is she?" Ruth whispered.

"I don't know," I replied, "but can you see her aura?" It wasn't the norm for me to see them clearly, but this one was vivid.

"Not really. There's too much light behind them. Can you?" Ruth asked.

"Yes, it's *pink!* Look around the edges, Ruth." She squinted as I explained, "Pink indicates purity." I saw the woman's aura intensify as she shyly brushed Gilbert's hand. "But I think in this case it means tenderness, compassion, and …"

"And what?" Ruth prodded.

"Romance!"

We had the barista put our drinks in to-go cups and we slipped away. We knew we wouldn't be missed.

CHAPTER NINE

A master plan had been hatched by the time we arrived home.

"You're the bait, Father John, and yes, we have McCollum's blessing," Will promised.

Father John didn't look convinced. "Maybe it should be Gilbert who makes the announcement."

"No, it has to be you," George said emphatically. "We've put a lot of thought into this, and it's either going to work or not work, but either way you have to be the one to offer the invitation."

December 11, 2011

Today we attended class as mere spectators. We mingled with the students and waited for the trap to be sprung. Gilbert stepped to the podium with an unusually large smile adorning his face. I suspected his newfound facial expression was because of the girl in the coffee shop, and I really was truly happy for him. I was willing to give him another twenty-four hours to spill the beans—and after that, I was going to ask him.

Father John had taken his seat in the center of the classroom, and in contrast to his usual demeanor, his head was down and his smile was missing. I knew a crowd this size could be intimidating.

"You have one hour and forty-five minutes to complete your final exam," Gilbert announced, "beginning... now! Please, remain quietly in your seat until the end of class, at which time your tests will be collected."

Gilbert walked to a far corner of the room, and I took the opportunity to join him and his super-sized smile. I stood beside him, mirroring his posture as he watched over his students.

"You're going to have to tell me about that," I said out of the side of my mouth.

"About what?" Gilbert answered, innocently.

"That!" I said, pointing at his face.

He just leaned back against the wall and continued smiling.

As time crawled, I took a seat next to Ruth and twiddled my fingers, thankful when Gilbert returned to the podium. "Time is up. Please print your name on the top of the first page and pass your test to the right."

Papers began to shuffle, and the student assistants walked down each aisle to collect them. "Please stay in your seats for another moment; the bell hasn't rung," Gilbert said. "I'd like to take a moment for comments and questions."

A small hand shot into the air, and a girl stood, "Professor Dutton, your class has been pivotal for me. I look forward to studying the dimensional parameters that characterize the physical universe in more depth with you next semester."

Ruth smirked as we recognized her as the one from the coffee shop. "I bet she really just wants to characterize the physical parameters of Gilbert's dimensions," Ruth said with a smirk.

A few others also stood to share their thoughts on Gilbert's first teaching experience, but the person we were waiting to hear from was still seated firmly in his chair, and the bell was about to ring.

"I'll take one more comment," Gilbert said with an emphatic tone in his voice. We all watched as Father John ever so slowly pulled himself to his feet. "Sir," Gilbert said, pointing to John and quieting the class with his a motion of his hand. "What do you have to say?"

"I would like to take this opportunity to invite you, Mr. Dutton, and anyone in this class—"

"Speak up, sir, I can't hear you. You'd like to invite me and—"

"Yes," Father John said, finally hitting his stride and raising his voice to a booming volume. "I'd like to invite you, Mr. Dutton, along with any interested student in this auditorium, to attend a midnight meditation." The auditorium filled with soft snickers and the rustling of young people readying their backpacks to leave the moment the bell rang. "My e-mail is posted on the bulletin boards at each exit," Father John shouted, trying to be heard over the noise. "Please contact me for information." The bell rang and everyone rushed toward the exits.

Ruth, Gilbert, and I looked up at Father John, who was quickly becoming the only person left standing in the enormous arena. We all crossed our fingers.

When the other members of the Brass Band rushed toward us, I was glad to see smiles on their faces. "Success," Mom shouted, as she ran down the middle aisle. "Students are writing down Father John's e-mail and taking the pamphlets that we left on the tables."

She handed Gilbert the camera that she had used to snap some candid shots of the students picking up Father John's information.

McCollum was very excited when the Brass Band took their seats in his quarters. "Gilbert, I have heard that you were successful, so may I ask what you have discovered?"

"Of course, sir," Gilbert replied, separating his papers and Mom's photos into two piles. "These are the points where we recorded flashes, which we now believe are occurrences happening in the auras of at least a few of my students. The second pile is pictures of the multitude of students who took information from the bulletin boards outside my classroom."

"So this is how they have come," McCollum said, looking up to meet Gilbert's eyes. He chuckled. "Even though I consider our group a very special collection of beings, I have to admit that we are not totally unique in our quest. Fortunately for us, there will be many others to help us diminish the dark, and it will take every single individual who is willing to join us to propel mankind through this window of enlightenment.

"Even with the enormous population that already inhabits this planet," McCollum continued, "there are many more who wish to be here. The waiting lines are long for *those entities* who want to be on Earth to participate in this monumental junction. And for those who believe animals don't have souls, I advise they look into a beast's eyes, for souls are coming in any form that is available."

CHAPTER TEN

December 31, 2011

My dreams of maimed bodies and brutal battles had subsided as of late, to be replaced by a blissful state of union with the soul I carried within me. Knowing that one day this being would live separately from me brought me both joy and a little sadness, because this feeling of oneness was extraordinary.

"Get up lazy bones!" Will teased affectionately as he bent to kiss me. "George, Ruth, and John will be here within the hour. I let you sleep as long as I could. Now you need to pack."

I sat up on the edge of the bed and placed my hands on my belly. It was beginning to swell, but not enough to be noticed by anyone other than the people closest to me. Going with our intuition, Will and I had become accustomed to referring to the baby as *he*. I could already imagine a miniature Will crawling around on the apartment floor. Then I thought of the dust bunnies that would attach themselves to his little jammies and made a note to myself to get into the habit of sweeping more thoroughly. Every bit of it made me very happy.

Today was the day we were to see if Gilbert's experiment would bear fruit. Father John had answered about twenty-five e-mails in response to the information he had left on the bulletin boards outside Gilbert's classroom. I was excited that the Brass Band and the boys in the household would finally be able to put faces to the *people of light—* the name we'd decided to give them rather than continuing to refer to them as flashes or X's on our drawings.

The doorbell rang as I threw my last pair of clean socks into my overnight bag. "I'm in the bedroom, Ruth," I shouted.

She let herself in and laughed when she saw me struggling with my suitcase. "Let me help, Hillary. I'll sit on it while you zip it closed." It was a good strategy. Ruth was pretty inventive when it came to travel preparations, and distributed her weight just where it was needed.

"Works like a charm," she said, and within seconds my husband's and my things fit snuggly into one slightly bulging bag.

"Honey," Ruth said mockingly as Will came back into the room. "Can you please carry this bag down to the car for me?" She fluttered her eyelashes as Will walked over to pick up our bag.

"Come on ladies," he said. "We want to get there early so we can get prime seats. I want to see all of the twinkly people as they enter the temple."

As it turned out, we weren't seated in the temple at all, but stationed in a greeting line as our guests began to arrive. McCollum had given us very specific instructions: "Greet them, make them feel welcome, and show them to the temple door … no further. Let them enter on their own, and by no means show any surprise on your faces."

"What do you think he means by that?" Gilbert inquired.

"Not a clue," George replied, innocently. But we knew that he knew more than he was letting on, because Will and Father John were both suspiciously absent.

At eight o'clock, the overhead lights were softened, and the sound of chanting began to play in the background. At 8:05 the front doors opened and our first guest arrived—it was Gilbert's new friend, and no way was he going to get away without introducing me to her. As she walked in, both of them began to blush. Her long dark hair was twisted atop her head, and she was undeniably beautiful in her oriental robe.

I cleared my throat in an attempt to interrupt the sparks flying between them. Other people were beginning to fill the entryway, and they were holding up the line.

Gilbert turned to me. "Hillary, this is my friend Indira. Indira, Hillary."

I took her hand in mine, and her skin temperature verged on being not warm, but hot.

And then I felt it—Chi, flowing from her to me. I looked into her face with surprise, and in return I saw serenity. "Nice to meet you, Indira," I said, and I really meant it. I was surprised at my reluctance to release her hand. I gazed into her eyes to see if I could discover why my heart had opened so easily. She smiled back knowingly, and let Gilbert guide her to the temple door.

Feeling a little stunned by the encounter, I watched Gilbert return to his place in line. "Her name means beauty and splendor," Gilbert said under his breath. "I think she may be the reincarnation of a Goddess."

We were both brought back to the present moment by the long line of guests who were streaming past. They took our hands in greeting, each more anxious than the next to enter the temple. By nine it seemed like all of our guests had arrived, and McCollum entered the lobby to talk to us briefly.

"You are free to take your places in the temple."

Ruth guffawed, "Father John's invitation drew quite the crowd."

"You'll be surprised how well this has worked," McCollum replied with a twinkle in his eyes, and as he turned to leave, I thought I heard him quietly laugh. "Next time you see Will, Dear One, please send him to me."

We returned to our rooms to gather our meditation pillows and shawls, and the Brass Band members, minus Father John and Will, entered en masse through the temple's side door. We were anticipating not being able to sit together because of the crowd, but to our amazement, we found that none of McCollum's boys were in the temple, and without explanation I understood McCollum's experiment clearly.

In the center of the left half of the room sat Will, deep in mediation. In the center of the right half was Father John, a blissful smile on his face, although we knew he was far, far away. And surrounding John were all the guests, sitting shoulder to shoulder as if touching one another was a necessity.

My eyes watered as my emotions overflowed at the beauty of it. It was then that McCollum's boys began to enter the temple, soundless with their bare feet, and took their place on the left side of the temple with Will. Unable to take my eyes off what I saw in front of me, I made my way slowly to where Will sat meditating. I tenderly placed my hand on his shoulder to encourage him to return.

"Is it time?" he asked, looking up at me.

"Yes, McCollum needs you," I whispered, and then his eyes followed mine.

"Just as McCollum thought!" he exclaimed. And when I turned around to ask him what he meant, all I saw was the back of him as he slipped out the door.

The energy in the temple was amazingly high, and I looked forward eagerly to my first encounter with my baby in this supercharged environment. I had to believe that this was what he had come for, so tonight would be his journey as much as mine.

Mom seemed to know exactly what I was thinking. She paused in front of me and touched my face before taking her seat between Dad and Dr. Edwards. The Brass Band also sat shoulder to shoulder, touching, instinctively knowing that tonight we were to exist as one. We let the energy join us one to the next, until our union was complete. Then I closed my eyes and let go.

It felt like only minutes before I heard a bell ringing to call me back into my body, and when I opened my eyes, McCollum was seated in a large white chair at the front of the room. He waited for a few moments, and then stood to walk among us.

"There is a story that deserves to be told," McCollum began, coming to a stop in front of Father John. "You, like all of us, have wondered what drew our paths to cross, and tonight, due to our ingenious professor, I know why … and now it is time for you to know, also."

Gilbert shifted on his pillow next to me, and I could feel him swell with pride at being singled out in such a distinguished group.

"I've invited a dear and very old friend of mine, who exists as part of The River of Knowledge, to be the one to tell this story."

I watched as Will entered the room, and as he walked toward McCollum's chair rather than joining me, I knew just who our special guest would be. Will sat, and while he closed his eyes and began to slow his breathing, McCollum continued to address the group that surrounded Father John.

"Mr. Emerald is one of my most prized instructors. He is also a person who has traveled throughout time with an extraordinary companion. Tonight, Mr. Emerald will relinquish his body, letting his consciousness cross over into the heavens and allowing his companion to inhabit his physical body. And because *this being* exists as all things and simultaneously spans all time, he will recount the details of a most improbable and miraculous story. So now it is my deepest pleasure to introduce you to The Teacher."

McCollum moved to sit with his boys, and all eyes moved to watch Will. Even though I had seen my husband slip away many times before, the sight of it still took my breath away. I'd learned to quiet myself and wait for that wind to blow through me, to feel that momentary quickening in my chest. For just that instant before The Teacher settled into Will's body, I could feel his power touch me as he condensed all that he was to the size of a mere human body. I watched as *he* placed the magnitude of what he was into Will's human frame, and the physical form become slightly larger to encompass the energy of The Teacher. When his eyes opened, I knew he was no longer the blue-eyed man who was my beloved husband, but the *all-knowing One* who comes from beyond and embodies all knowledge—past, present, and future.

With a massive intake of air, The Teacher rolled his shoulders and stretched to arrange himself in his new anatomy. Standing slowly, he locked eyes with Father John and smiled. Then, scanning the guests who surrounded John, he began to walk with his head bowed in thought. When he finally came to a stop, he had gathered all of the information he needed to begin his story.

"There was once a group of peaceful Buddhist monks who lived high in the Himalayas, deep within the borders of Tibet. For centuries they lived in seclusion, only occasionally venturing from their monastery into the nearby villages. This sect of monks spoke very little when they were in public, so they were shocked to discover that a rumor had begun to spread among the villagers that they had in their possession a brass bowl that held great power. The villagers weren't of malicious mind, but the whispers grew, and a tale spread about a magic vessel that had been created by the Gods long before the Earth began. When asked, the Monks fervently denied the existence of such an artifact, and in their innocence they believed their denial would be enough to stem the curiosity of treasure seekers and other, darker souls who longed to possess it."

I felt the Brass Band members become restless, all of us realizing at once that it was our bowl The Teacher was talking about.

"When negotiations failed in 1950 and The People's Republic of China began their invasion of Tibet, these monks thought that their remoteness would keep them safe, and that the stories of the artifact they held within their walls had long since died away." The Teacher returned to McCollum's chair and sat heavily. "Alas, they were wrong. The rumors of the existence of a *mystical brass bowl* drew armed treasure hunters among the Chinese army higher and higher into the mountains, until one day they arrived at the village below the monastery, and the monks knew that it would only be hours before their gates were forced open. With no time to ponder, the bowl was placed in the hands of Wangdak, the fiercest of the monks, and with no plan beyond the knowing that he would forfeit his life to protect it, Wangdak changed into peasant's clothing, climbed over the back wall, and disappeared into the village below. With the sacred artifact wrapped only in a tattered blanket, he noticed that it began to quiet the further it was taken from its home, and he feared it was dying ... never to sing again.

"The villagers were frantically packing wagons and beasts to make the long trek down the very narrow trail to the valley floor before the army made their only route of escape impassible. They knew that if they stayed, the soldiers would confiscate their food, and they would have nothing to carry them through the winter.

"Wangdak hid his sorrow when he heard of the butchery at the monastery. He silently prayed for his friends' souls, but did not dwell on the manner of their deaths. He could ill afford to be singled out by the Chinese as he made his two-day descent to what he hoped would be freedom, hidden amid the peasants he depended on for his survival.

"Then one morning, the worst happened, and the army was upon them at dawn, demanding information and a pledge of loyalty in exchange for passage. Wangdak only had time to place his precious package into the back of the wagon ahead of him, with an apology for his failure to protect it and a promise to spend eternity attempting to find it again, Wangdak turned to face his destiny."

The Teacher paused, taking a moment to look around the room and to gather more memories. "Wangdak was identified as a monk the moment his headscarf was removed, and was decapitated at the edge of the trail. The bowl found its way to the valley floor and into a shop. A discerning collector then purchased it and moved it to his private collection in Europe. After his death, a gentleman from India acquired it at an estate auction. Feeling the bowl should return to an ashram, he traveled back to his homeland and used it as an offering to his guru. That Guru was invited to attend a conference in the United States as eastern philosophy began its journey to the West. He brought the bowl with him, and it found its way into the safekeeping of a household in Kansas, and eventually came into the hands of a being of great light by the name of McCollum, who in turn placed it under the protection of my oracle, Mr. Emerald, who he believed could bring its powers back to life."

There was an audible exhalation in the room as we began to understand just how we were all characters in the journey of this amazing artifact.

"So, what happened to Wangdak and his promise to find the mystical brass bowl and return it to the ones who had brought it life? The answer lies in a man who came to this lifetime in search of something Godly, but never quite found what he sought. Last year, in despair, this man answered an advertisement placed in the *Emporia* newspaper by another beautiful soul who sits in this room with us tonight."

I was unable to hold back my tears back as I heard Father John begin to sob.

"My Oracle's group embraced this lost and weary seeker, even though they knew he was not of their Druid decent, trusting that if fate had brought them together, all would be revealed."

I saw that not even McCollum could keep his tears of joy from falling, because he knew Father John had finally found what had been so elusive.

"Now that the journey of the brass bowl has concluded, let me return to the fate of those monks high atop that mountain," The Teacher said lightheartedly, which eased some of the tension in the room. "The news is not good. The gate was shattered, the temple ransacked, and every last monk was killed!" The Teacher raised his shoulders in a shrug, with a mischievous smile on his face. "But like all good people of the light, they also had a plan in place to return at the time of the twilight of the Kali Yuga, the window for enlightenment. They would reenter this Earthly plane unseen by the dark forces that had tried so hard to destroy them.

"I want you to understand this plan was absolutely ingenious." The Teacher laughed loudly, energizing us all. "It took courage and absolute faith, knowing from the beginning that not every soul would survive the journey, but enough of them would."

Lowering his voice to a whisper, The Teacher began the tale of their remarkable plan.

"Where better to return unnoticed than back into the viper's nest! So, these brave Buddhist monks, armed with the belief that a beacon would be set with the strength to reunite them, began incarnating into China as baby girls, during a time when that was most often a death sentence. The one-child law in China made women societal outcasts if they gave birth to and kept a female infant. For this reason some 37 million baby girls were secretly killed.

"But because mothers everywhere have an innate need to protect their offspring, Chinese women did what was necessary to save these innocent beings. They decided that if they were not allowed to love these babies, they would make sure they were loved by others and parents from across the oceans came for them." And as The Teacher, the Brass Band, and McCollum's boys gazed into the faces of the Asian girls who surrounded Father John, The Teacher continued.

"The children I speak of were loved very well indeed … by

Americans who fought reams of red tape and overwhelming governmental bureaucracy to claim them as their own. The monks' plan was well underway, and the magnetic power of the light was drawing them ever closer to their destiny!"

The Teacher stood, spreading his hand in introduction, "So Wangdak, meet your brethren, who laid down their lives so the bowl could be saved. And my dear Buddhist monks, meet Father John, your beacon who has always stayed true to his promise to reunite you with the brass bowl."

From behind McCollum's chair a voice sang, softly at first, then swelling to a crescendo, which brought the room to its feet. The Teacher bent to retrieve the bowl from its hiding place and handed it back to the monks who had given their lives to protect it.

CHAPTER ELEVEN

December 31, AD 38

I kneel alone in front of the altar as the sole survivor of my people—other than the one I carry within me. My belly is heavy with Liam's child, and my time grows short even though it is not yet time for his birth.

I have returned to my Druid home on the island of my birth, no longer having a reason to keep its location hidden. The families and priests who once occupied this enchanted place no longer live here. They are as dead as my dear Liam.

I hear the door open behind me and am not surprised. Long moments ago I heard the sound of Roman armor and weaponry entering the village, and wondered why my time of death was being postponed.

"Greetings, Hilsbeth," I hear in the familiar voice of General Marcus Flavius. "My soldiers are afraid to enter the holy house of the Druids for fear of being eaten alive by demons. Their foolish fears please me, for their hesitation enables me to have a moment alone with the greatest of the Druid warriors, the one who invades my dreams."

I rise to my feet and turn slowly to meet his gaze, still dressed in my full battle regalia except for the chest plate, which no longer fits the swell of my belly. "Marcus Flavius, it's actually nice to see you, for you are the only human left on this Earth whom I know, and who knows me." I falter only slightly as I feel the depth of my loneliness, and place my hands on my belly to feel the movement of the baby.

Vicki Renfro

Marcus Flavius takes a step toward me, and then another. "If we had existed in another place and time, I would have made you my wife, and your baby mine."

I am stunned by his frankness, but I know there is no time left to be anything but honest. "The times I entered your dreams were not for love, but to gather military information," I confessed.

"I have always known that, but have never desired you less because of it." He closes the space between us and places his hand gently on the side of my face. Hungry for human contact, I close my eyes and just feel the warmth upon my skin. "Hilsbeth, this is the end. There is no path left for either of us."

Knowing he speaks the truth, I open my eyes to take this world in one last time. "I have built funeral pyres for everyone I have ever loved, so their path into the next world would be lit. You are the last who can do me this honor."

A tear escapes the General's eye as I feel a sword pressed into my hand, "I will do you that honor, my lady ... with your promise that I am not responsible for your death. You will not have but a few minutes once I exit this temple because the fire must ignite immediately to keep any curious soldiers from entering and seeing you are with child ... for it would be cut from your living body and sent to Rome for a horrid display of the last Druids."

The thought breaks the last of my heart. "I promise you, Marcus Flavius, and I thank you for leaving me with my honor."

Marcus kneels to kiss my hands with astonishing reverence, and walks out the door without looking back. I hear the crackle of the flames igniting in the thatch overhead, and feel the heat explode within the temple. I draw upon the secrets held within these walls for final strength, and with sorrow I realize that with my death they will be known no more. I wedge the hilt of the general's sword between two stones at the foot of the altar, and fall on the sword of Rome.

Jan 1, 2012

I felt the fire's heat on my face, and a searing pain ran through me as my eyes flew open. I was sitting in another of McCollum's temples, most of the guests long gone. Barely able to catch my breath, I reached for my belly and felt Will's hands cover mine.

"I can see in your eyes that you have reached the end of the story," he said tenderly, as he touched my face to catch my tears. "You returned to our Druid village."

"Yes, I experienced my own death, Will. I failed the Druids. None survive, not even our son!" I whispered in a sob.

Will gathered me up in his arms. "Maybe looking back is the wrong direction, Hillary. You chose to come again, into this lifetime. Bring forward what you are, and let the other thing remain in the past."

"Do you know how I died?"

"The Teacher has told me everything, and it was difficult to listen to," he admitted remorsefully. "My most profound regret is that I was not the man standing in the temple with you."

I began to defend myself, but Will's finger gently touched my lips, and the memory faded. "I'm glad you didn't die alone, my dearest Hillary. It just gives me another reason to be thankful for Bennett Taylor, and another reason to envy him."

I looked at Will inquisitively.

"As hard as I try, I'm not perfect." he smiled. "I'm sometimes jealous of the other who has loved you nearly as much and as long as I have."

"Really?"

"Yes, really!" he said, reaching for my hands and pulling me to my feet.

"You must have stayed with me for hours," I said, as I noticed the total silence of the household.

"Yes," he replied, as he carried our things up the stairs and down the hall to our room. "And by your side I will remain forever."

I slept with both hands on my tummy, and thought of the baby I had lost and the one that I would soon give life to. The despair of the past and the joy of the present both bubbled up within me, and tears ran down my checks as I silently cried for both.

Shortly before dawn I rolled over to touch Will's face. "I love you, Will Emerald. Then, now, and always."

Will looked into my eyes to respond, but something interrupted him. Sitting up to listen, I could tell he was puzzled. "What on earth is going on?" he said as he jumped out of bed and tossed me my clothes. "Get up, sweetheart!"

Then I heard it too: a rambunctious chorus of bells, and I felt excitement rise up inside me. Will opened the door to see Father John dancing down the hallway, his face beaming, ringing a bell held high over his head as he danced. Following was an equally joyful group of young ladies, long black hair flying as they spun and danced their way forward, ringing their bells as a call for us to join them in morning practice.

I grabbed my shawl and pillow and ran to find a place in the line that was forming behind them. They danced down one hall and then up the next, until the parade concluded in the temple. Taking my normal place between Will and Dad, I sat down and watched Father John's group exit the rear doors. Turning my attention to my surroundings for the first time, I noticed the temple had been redecorated. Ribbons of Tibetan prayer flags streamed in every direction, crisscrossing the ceiling and draping McCollum's chair.

It was probably an hour before a single bell rang. The scent of fragrant sandalwood and swirling incense preceded the procession as the doors opened.

I was struck dumb by the splendor of what I saw. First through the door was a tall monk, grey hair shorn to the scalp, dressed in a deep maroon robe, the diamond stud still glittering in his ear.

Totally unprepared for what followed, I sat with my mouth agape. I knew these were the Chinese girls who had arrived the night before, but this morning they were transformed. One by one the Tibetan monks entered, each dressed in burgundy, shaved heads bowed in prayer. They were magnificent.

The onlookers let out a spontaneous *ahhhhhhh* as the last and smallest monk of all entered the room carrying the brass bowl on a brocade pillow. I heard a few boys laugh softly as the bowl raised its voice in festive song—they had lived with the bowl most of their lives and had never heard it make a peep. When the monks began to chant, I had to hold onto my pillow to stay grounded. I'd always loved the CDs of the Tibetan monks chanting, but this morning it was as if I were hearing it for the first time.

The smoke from the incense wafted into the air, and the chanting enveloped us. I linked hands with Will, him with Ruth, Ruth with George, and so on to Gilbert, Dr. Edwards, and Mom, the circle ending with Dad softly laying his hand on mine. And with that final connection, we became free to join the other etheric beings who had come to join the celebration.

When I arrived back on the plane known as plant Earth, everyone around me was well into the yoga class. The instructor moved slowly from position to position in total silence. It felt like a ballet as I allowed my body to move with the Shakti, that incredible energy with the ability to increase my life force. I embraced it, letting the total stillness move in and around me. This kind of yoga is done silently, in preparation for an expanded state of consciousness. It is only you and your breath, moving deeper and deeper until the letting go is inevitable.

The last movement was to slip ever so slowly into a lying position for shavasana, the meditation that the practice of yoga prepares you for. The release from my body came quickly, for both me and our baby. As my consciousness began to lift upward, I felt my son break free and race ahead of me to the place of nothingness and everything.

I had a tinge of regret when I felt myself snap back into the human world. I instantly looked for Will, and there he sat, just watching me with those wonderful blues eyes … and my insides turned gooey with love.

"I was with you," he said, not quite back in his body. "I followed you and our son, and as he will be a teacher for you, so he will be for all of us." That was all he said before he slid back into meditation.

Relaxing, I arched my back in a nice long stretch, letting my head fall backward, and listened to my bones pop—they sounded like a mallet running over a xylophone. Will's words came back to me, and I knew he was right, for I had just experienced our son's understanding of things which were far beyond mine. His consciousness was already expanded, and I was caught off guard by a tinge of sadness at the thought of being left behind. So I did what Will had told me to do on the morning when he'd first taught me to meditate. I closed my eyes and softly repeated to myself, *I am so happy, I am so happy, I am so happy* … until I found it within me.

I opened my eyes to find the brass bowl gently cradled in my lap and Father John sitting cross-legged in front of me with a blissful look on his face; that look suited him.

"Isn't it interesting how you always end up in the perfect place," he said, his eyes twinkling. "I'd spent all my life searching, only to end up feeling like a round peg in a square hole. And yes, sometimes it drove me to despair. That's the point I was at the morning I opened the *Emporia Gazette* and read your father's ad. I figured my intellect had carried me as far as it could. The only thing left for me was absolute and utter surrender. And isn't it the darnedest thing that *letting go* was what allowed me to find my true life's journey."

Assuming he was drawing a parallel between his journey as a Buddhist monk and mine as a Druid, I nodded for him to continue.

"The Teacher told us an astonishing tale last night about a faraway monastery that both lived and died to protect an object they deemed irreplaceable." His eyes drifted to the newly initiated monks. "And during the telling, I was propelled back in time, just like you are in your dreams. I relived every moment and passed my bodies willingly, as did all the brave souls who lived on that mountaintop … and no matter the agony, it's now been overshadowed by the wonder of being together again."

I understood completely what Father John was talking about because I, too, was dealing with the agony and wonder of it all.

"So have you talked to him about it?" Father John asked.

"Who?" I responded, totally baffled by this seeming non-sequitur.

"The American Indian," he answered, as if I knew what he was talking about.

"What Indian?'

"The one who sits at your side? I've sensed him often, but last night as The Teacher spoke, I was able to see him quite clearly."

"No, I've neither seen nor talked to him," I answered honestly.

Father John's resolve was not weakened by the fact that I was totally oblivious to what he was talking about. "Even if you can't see him, rest assured that he watches over you with great fondness. Maybe he will reveal himself on the next full moon." Father John patted my hand. "The bowl may help you. You only need to ask."

I placed my hands on either side of the bowl. I could feel the steady vibration of its blossoming life force, so I turned to look for the

Indian who sat beside me, and only saw Gilbert sitting huddled in the corner with his forehead pressed tenderly against Indira's. While most of the girls had taken on a boyish look with their newly shaved heads, Indira's lovely femininity was not lost. She glowed—literally—with the light I had seen in Gilbert's classroom.

Smiling, I turned back to continue my previous conversation. "Do we still call you *Father*?" I asked, since everything about him was screaming Buddhist monk.

"I suppose at some point in time I will make a change, but not now. Today, I am just going to bathe in the joy of finding the place where I fit." He placed his hands on his knees, and with the agility of a teenager, levered himself to his feet and walked away.

"Sad," I heard a voice say softly. Will was back in his body and opening his eyes.

It took me a minute to recall Will's last fading words as he slipped back into meditation. I reengaged my mind to locate that conversation. "I'm okay now, just a momentary glitch in the matrix," I teased.

He gently slipped the bowl out of my hands. "Now that I am back and you're no longer in great need of this, let's see if we can squeeze it between Gilbert and his new lady for safe keeping while we enjoy breakfast."

My stomach growled in agreement as Will lifted me to my feet. "Our son," he said introspectively. "I like the sound of that. By summer there will be three of us in our family.

Breakfast was the normal fare, but it tasted much better than when I ate it at home. The magic ingredient here was the chanting the cooks did while preparing it.

The Brass Band gathered at our regular table, and we were joined by Indira after the bowl was safely tucked away. To tell the truth, we were all excited to hear what her experience had been since arriving, but we skirted the topic, not wanting to pry.

Gilbert was the one who finally broached the subject. "Indira, my friends are far too polite to ask, so maybe you should just start at the beginning. It will put them at ease."

Indira smiled with a composure that would make both her Chinese and American parents proud. "In 1979 China invoked the One Child Act to reduce the population, and the program was necessary. But because China's social indoctrination only gives value to the male, it caused baby girls to be discarded by the millions during the 1980s. I was adopted from an orphanage in Chongqing as an infant, so I have no memory of abandonment." She lowered her eyes momentarily as she explained that many had spent years in desperate conditions waiting for someone to come for them. "I have only known love in my life because my parents came. They traveled halfway around the world to save me. I've always been thankful for my good fortune."

Gilbert took her hand to give her courage to continue. "I've carried a bit of survivor's guilt associated with, well … how come I was chosen to live when so many died? Last night was a glimpse into the karma that propelled me on this particular journey, and it helps to know that there was a plan for my survival, as impossible as it sounds. I must have picked a loving woman to be my birth mother… one I knew would deliver her newborn girl safely to an orphanage, rather than discarding her in a trash bin."

"I'm okay, Gilbert," Indira said when she saw Gilbert flinch in pain. "These are questions that I have been mulling over for most of my life, and for the first time I have answers. I've always felt tugs at my soul, pulling me here and pushing me there, and I've gladly followed, not knowing why. That's how I ended up in Kansas."

"Where do your folks live?" Ruth asked, with obvious relief. Not being able to ask questions was against Ruth's nature, and now that the subject had been broached, she could set her big personality free.

"Evergreen, Colorado. Chinese people make up the second largest ethnic group there because so many couples adopted from China." She beamed with the memory of it. "Colorado has always been my home. I love the mountains, the adventure of hiking to the tops of them and gazing at the awe-inspiring vistas. It's the reward reserved for those who dared to make the journey, and it's never failed to take my breath away. So when I announced to my parents that I wanted to attend a university in Kansas, they were more than amused. I had a thousand excuses, but the truth was that my soul was once again being pulled, and even though I didn't know why, I had to follow."

Enthralled by the story of another group's plan to journey through time to meet again, George had to ask, "When you signed up for Gilbert's class, were you aware of the other girls—well, monks—who were also in that auditorium?"

"No, I don't think so. I believe I was being drawn to Father John, because the day he stood up in class and offered the invitation for this New Year's Eve meditation, my heart opened so fast it almost hurt. I knew at that moment that something incredible was happening to me."

My curiosity forced me to ask if she remembered any of the other girls from when they lived together in the monastery, or if they remembered her.

"Right now, all I know are the things I've been told, and some things I have gleaned from my dreams." Smiling at me, she continued, "Gilbert eased my mind by telling me about you, Hillary. He believes we have a lot in common, but I'll let you be the judge of that. You see, I began having dreams my freshman year about a very strange place on the top of a mountain."

She paused to look at me, and I knew we were kindred souls.

"It took me a while to remember my dreams," I admitted with a sigh. "And when I finally did, I wanted to forget them."

"I knew mine held significance, but the brutality was more than my heart could take," Indira replied. "But now that I am here among the other girls—monks—I hope to remember the love that we shared. My heart rejoices at the thought of what is to come, while at the same time I feel sorrow, knowing that not all of us were able to complete the journey that we had planned. If death befell them, I pray that it was swift and that all of them will find their way back to us." Her eyes began to water, but she wasn't embarrassed. "You see Hillary, we are much alike, but I find myself at the beginning of my learning, while you are well along the path."

I was momentarily speechless. Was I really well along? "What happens next?" I managed to ask, as my insides fumbled with the implication of her compliment.

"We will begin our lessons with McCollum, and because there is no one among us with conscious memory as McCollum holds for the Druids, we will also be led by The Teacher."

Now I felt an emotion I would never admit to anyone—jealousy. I mean, Will and the boys were one thing, but Will and a group of very attractive girls gave me a totally different feeling. I found myself both surprised and ashamed by my initial reaction, but managed to hide it until I could with deal with it later.

Father John joined in to explain: "Until we understand the part we are to play at this gateway to enlightenment, we'll need The Teacher to help us by filling in the blanks, and to nudge us in the right direction."

"I believe the training that you've had with The Brass Band will help you move along very quickly," Will added. "After all, you and your group are only one lifetime removed from your incarnation at the monastery, and you were all highly evolved."

"We are one thousand nine hundred and sixty some years beyond our lifetime as Druids," George said, laughing. "We're incredibly lucky to have McCollum as our beacon and teacher."

"I've never thought of McCollum in that manner before, but you're correct," Dr. Edwards agreed. "I find it amazing that he came into this lifetime with so few veils that he was able to recall every detail of the Druid plan, recognize each of our souls, and draw us to him at this precise point in time. It's really mindboggling, and pretty much a miracle in my mind."

I excused myself to go to my room to rest. I was no longer experiencing morning sickness, but I was tired a lot. Ruth walked upstairs with me, eager to have a shower while there was still hot water.

"The parallels are interesting, don't you think?" Ruth asked, when we were out of earshot. "I mean, you and Indira, the McCollum and Father John beacon thing, and the plan to come back now! I wonder who my counterpart will be? I suppose Indira had a right-hand monk." She laughed.

"No one could possibly be as irreplaceable as you," I remarked. "There is only one you, Ruth Witherspoon!" I roared as I disappeared into my room. "And thank God, you're mine!"

The Brass Band had one last meeting in McCollum's quarters before we adjourned to begin the New Year. The fire was roaring, and we all took our seats as McCollum began.

"Our army is growing in strength, for the Tibetan monks bring much power with them, although it is not yet honed. The battle is well underway as the dark forces try to close the window from which enlightenment will dawn. I thank you, Father John, for your wisdom in bringing us your precious brethren. Now, we must scrutinize our position and bring forth the light in a fashion that will cause the darkness to fall away."

To my great relief, the retreat ended with me still on my feet, without an embarrassing replay of what had happened the previous year. At no time during the retreat did my soul try to flee the premises, requiring the entire gathering to chant for its safe return. I was able to walk out of the celebration under my own power. So as far as I was concerned, 2012 was going to be a very good year.

CHAPTER
TWELVE

January 6, 2012

Will's duties as The Teacher for our new monk counterparts began immediately. That left me with the entire day to myself. I was excited to have some time to rest before school was back in session, so after Will kissed me goodbye, I closed my eyes and slipped back into a deep restful sleep.

Bang, bang! I woke, groggily wondering why Will wasn't using his key, but when the banging didn't stop, I regained my senses enough to put on my robe and look out the peephole.

Ruth was on the other side, red faced, her fist raised for one final assault on the door. "Hold on, Ruth!" I yelled, attempting to unlock the door before she hurt herself.

Ruth entered like a bull charging a matador. She was as mad as I'd ever seen her. "You won't believe it! Your creep has decided to be *my* creep, too. I was just on campus and—"

"My creep? Are you talking about Jack Black?" I asked, praying that he hadn't done any more than really piss Ruth off.

"The guy's like a freakin' tornado, suckin' everybody up around him and spitting them out broken. Some of the people I used to respect around campus are hanging out with him now and vomiting the same vile crap that Black promotes," Ruth shouted, slinging her two-ton purse against the back of the couch. "He has a squad of goons terrorizing students! He saw me, and if it wasn't for the flock of crows in a nearby tree, I think he would have come after me!" She couldn't resist laughing. "Black wasn't sure if the crows were guarding me or not. After that attack by Gus, I think he's a little spooked. For all I know, one of them might have *been* Gus, because they sure made a racket when he looked my way." Ruth threw herself into the overstuffed chair and took a deep breath. "Okay, I feel better now."

My eyes must have looked like saucers, because Ruth immediately began backpedaling. "Okay, maybe *terrorizing* was a little bit strong. I mean, his goons weren't beating students up or shoving their heads down toilets, nothing like that. It was all emotional intimidation—maybe just bullying. Keep in mind, Hillary, I'm a drama major."

I pulled my robe tight around me and sat down; she had absolutely caught my attention.

"I've become more sensitive lately," Ruth said, as casually as if she were talking about which shoes to wear. "I could feel the hatred radiating from Black and his thugs even if it's not apparent to others. So I wrapped myself in white light. I should have included the birds. too. Black recognized me and began to come toward me with his dark, depressing self, but then he decided to turn back. I think he ran into my force field and was too embarrassed to admit that he had no power over me." Ruth sighed, relaxing back into the chair and crossing her arms and legs dramatically.

I opened my mouth to speak and found it took a couple of tries before I could actually formulate words. "I am so proud of you, Ruth! Were you frightened?"

"No, not at all," she said, changing the subject. "And before I forget the most important thing—"

"Ruth, the most important thing is that you are safe and—"

"We can talk about it in the car," she interrupted. "My parents have been dying to meet George, so Mom's invited us up this weekend. We'll drive up Saturday and drive back Sunday evening. Don't tell me no, Hillary," she said, emphasizing her need for me to be there when her parents met George by giving me her infamous *please, please, please* eyes. "All four of us on a road trip—it will be a blast. Just pack casual. It's just dinner at home." She heaved her purse back over her shoulder. "We'll leave around 9:00 a.m. tomorrow," she added with a wave over her shoulder as she walked out the door.

I walked back to my warm bed and crawled in. I wanted to make the most of my last day of rest, but it took a while to erase Jackson Black from my mind.

January 7, 2012

We didn't talk on the way to Kansas City … Ruth did. She was a ball of nerves and excitement, rolled up into one energized package. George and Will just kept looking at each other on the verge of laughter, but they held it in, not wanting to push her over the brink. We pulled to the curb a block from the Witherspoons' front gate so Ruth could do some breathing techniques to calm herself down. We all joined in with her for encouragement, and ten minutes later, we pulled up to the gate and she punched in the code.

The look on George's face reminded me of myself the first time I'd taken the long drive from the gate to the front door of this mansion. It's rather impressive even if you've been told what to expect. Ruth's parents were on the front steps, shivering, as we pulled up to the house, so we quickly jumped out of the car to usher them back inside to warm up.

Ruth made short business of Will's introduction. "Mom and Dad this is Will Emerald, Hillary's husband." There were handshakes all around, and then she pushed George to the forefront. Standing on tippy-toes, she peered over his shoulder to see her parents' expressions. Smiling like an idiot, Ruth said absolutely nothing, so George made his own introduction.

"Mr. and Mrs. Witherspoon, it's nice to meet you. I'm George Elliot."

The room was silent … I mean dead silent! Ruth must have used up all of her words on the drive, so I stepped forward. "Will and George are best friends; they grew up together. Things couldn't have worked out more perfectly for Ruth and me."

By now, Ruth was coming out of her stupor, but it seemed like her parents were fading. I motioned for Will to take Mr. Witherspoon's arm as I helped direct Mrs. Witherspoon into the sitting room. "Call me Bob," Mr. Witherspoon said, as he lowered himself into a chair. The big man had a healthy pink complexion that was getting pinker by the minute. "This is my wife Joyce," he continued, as Mrs. Witherspoon dropped onto the sofa while attempting to give a Miss America wave.

I heard Ruth begin to sputter. "You guys stay put," she directed her parents, "and we'll bring you some coffee." Her mother nodded yes, and she curled up and closed her eyes. The snoring from the other corner indicated that Bob was long gone.

We all burst into laughter when we reached the kitchen. "I didn't know my parents drank," Ruth remarked, "but they seem sloshed."

"Nope, that's not it," George said, pulling Ruth in for a hug. "Remember how McCollum talks about the *general public*, and how he dials the energy in the house way down when a workman or a visitor comes in?"

"Yessss …" Ruth responded slowly.

"Well, we were all very wound up when we came in, and I think our combined energy kind of bowled them over," George said, gesturing to the other room. "Let's dial it back a bit, so I can impress your parents with my charm."

Ruth pinched his checks and kissed him on the lips before jabbing him in the ribs. "I've been trying to increase my life force for so long that it didn't occur to me that my parents are the general public. How about that!"

I had the coffee ready and six mugs on a tray. "How do Bob and Joyce drink their coffee?"

"Black!" George and Will said together.

"I'll bring some half and half for when they begin to come around," Ruth added.

Ruth and I took over cooking dinner. The staff had the night off, and we wanted it to be edible. We set the table in the formal dining room and turned on some upbeat music to help Ruth's parents stay energized until they got a little more used to us.

George was very charming, and I knew the Witherspoons loved him, even though they spent most of their time napping. That left us with a lot of Jacuzzi time, which didn't disappoint me at in the least, although my feet were the only part of me allowed in the water because of my pregnancy.

Ruth's sister, Sissy, dropped by while we were enjoying our morning dip and sat next to me, dangling her feet in the water. It was interesting that she was just fine around us. I figure it was because Will and George were mostly submerged.

"Oh Ruth, I forgot to tell you," I said, "I talked to my Mom last night and Gus was cozy in the nest box that Dad built for him in our barn. He had nothing to do with the reaction of the birds on campus." I knew I didn't have to worry about Sissy overhearing because she was deep into a philosophical conversation with George.

"Must have been a reaction to the bad juju being flung around," Ruth concluded. "I think I'll start carrying bread crumbs so they'll stick around, because they sure work great as a Jack Black repellent."

"Hey Hillary," Sissy interrupted, as bubbly as ever. "I saw Bennett the other day. He's home for the holidays and as hot as ever.

He said to tell you congratulations on your marriage."

I could feel Will bristle as she turned innocently to him. "He thinks you're the luckiest guy in the world." Will smiled and said nothing as a huge grin spread across George's face.

After lunch the men retired to the library while Mrs. Witherspoon asked Ruth and me to come to her room. We followed her up the stairs and down an incredibly long hallway and through a set of dramatic double doors. The room was about six or seven times larger than my bedroom and elegantly appointed with a comfortable seating area. Joyce motioned for us to be seated by the fireplace while she retrieved something. We watched as she removed a picture from the wall, revealing a safe. She began dialing a combination into it. Opening the safe, she pulled what looked like a very ancient box from it and shoved the door closed, spun the mechanism, and rehung the painting.

Hesitantly, she sat down across from Ruth, taking a few uncomfortable moments to find the right words. "This is something that I imagined I would pass on to you shortly before my death, but after spending time with you this weekend, I believe it is meant to be yours now." Looking shyly up at Ruth, she continued, "It has been passed down through my family for centuries, from mother to daughter, never being in a male's possession. I imagine when it all began, the women knew what it was used for, but over the years the meaning has been lost, and now only the tradition remains. I've always kept it locked away, not because I think it is of great value, but"—she searched for the proper words—"but because it has power. It makes me feel … well, funny. It gives me a warm feeling in my chest and makes my brain go fuzzy. I really don't understand anything more than what I've said, except … well, the funny feeling I get inside of me when I'm near it is very similar to the one I get when you come home to visit."

Ruth remained entirely motionless as her emotions began to

overflow.

"I'm not frightened by you, dear," she said, reassuring Ruth by taking her hand. "You are everything your dad and I could have ever dreamed of. You are intelligent and witty, beautiful and inspiring, confident, and full of life. And darling, that's why I know this is yours."

Ruth's mother handed her the container to open. It was a box within a box, and as Ruth lifted the even more ancient box from within, I could also feel the power.

"Open it, darling," Joyce urged, and with gentle fingers, Ruth opened the second box. Inside rested a simple piece of wood that was twisted into a knot. It looked like a Christian cross, but felt much older.

Leaning back in her chair, Ruth's mom seemed to be bathing in the energy, unafraid because of her daughter's presence. "It feels good, doesn't it," she said with eyes closed.

"Mom, this is magnificent. Tell me the story again. How did it come to you?"

"Your great, great grandmother, who was my great grandmother on my grandfather's side of the family, was Italian. That's where your beautiful olive complexion comes from," she said, gently brushing away Ruth's tear. "My grandmother said someone might steal it, and warned my mother to keep it hidden. I've never understood why. I can't imagine it has much monetary value, but I followed in the family tradition and kept the secret."

Ruth said, "I believe that the women who passed this down through the centuries were right, Mom. This is something very special." Placing it back into its box and closing the lid of the larger box to keep it safe, Ruth lifted it to her heart. "I'll uncover its secrets, and tell you all of them because you deserve to know. You've been its guardian, which makes you a very extraordinary woman." Ruth almost lost it, and her voice quivered. "Mom, you are a very special person."

I watched as they both cried, touching each other's hands and faces in complete silence, and I knew I was witnessing an ancient ceremony, an elder relinquishing her power and passing it into the hands of a more powerful guardian.

On the way home Ruth was not her normal, talkative self—she was completely silent, holding her box on her lap. She spoke her first words around Topeka. "Do you think it was passed down through my family and was destined to be mine?"

"I suppose if nothing is really an accident, then yes, regardless of the artifact's path, you are the one that it was meant for," Will answered thoughtfully. "If the brass bowl was on a parallel journey that intercepted Father John's, then why would this be any different?"

Again the car was quiet.

"But am I the final owner, or am I to pass it along to another?"

"I think you will pass it along to our daughter," George answered, without giving it much thought.

"Our daughter," Ruth came to attention. "Our daughter!"

"Yes, Ruth, do you think that after you've been my mate for centuries I'd suddenly decide not to spend the rest of this life with you?"

Ruth blubbered, said, "I love you, too," and nuzzled into his neck and began to cry … again.

I honestly didn't blame Ruth for becoming overly emotional. But just the same, I was glad to be on our way home.

January 9, 2012

George put an exhausted Ruth to bed early and then came up to spend some quiet time with Will and me. There hadn't been much time lately to just sit and talk. The appearance of the Tibetan monks was keeping Will—or should I say *The Teacher*—busy. After all, the monks were college students in this incarnation, and a lot of what they were learning was still new to them in this lifetime.

I made tea and joined Will and George at the table. "How's Ruth doing?"

"Emotionally drained, but great. I talked to her for a while before she fell asleep and she told me some pretty major things."

"Major in what way?" I asked, knowing that George and Ruth kept no secrets from us.

"Ruth feels like the gift from her mom puts her on an equal footing with the other Brass Band members. She's always felt a part of it, but not an equal until now." George waved off our rush to comment. "I know, I know. It surprised me, too. But the idea that that box came through time to be with her raises her self esteem, and in her mind, moves her up a notch from your guardian."

I grimaced at my insensitivity. "I had no idea, George. I'm so sorry."

"I'm with her every day and had no idea. There's no need to feel bad, Hillary. She's found you willingly throughout the centuries because of love, not duty. Now she has a journey that is totally about her, and when she figures out what that artifact is used for, she's going to take full advantage of it." George looked delighted with the new situation.

"Can we help?" I asked, trying hard not to feel like a terrible friend.

"No, I don't think so," George answered in his gentle manner. "I think she'll ask if she wants our help. I think this is going to be very enjoyable for her."

It was then that I felt it for the first time, a little pinch that made me close my eyes. I placed my hands on my abdomen and waited for the sensation to pass. I thought I might have overdone things while we were in Kansas City, so I excused myself, saying I needed to get some much needed sleep. But I really wanted a moment alone with my baby.

I slipped into bed with my hands open, palms up, and began

looking for that amazing feeling that was my son. "There you are," I said, as love enveloped me and I slid into sleep.

CHAPTER
THIRTEEN

AD 38

I sit astride my warhorse in the silence. When dawn breaks and the shadows disappear with the night, my men will face the greatest army Rome has ever assembled. Standing beside me are the three Druids most dear to my heart: my beloved Liam, Rutiah, my guardian, and Georog, the only one of them who is truly trained for battle.

My legs tense as my mare lurches forward. There is a painful explosion of blinding color inside my head, and I fear I have taken a fatal blow to the skull. Half dazed, my eyes fly open in search of the enemy.

I can see the flora around me in exceptionally sharp detail. I can see each fracture in the fragile leaves that litter the ground beneath my feet, and I see every minuscule branch of the forest that surrounds me so vividly that it is startling.

Every thought is crystal clear, as if my mind is perfectly balanced on the point of a pin. It is then that I become aware of the most amazing phenomenon.

This is my very first dream, the one that I've been waiting for. But this time it's very different from when I dreamed it in my dorm room freshman year, because now I am looking back from the other side. I am totally conscious in this ancient world of primitive warfare and bloodshed. I can feel the heavy weight of my chest plate and smell the damp forest … but today I know that I also exist in 2012, and today I am determined to change the path of the arrow that killed my beloved Liam.

I hear the clank of Roman armor as they take their positions across what will soon be our battlefield. I close my eyes to pray to the Gods as I have done a hundred times before, but this time I am aware of what the future brings. I silence my mind, open my hands palms up, and release my power.

I hear the flint strike as our shape-shifters bring their fire to life, and listen to the subtle change in Gillian's breathing as he begins his ritual to share nature's powers. I feel each hair on my arms move as the wind dances with the sunrise, and I catch the sound of a nervous horse as its hooves tap upon the stone underfoot, and I know that the great General Marcus Flavius has arrived.

I listen to the shaft of a Roman arrow sliding past the others as it is pulled from its quiver, and recognize the sound of stretching sinew and the snap of the arrow's release. Time strangely begins to slow as I tilt my head to pick up every movement of the air. I extend my arm and close my fist to feel the broad head of the arrow slide across my palm. Tightening my fingers, I feel the grain of the wood slipping past, until the fletching touches my hand.

In that one moment, my mind races through the entirety of my soul's journey—its creation, its lives and deaths. I see the pain of human existence, which I have both endured and caused; the love that I have received and willingly given; the heartbreak, the cruelty, and incredible beauty of it all. And I realize that it has always been perfect.

I open my hand and I let the arrow fly!

January 19, 2012

Will felt the violent jerk of my body as I reacted to the force of the arrow that had been driven through his body. My eyes flew open, the stench of Liam's blood still filling my nostrils. I screamed as Will gathered me up into his arms. A torrent of tears flowed down my face as

Will whispered words of comfort.

"Hillary, I'm here. The Wolf's Moon is setting," he said, soothing me as he rocked me in his arms. "Shhhh, you're safe now."

I begged Will to call McCollum and tell him we had to gather in his quarters at dawn. "I need to talk with all of you. I … I …" and that was all I was able to say before I broke down, wholly out of control.

As we knocked on McCollum's door, I could hear the boys chanting downstairs. Their voices began to calm my soul, but could do nothing for my eyes, which were all but swollen shut from crying. Will kissed me softly on the forehead, and I felt his familiar hum circulate through my body. I knew he was supporting me with his life force, which brought on a new round of tears.

When McCollum opened the door, I caught the scent of an exotic tea brewing. I looked around, noticing it wasn't the unusual arrangement. There was a large table in the center of the room where all the Brass Band members were already seated, obviously waiting for our arrival. In a daze, I sat where McCollum led me to sit, but I had nothing on my mind other than making my confession.

As the sunlight lit the room with brilliant streaks of yellow, I began to recall the previous night's journey. The room grew silent. I closed my eyes, took a deep breath, and positioned myself atop my horse. I was Hilsbeth again, and as everything slowed, I could once again hear the hooves of the General's horse dancing on the loose stones before the battle began.

"This is where everything began for me, the very first battle I ever remember dreaming about," I explained, rubbing my hands over my face. I knew the depth of my sorrow was breaking my mom's heart, and that it was taking every bit of her willpower to stay in her seat. Dad wrapped his arm around her, drawing her near as I continued my story.

"I've never seen it as clearly as I did last night," I said. I looked around the room, into the faces of my beloved Druids. "I heard you strike the flint as you lit your fire, Dr. Edwards, and the sound of your breathing as you settled into the fork of a tree, Gilbert." I looked up and found compassion in his eyes. "I knew our young and old were safe because I could feel Kathryn and Terrance within me." Mom sobbed softly as I forced myself to continue. "I shared Georog's fear and watched as he placed himself in front of Rutiah to protect her. I was humbled by the extent of your love." I said, locking eyes with Ruth.

I could feel George doing the same thing now, moving closer to Ruth in case she needed him. I could hear Will's heart beating now just as I had heard Liam's on the Druid battlefield—strong and powerful beside me. Horrified by my choice not to stop the arrow that killed him, I opened my hands, palms up, and felt my arms assume the outstretched position Hilsbeth used when gathering her power. I silently prayed to the same Gods Hilsbeth had prayed to on that dreadful morning, and then I tried to explain my realization that by changing *that* moment, I would change this one. I tried to explain that I didn't believe my selfish attempt to move Hilsbeth's powers forward into this lifetime was worth the risk of losing what we shared together.

"I heard the arrow puncture Liam's chest, and I heard his heart burst, the gurgling of blood, and his … his last gasp for breath," I confessed, as my world fell apart.

I felt a hand in mine. Will lifted it and placed it against his chest. "It still beats, Hillary. I cannot be killed."

I opened my eyes and met Will's infinite blue gaze. Then I let myself collapse in the joy and pain of it all.

As my sobs subsided and I became fully Hillary, leaving the battlefield behind, I felt a hand gently lift my chin. "Dear One, you have reached a monumental moment," McCollum said, smiling into my swollen face. "Now, you must let yourself heal and forgive."

It's hard to explain what happened to me next. It was a straightening of my spine, a weight being lifted off of my soul. My breath consisted of something other than air. It felt like power!

"Even though I have watched you silently suffer, Hillary," McCollum continued, "I could not allow myself to ease your pain, because when your dreams allowed you to become Hilsbeth, Hillary was also growing in wisdom. Your memories united the Brass Band in a way that could not have happened without your intimate knowledge of each one of us. You alone brought to life the visions of times past, which gave everyone a way to move forward on their path in this lifetime. The Brass Band's belief in you gave them the courage needed to see themselves as powerful beings."

I instinctively placed my hand upon my belly and felt a change in the spirit within me. *I'm sorry I woke you*, I spoke silently within my mind, mentally rocking him back to sleep. "Rest now and grow strong until the day you walk with us in this world." I felt his energy soften before I let my mind return to McCollum.

"Some will never have conscious memories of their Druid lives—only the amazing stories you have provided—and because of that, this morning we celebrate you as both Hillary and Hilsbeth!" McCollum waved to Jimmy, his young nephew, who had been sitting quietly on the bed that McCollum sometimes made for him near the fire on nights when he could not sleep. He immediately jumped to his feet and rushed out the door.

"We move beyond those moments in time that we cannot change, to the ones that we must change!" McCollum stepped aside as the door opened and a number of young men entered with trays overflowing with fruit and pastries, setting them on the long-forgotten table in front of me. The candles were lit and the coffee cups refilled and McCollum began to regale us with joyous stories of our Druid lives long before the Romans came.

CHAPTER FOURTEEN

January 20, 2012

I awake to the roar of a motorcycle and hear a female voice. "Oh good, you remember me, Hillary," the lady in leather says as she strides toward me. "I was afraid you might have forgotten me."

"How could I forget the one who told me someone wants my husband dead?"

"Did I say it was your husband's life that was in danger?" she says, taunting me. "I can't remember which 'he' I was referring to."

Her gaze lowers, and my hands automatically cover the son who sleeps within me.

"You and yours no longer interest me," she says, circling me slowly as if I were prey. "That's for you to deal with, little girl."

"Mine to deal with? Tell me what you mean!" I demand. I take a defensive stance, but I feel something slipping away within me.

She just laughs. "My concerns lie in a completely different arena, and I believe you can help me. Be a good girl, Hillary, and tell me where the brass bowl is."

Caught completely off guard, I just stare at her.

"The brass bowl, Hillary ... where is it? I have searched the world over for it, and now it's so close I can smell it," she sneers. I watch her face turn red as her blood pressure rises, and the silence between us grows deafening. "It's taken me decades to get the scent

again, and I'm as close now as I have ever been."

Dr. Edwards' words haunt me: "I find it difficult to believe that a bowl that manifests and sings wouldn't have been historically significant."

"Where is it, Hillary?" she yells as she throws me to the floor.

January 20, 2012

I woke up alone and terrified. "Will where are you?" I cried as I grabbed for my cell phone. "Ruth, oh Ruth … Please hurry!" was all I could manage.

Ruth was at my side within minutes. "What's wrong, Hillary? Tell me what's wrong?"

"It's bad, Ruth. I had a terrible dream. She made me think Will was in trouble … then my son." I couldn't think. "I can't feel a life inside me! Oh, Ruth, something is wrong!" I cried. "There's blood."

"Hold this," Ruth insisted, as she wrapped my fingers tightly around her precious artifact. "We need to get you to the hospital right now." She draped my robe around my shoulders, and arm in arm we made our way to her car.

Ruth came with me into the examination room and helped me change into a gown. I lay down on the table, uncomfortable on the crunchy white paper, my head resting on the tiny pillow. Ruth held my hand while we waited for a doctor.

"It's always belonged to women," Ruth stated simply, "so I figure we should keep it with us." She placed her little relic on my heart chakra.

I managed a weak smile. "I'm just glad you're here, Ruth."

Ours eyes met, and words weren't necessary. She squeezed my hand and I held on tight as we closed our eyes and opened our free hands, palms up. We both knew what we were searching for.

When neither of us felt another living soul in the room with us, Ruth held me and we both cried. When the doctor entered and completed his examination he let his head fall. He broke the news to me in the same way I imagine he had to many other prospective mothers before me. "Your pregnancy was not successful, but you are young..." I stopped listening because this horrible news was merely the final confirmation of what we Ruth and I already knew.

The door opened, and a crestfallen Will entered. His heart was ripped into a million pieces, but his only thought was for me. He gathered me up in his arms and I melted into grief.

"Our baby is gone ... he left," was all I could say as my chest heaved with despair.

"Shhhhh, Hillary ... we'll be okay," Will said, consoling me, brushing my hair away from my face to kiss away my tears.

I thought of all of the death I had seen in our Druid lifetime. I had lost my friends, family ... everything. But nothing prepares a person for this kind of despair. It was unbearable. The doctor asked if I needed a sedative, and I surrendered because my anguish was so bottomless that I couldn't breathe.

When Will and I arrived home and opened our apartment door, Mom was there, sitting silently with her hands crossed in her lap. She rose to her feet and took me in her arms. "There, there," she whispered, because words were meaningless. Will released my hand and Mom took me into the bedroom.

She had changed the sheets and placed a bouquet of lavender on the nightstand. I moved mindlessly and let her fold me into the blankets and tuck them in around me as she had done when I was a child. She gently touched my check as tears began to stream down hers as well.

"Mama," I said, calling her by the name I used when I was a little girl. "What do I do now? I don't know how to make the hurt go away."

Bending, she kissed my forehead. "You will make it through this because you are a very strong young woman," she replied, and she sniffled. "And I will be here with you." She handed me a pill with a glass of water, and I went willingly into oblivion.

As I began to resurface, I could hear Mom whispering into her cell phone. She was talking to Dad, who was still at the farm. "She's very sad. Between losing the baby and the realization that she had to let Liam die, I believe her feelings of sorrow have just overwhelmed her."

When I rustled the bedclothes, she immediately got to her feet and motioned Will into the room. She left the room as Will walked to my side, looking as bewildered as me. "How are you feeling?" he asked, and then clarified: "Physically, I mean." He knew that emotionally, I was wreck.

"Better," I replied. "How are you doing?"

"I'm sad, sweetheart," he said with his heart in his throat. "McCollum called earlier to find out how you were doing and to ask if I would be able to visit with him tonight. I thought as long as your mom was with you, it would be okay if I went to see him later on."

"You go, Will. I'll be okay," I assured him.

He sat on the edge of the bed and as I buried my face in his chest, I heard a catch in his breathing. He wasn't one for crying, but today he let himself go. He slid in beside me, pulled the covers tight around us and held me as if it were the end of the world.

January 27, 2012

It had been a week, so I wasn't surprised when the members of the Brass Band began to gather in our living room as the sun set. They had been part of every important moment in my life for the last two years, so I supposed they wanted to make sure I was recovering okay and offer me condolences. And then I saw Dad walk though the door.

"Hi, Dad," I said. This was the first time I had seen him since New Year's Eve, and his eyes were filled with compassion.

"How's my girl?"

"I'm good, Daddy." But even though I was able to put on a strong face, he wasn't fooled. He placed his hands on the sides of my face and looked directly into my eyes.

"I know you're good, kiddo. You're one of the most amazing people I know, but don't let your strength keep you from fully feeling your emotions. Deal honestly with what you're going through and lean on the people who love you."

"I will Dad, but right now … I'm just not ready to talk."

"I'll keep you in my meditations," he said, "wrapped in white light because your soul is still music to my ears."

The memory of Dad as a Druid came to mind, melting the hard façade I was trying to build. I remembered the hours he'd spent in the temple, lost in the ether… tethered to Earth by the thinnest of threads. When he wasn't meditating, he was in his garden, digging in dirt to keep himself connected to the physical world. He was much the same in this incarnation, a farmer in search of consciousness.

I looked around the room, and seeing Ruth brought back the vision of the young girl standing at the gate of our Druid community. Arriving at dawn, she'd asked McCollum's permission to become my apprentice. Now she sat with George, a Druid warrior who'd fought by my side. I could see each of them so clearly, as if the barriers between the two worlds had dropped momentarily: the young girl who danced herself into trance, the boy who bent nature, and the alchemist who became a shape shifter.

The door cracked open and our last member came in. "Hi Father John. How goes it?" I asked … and my veils snapped back into place.

"Remarkably well, Hillary. The monks and I are taking much the same path as the Brass Band, and with The Teacher acting as our McCollum, we are making great strides."

"Speaking of The Teacher," Will said, squeezing my hand, "that's who will be speaking at our gathering tonight. McCollum has asked me to step aside and let The Teacher take the helm, so get comfortable everyone. McCollum has informed me that this will be a significant evening."

I turned and whispered into Will's ear, "Lords know, I could use the distraction." I was having a hard time getting back into the swing of things. The loss of our son hung heavy on my heart, even though I had carried him for only a few months.

"I'm sorry I can't be with you tonight, but I'll be back soon," Will said. "McCollum is having me do this for you."

I looked at him questioningly, "For me?"

"I don't know anything more than I'm telling you, Hillary."

His eyes were full of concern, so I reassured him with a smile and a kiss. "Like you said, you'll be back in no time at all, and what on earth can happen to me when I'm surrounded by this group? Don't worry, sweetie—I love you," I said as he reluctantly left me to take his seat at the front of the group.

Will's head drooped and his breathing slowed. I could feel George's excitement as he grabbed Ruth's hand in anticipation. It reminded me of that very first evening when I'd met The Teacher. George had said then, "No matter how many times I see this, it never gets old."

I closed my own eyes so I could feel the wind blow through me. I listened to Will fill his lungs with it. His body swelled as he drew in the energy of another *being*, and when his eyes opened, I knew my husband was no longer here.

The enlightened being stretched the arms of his newfound physical form and relaxed into it. Then with a smile, he raised his head, "Good evening."

The Teacher began to speak as he looked around the room to see who was in attendance. "This is a very remarkable evening indeed, because I also will be moving aside. Tonight there is a being who has a story for you. His tale crosses centuries, dimensions, and time itself."

I felt Dad take my hand in his, patting it as he used to when I was a kid.

"I'll let him introduce himself," The Teacher said, as another face replaced his. Will's facial musculature rearranged itself, along with his carriage and personality. The notion that our new visitor was an American Indian struck me instantly. He had become rather angelic in stature.

He looked slowly around the room, until his eyes stopped on mine. "Do you recognize me, Spirit Lady?" he asked with great tenderness. "Not necessarily in this form," he clarified, "but do you know my energy?"

My heart raced, not with recognition, but with apprehension as I shook my head no.

He placed his hands on his knees and took a deep breath as he prepared to talk. "I am the One who has traveled though time with single-minded determination. I am the one who has come, Spirit Lady, to reunite the two parts of your broken soul."

I had thought nothing could surprise me anymore, but that sure did. I let go of the death grip I had on Dad's hand and took a deep breath to calm myself so I could focus on what was being said.

"I first came across your sweet spirit thousands of moons ago," he continued. "You were floating above the brutal aftermath of a battle in search of something, but I know not what. You were so loving and respectful as you looked into the face of each fallen soldier, blessing each as you moved to the next, that I was profoundly touched, and my spirit wept for your loss. I was so captivated that I followed that lost part of you for a millennium, always gently pulling you toward the light, but never persuading you to leave the fallen soldiers."

He looked at me with an inquisitive expression. So I said, "No, I don't remember, I'm sorry."

"That is why I have come to you on this night of the no moon. The sky is completely dark, and there is no pull upon your soul." He smiled to put me at ease. "Like you, I have lived many lives and been all things, but tonight, when your mind is unclouded, I wish to tell the story of my last life here on Earth. Then all will become clear."

I nodded okay and watched him assume a more confortable position as he began his story.

"I was born into the Cherokee Nation during the dead of winter in the year 1922. My parents named me Eugene Atohi, which means 'He Who Laughs.' It was a very appropriate name for me because I found much happiness as a child, even though I was surrounded by incredible poverty. On my reservation alcoholism ran rampant, and most young men assumed their futures were bleak. But as I grew, I discovered the Great Spirit had placed a unique talent within me. You see, I could understand the voices of small animals that scurried in the prairie, and I knew what the wild horses whispered.

"Rumors of my talking with beasts spread quickly throughout the region, until one day a nearby rancher wondered if there was any truth to the gossip. He found me one afternoon, with my arms to the elbow inside a mare that needed help birthing a foal. After a short, one-sided conversation, he took it upon himself to find out the truth by hiring me." Smiling with malice, Eugene admitted, "My job never became anything more than cleaning the manure from the horse stalls, and I tired of it swiftly. But it was a job in the white man's world, and for a short time it allowed me view the world from a different perspective.

"Oklahoma was dry, and the sun beat down hard on the cracked earth during the summer my adolescent body finally changed into that of a man. My reputation had grown along with my physique, and within the tribes I was respected for my animal magic. So at the tender age of seventeen, feeling I had outgrown my humble beginnings, I decided to leave Oklahoma to prove my worth in parts unknown.

"I jumped a train headed toward Texas, dreaming of the land of longhorns and cowboys. As an Indian, I'd grown up thick-skinned and gotten used to being less than the dung stuck to a white man's boot, but now I was the best horse trainer in the Cherokee Nation. I was the one who communicated with horses, and foolishly I believed that I would be able to gain respect. You must understand, my family had survived *the Trail of Tears,* and by God, I was going to stand among the white men as an equal." Eugene laughed at his own naiveté.

"My first job was shoveling manure—again! I was kept away from the corral … until one day the white boys had a stallion too wild for them to handle. They thought there was a good chance the horse would kill me, so for a good laugh, they threw me a rope and made a dare against my manhood. I accepted both!

"I calmed the horse with my Cherokee tongue, answering its erratic movements with the gentle touch of my hand. Once I was on its back, I never let loose. The horse and I knew that all the limits had to be tested before we could come to a place of mutual esteem. I was a master of my craft, but so very innocent, oblivious to the situation I was creating for myself. I thought my performance would earn me inroads among the other ranch hands, but instead it earned me scorn. They weren't willing to be shown up by a stinkin' redskin, so at nightfall I was dragged from my bunk, hog-tied, and driven to a place so dusty that I choked when they threw me face down from the bed of their big, shiny pickup truck. I curled into a ball, bracing myself for a kick in the ribs—but that would have been humane in comparison to what they had in store for me. They left me locked in a metal shed, not more than five by five foot, with my hands and legs still tied. I heard the roar of the truck engine, and a moment later I was totally alone in the dark.

"They left me there for days. I wasn't sure what would kill me first, my body slow cooking in that sweatbox during the days, or the fear of facing my own mortality. I spent what seemed like an eternity with nothing to keep me company besides the eerie cries of the coyotes …

and the bugs I learned to call *dinner*."

"On what might have been the third day, I heard a truck in the distance. I wasn't afraid—at this point I would have welcomed death. The door to my prison flew open, and two tall shadows fell across me. One came near, nudging me with the toe of his boot to see if I still lived, while the other got ready for the fun."

"After they roused me with a bucket of water, I rolled onto my back, too weak even to sit up. 'Let's drag him outside and let the coyotes take care of disposing of the body,' one hissed, as I heard the click of a gun chamber rotating.

"'We're not leaving him for the coyotes until I'm finished with him," the other said. I felt my mouth being pried open. With no strength left in me to resist, an old wet rag being stuffed down my throat, and as my life ebbed, the men howled with laughter. They left me for dead, leaving the door open so the animals could drag my carcass away.

"I woke in a hospital bed on the Alabama-Coushatta Reservation. My body rapidly healed, but my spirit did not, for it had broken apart when my dreams died. I lay in bed letting my muscles atrophy, until the morning a tribal medicine man walked into my room.

"That ridiculous man insisted on taking me back to where I had been found. And because I had no strength to resist him, I once again found myself in the back of a pickup truck that pulled to a stop in front of my five-square-foot hell. Forced from the truck, I fell to the ground and drew a circle around me where I lay. Leaving me food and water, the medicine man ordered me to stay within the circular boundary until his return. Unbeknownst to me, I had just begun my vision quest.

"On my third night, the night of the waning moon, the darkness closed in so tight it was suffocating, and I heard the same eerie coyote screams that had haunted me when I lay dying inside my metal box. I was so terrified that I actually wished I had that thin piece of metal between me and the animals that would soon rip the flesh from my bones." Eugene chuckled at the irony.

"Fear engulfed me as I scrambled on hands and knees around the perimeter of the circle that now imprisoned me, consumed by the feeling of being watched. My heart hammered in my chest at a speed that should have killed me, bumping against my ribs and clogging my ears with a deafening rush of blood that made it impossible to hear.

"It was hours before I finally came to my senses, deciding that if death were upon me I would face it on my terms. I crawled back to the center of what was left of the dusty line the medicine man had drawn around me. There I strived to become the man I had once been destined to be. I sat cross-legged, as I had during ceremonies on the reservation, and mentally reinforced the area that I had decided belonged to me.

"I saw the glow of his eyes before I heard his low, throaty snarling. I fought to remain motionless as the lone coyote paced slowly back and forth, just a fraction of an inch from my line. He was considering what to do about me. I knew this because I could hear him as clearly as if he had been speaking out loud to me.

"'We are the same, alone and outcast,' I said telepathically, causing him to stop dead and scrutinize me cautiously.

"'I am alone of my own choosing,' he answered. 'And it is yet to be seen if I am an outcast.'

"The yelping of the pack was growing near. 'Will they cast you aside if you don't kill me?' I asked bluntly, knowing I had no time for casual conversation.

"'I am the one who decides who I shall be, not them, and I will not give them the power.'

"'So exactly who are you?' I asked the creature, as I watched his paw step into my circle.

"'I am a reflection of you, my friend.' His eye never left mine as he walked toward me. 'Sleep,' he ordered. 'I will watch over you while you find the parts of you that you have willingly given to others: your worth, your will, and your power to become ...'

"His voice faded as my eyelids became so heavy that I had no choice but to let them close. My head nodded forward, and I felt the warmth of the wild animal as he curled up against me. My mind let go, and I sank into the first deep sleep I'd had since the day the medicine man unceremoniously dumped me from his truck.

"I saw my parents and knew it was a dream, but my clarity of mind was remarkable. I watched myself grow from a babe into a man, and became aware of the inter strength that had driven me from the moment I emerged into this world. It was what had subconsciously pushed me to become more than what was expected of a poor, uneducated boy like me. It was that strength that enabled me to see clearly what had happened inside that metal shed. Without my blinders of judgment, those two cowboys' souls were laid open for me to see.

"One followed in his father's footsteps, brainwashed from childhood into bigotry and intolerance. His overpowering rage was such a part of him by adulthood that the idea of love was not appealing to his psyche. I saw the agony that kept him a captive to his past, and it taught me the necessity for me to release the anger that was also holding me captive.

"Then I saw the other, the one who had roused me with a bucket of water and stuffed the wet rag down my throat. I was astonished by the realization that he had been trying to save my life the only way he knew how. He knew I could not survive without water, so in what I had judged to be cruelty, he actually gave me the fluids that surely saved my life. And somewhere in the darkness, I found forgiveness for all of the people who had wounded me, and I began to heal.

"The coyote had disappeared with the dawn, never to be seen again. The fourth night was silent and uneventful. I slept visionless and alone. On the fifth night I finally forgave myself for what I viewed as my failures, bad judgment, and a multitude of inadequacies, and this self-forgiveness is what gave me back my will to live. I fell to my knees with gratitude for the second chance I'd been given, and felt all my forgotten dreams return. It was then that my Spirit Guide appeared to me for the first time." Eugene Atohi tilted his head, locking his eyes on mine.

I imagined Will somewhere behind that look, but intellectually I knew that no matter how much I wanted him to be with me, he wasn't here. Dad patted my hand to reassure me.

"There are several different kinds of Spirit Guides," Eugene patiently explained. "Mine is the archetype, who appeared to me in whatever form I needed to guide me along a particular path. Yes," he smiled broadly. "The Coyote was one of those forms. You, my dear Spirit Lady, also have a spirit who guides you, but yours falls into a different category. Your guide is an Ascended Master. He once lived in physical form, but in death moved to a much higher plane." His eyes twinkled with delight as he continued his story.

"My guide explained that *my vision quest* was complete because I had within me all that I needed to be whole. So on that last night, just as the day began to dawn, I sat blissfully alone in my circle, and I called the broken parts of my spirit back to me, for I had overcome what had stood in my way.

"I was a very old Indian who had lived a very full life on the day my soul walked away from the physical world for the very last time. It was there, in the astral plane where time doesn't exist, that we first met, and I discovered that you were in much the same condition as I had been in that hospital … with your soul broken. It was then that we struck our bargain. I would show you how to make your soul whole again, if you would give me *the spark of life* one last time before I began my final journey. For I had expanded beyond the need to be birthed into a physical form again."

The dark moon quieted my mind as the magnitude of what he was saying began to dawn on me.

"Knowing our spirits were forever linked to each other, I traveled back to the time you became broken, Spirit Lady. I saw your inner strength, and the commitment to duty that bound your body to Earth … as I watched the other half of you follow the one you were bound to by love.

"It was impossible for me to physically take you back to the location where your soul had initially been broken and draw a circle around you like my medicine man had done for me, but as I saw your heart ignite with the decision to incarnate again, I knew at once that when you were in human form I could finally fulfill my promise to you.

"I waited for the dawn of your womanhood. Then together with me as your Spirit Guide, we began your *vision quest*. At each full moon, when your veils were the thinnest, I helped you travel back to *the broken time*. As each moon rose in the black velvet sky, we returned to your past, and you slowly began to remember. And when we reached the point in time that you believed you had to change, you displayed great wisdom. You saw that moment with utter clarity... without your blinders of judgment. You let your Druid lifetime stand on its own, and although your heart broke, you did not. You forgave yourself for all you had held yourself responsible for, and you called the broken parts of your spirit back to you."

I heard sobbing, and was surprised when it wasn't me. In fact, I felt pretty steady at the moment, for as I experienced the past and present, so could I feel the support of both Liam and Will.

"There are always bargains, Spirit Lady," Eugene said. "As was there a bargain between the archer who shot the arrow and Liam who died. It was a balancing of an old karmic debt, which freed you both to be together again. I know it seems impossible, but these things take place deep in the subconscious, and few people are aware of their existence at that level. "

Eugene Atohi paused momentarily, and his dark eyes sobered as he thoughtfully continued.

"I am in deepest gratitude for my time with you," he said, bowing his head in respect, "for it was my soul that has lived within you. To complete the fulfillment of our bargain, you gave me a final moment of life and an opportunity to be loved with a purity I never realized existed. All of this will nourish me on my journey toward the Great Spirit. My only regret is that you were unaware that our time together was limited, for it was never my intention to be born again. You see, being human is a very seductive thing, and I could not risk being pulled away from my path, for I am your Ascended Master.

"Now, Dear Spirit, we have one more thing to accomplish together."

A momentary dread ran through me as I wondered if I'd be capable of what he might ask of me, for if my vision quest had been going on for almost two years, what could I do in just a single moment?

"Close your eyes," he asked softly.

I pushed my insecurities aside, closed my mind to the ticking of the clock and the sound of the refrigerator motor, and let only the voice of my Indian guide into my consciousness.

"Draw your energy inward, bring it to a single point of light between your brows, at your third eye. Now open your mind, Spirit Lady, to what you desire in life, and use your light to make it so."

I felt him touch my third eye, and basked in the sensation. Then, opening my eyes to tell him that I had felt the light, I saw Eugene Atohi's face fading away. Unable to hold back the tears that had been so close to the surface, I began to cry, not wanting him to leave me only an hour after I had discovered he existed.

Everyone in the room sat motionless as The Teacher resumed speaking. "I imagine there will many questions, but for tonight this must be enough. William Emerald has been away from his body far too long, and must return before we drain his lifeforce beyond repair. Please know the depth of Eugene Atohi's love for you, Hillary, and as he moves beyond this physical plane, there will always be a golden thread that will remain tied between you. Now, I bid you goodbye."

The Teacher crumpled forward, and as Will struggled to reclaim his body, I crawled to him and we wept together.

CHAPTER FIFTEEN

January 28, 2012

The Brass Band quietly left our apartment, while Will carried me to our bedroom. We would all meet downstairs for morning coffee, but I knew the others would also meet tonight to discuss whether they had heard what they thought they'd heard.

With great tenderness, Will placed me on the bed and crawled in to wrap himself around me.

"Did you hear any of it?" I asked, not knowing exactly how giving your body to someone else, twice removed, worked.

"Usually I go to another plane to meditate, but tonight it was important that I stayed. So, I wrapped my essence around you to anchor myself to this level of existence."

"I felt you," I confirmed, as I recalled the sensation of his life force supporting me. "I knew you wouldn't leave me alone if it was within your power to stay."

"We are bound together, Hillary, you and me," he whispered, pulling me closer. His body heat warmed our cold bed, and when I was on the verge of sleep, I asked if he would just hold me like this forever.

Will was still holding me when the sun came up. His body was hot, and as I snuggled in, I also found that he was hot for me. Smiling at the fact the he could still want me with my swollen eyes, red, stuffy nose, and less-than-stylish hair, I figured it was honestly true love.

"What?" he asked, knowing that I had a burning question from the tightening of my brow.

"I've lost both the babies—ours and Hilsbeth and Liam's. Do you think we will ever have a family?"

Before I could begin crying again, he took my face in his hands. "We've had many," he said, totally surprising me. "Did you think our life as Druids was the only one we've ever had?"

"Well … I've never thought about it that way."

"Let me assure you that we have birthed many children into this world, and when the moment is perfect, a soul will come to us and you will be an incredible mother." With amusement, he added, "Until that time comes, we will just have to practice."

After a long soak in the shower, my puffy eyes where almost back to normal and I felt calm enough to face the people waiting for me downstairs. I was used to being the center of attention after each full moon, but this was much more personal.

Will had gone ahead of me because he needed coffee, and I suppose to give me some time alone to gather my thoughts. When I arrived downstairs, it wasn't the solemn affair I was expecting. It was much more of a party. Ruth was serving coffee cake while George passed out huge, steaming mugs of spiced tea.

"Good morning, Hillary! George boomed. "Just in time for a cup of my newest blend." He pulled a chair out for me at the head of the table and attended to me while he carried on a conversation with Father John. "I never had a clue," he said, as he pondered whatever Father John had said, "Not a clue."

"About what?" I asked, surprised by the fact that my arrival hadn't made the room go silent.

"I just told George that last night wasn't the first time I'd seen your Indian!" an animated Father John said. "I saw him sitting beside you on New Year's Eve. Actually, I figured he was one of your guides even then. Remember, Hillary? I asked you about him. I just had no idea what a profound vision it was. I feel very honored."

"I can't believe I never saw him," George mumbled, as he sat the teapot on the table.

"In a way you also saw him that night," Will said turning to me, as he sat down to join the conversation. "Remember shavasana … the vision you had of our son?"

"Yes, I remember." I knew Will was right, and I smiled at his obvious conclusion, but inside I still felt an enormous loss that mere words could not erase. I listened to everyone's interpretation of the previous evening with a lightheartedness I didn't feel. For the first time among these dear friends, I was a fake.

February 2, 2012

Gilbert found me in the Union. I was trying to become invisible because it was easier to hide from my friends than to lie to them.

"I'm glad I found you," he said with enthusiasm. "Indira is on her way, and you are the reason we're meeting."

"Me?"

"Yes, you, my dear Hils," he answered, as he handed me a cup of coffee.

I warmed my hands by holding the coffee while I tried to pry more information out of Gilbert.

"It's not my place to tell you," he said, but he looked past me and smiled, and I knew this meant that Indira had arrived.

She was very distressed to see me, and not at all comfortable.

"We have to tell her," Gilbert insisted. "Sit down. It will make it easier."

I smiled and waited, giving Indira time to formulate her thoughts.

"Father John needs to be here, too," she insisted. "If you call him now, he might be here by the time I return with my tea." Indira stood and walked away. I unfocused my eyes so I could see her aura, which left a pretty pink trail even when she was upset.

I was on my second cup when our long-legged friend walked through the big glass doors. He had become very comfortable in his new college life, and had moved from a totally black wardrobe to one that included blue jeans. He also had a surprising number of friends who hung out at the Union besides us. I heard them call out his name as he walked down the center aisle, causing him to stop at more than one table to say hello. He finally spotted us when Gilbert, in an attempt to move things along, raised a cup of coffee into the air that he had prepared to Father John's precise taste. Father John gave us a nod, having evidently received the message, and excused himself to take a seat at our table.

Without prelude, he took a big swig of his coffee, turned to me, and began the conversation Gilbert and Indira had been so anxious about.

"You know that I can see Eugene Atohi?" It wasn't so much a question as a statement. "The last few times I've seen you, Hillary, I've also seen him sitting beside you."

A little confused, I searched my memory for when those times might have been. "Yep, but not since the dark moon. He's on a journey with the Great Spirit into the beyond."

"He postponed his trip," Father John stated flatly. "He won't leave you."

Indira grew pinker as she opened her heart to make this news easier on me, and I could tell by the lovesick look on Gilbert's face that he found it irresistible.

"I have also been in contact with your Indian guide," Indira added, giving more weight to the discussion. "But only during my meditation with the brass bowl. He's worried that he has once again damaged your soul. He sees how sad you are … even though you have been hiding it from us."

"Me?" I began to deny it, but then stopped—I knew this was a time for honesty. "Yes, I've been depressed since losing our baby, but I'm not broken. Please assure him that my vision quest will forever remain with me. I'm whole."

"Oh, nothing's going to be that easy," Gilbert said. He grinned tightly.

My dear friend Gilbert had helped me through enough rough spots for him to recognize when I wanted to be alone, so he broke the news of the impending gathering to me quickly. "Indira has come up with a plan that will work like a slingshot to send Eugene on his way. It will be a stupendous send off," he said, in an effort to make it sound fun.

"Don't worry, Hillary. Gilbert's exaggerating. It's more like a nudge," Indira said shyly. "It will be a very gentle release."

"I know you guys want to do what's best for me, but—"

"I originally envied your life," Father John interrupted, "because you know both the past and future. But until this moment, I hadn't truly understood how very difficult it must be for you to reconcile one with the other. Most of us don't remember a speck about those lofty contracts we made before we squeezed ourselves into these little human bodies … but just because you know doesn't make any of it easier on you."

Father John looked into my eyes for a long moment before saying, "Please Hillary, except my sincerest condolences on the loss of your son."

My hands flew to cover my mouth, and I squeezed my eyes shut as tight as I could in an attempt to stanch the tears. I knew I was profoundly blessed, and he was accurate in his assessment that I was unable to reconcile the loss of my baby with the reason for my dreams.

It was too abstract for my heart to grasp.

The table fell silent, letting me have space to feel the grief that I'd been so desperately trying to hide. It took a few minutes, and Gilbert gently wrapped his arms around me. Eventually I mustered the strength to ask when the ceremony would take place.

"At the Dark Moon," Father John responded softly. "It's auspicious timing, and our Indian friend will appreciate it."

I looked at my watch. "I've got to go to work," I said, picking up my books before I totally lost it. "Text me the details." I hurried toward the door, and the sanctuary of the library's glass-floored room.

February 7, 2012

Since the evening we spent with Eugene Atohi, my nights had been devoid of dreams. Although this made my sleep restful, I missed the visions of my Druid life. I had become a bit addicted to the adventure and the growth they brought to me. I now worried I might never have them again. So with anticipation of tonight's lunar pull, I closed my eyes as the fullness of the Storm Moon rose and waited for sleep to carry me away.

AD 38

"So Hilsbeth, to what do I owe this visit," McCollum asks, as he cracks his door slightly open.

"I'd like to speak to you of sadness."

One eyebrow lifts as he grants me entrance. "Is it you we speak of?" he asks as he invites me into his quarters.

"Yes," I reply, as my face heats with embarrassment. I walk directly to the fireplace where the logs smolder, and poke them into life. Warming my hands in the newborn flames, I keep my back turned so he cannot see my tears as I begin to talk.

"I find myself shrouded in sadness and paralyzed by the depth of

my negative thoughts."

I turn and lift my chin to gaze into his infinite blue eyes, ready to receive his profound wisdom, when he answers, "Then don't have the bad thoughts!" Smiling at the confusion on my face, he continues. "I don't mean to make light of your situation, but it is you who controls it. No matter the depth of sorrow, the choice to continue your life in joy or sadness is yours alone."

I find myself wanting to argue in defense of my despair, but McCollum will hear none of it.

"There will always be reasons, Dear One, and that is precisely the point I am making. You are the chooser. You have the option to drown in misery or find a way to live in joy." McCollum takes my hand to leads me across the room and simply says, "Change your mind! Decide to be happy! Delight in life, Dear One, because you hold the ultimate power and all decisions are yours alone to make!"

He pushes me toward the door, and as it closes behind me I hear him say, "You are the ruler of the realm of your existence. Choose well!"

February 8, 2012

"Did you sleep well?" Will asked, rising onto one elbow. "It's been a while since I've seen that smile."

"I talked with McCollum last night … the Druid one."

"I hope he eased your pain," Will replied, as his eyes searched mine. "I understand what you've been going through, because I'm sad and disappointed, too. We expected this experience to end with a baby boy, but Hillary, your soul has been healed, and you took a remarkable journey with an Ascended Master. And as for the rest … Hillary, we have time to try again."

I looked into his beautiful eyes, thankful for the karma that had brought me back into the arms of this loving man. "I love you, too, Will,"

CHAPTER SIXTEEN

February 10, 2012

Work had become a bit boring since Dr. Edwards no longer requested information from our library. He was now researching the origin of our brass bowl in texts much older than any that could be found within the walls of our university library. I longed to run into him in the glass-floored room, but I knew those days were probably over.

I got home from work at sunset and was surprised to find the house empty. I'd only been home about ten minutes when I heard a knock at the door. I hoped it was my husband, who constantly forgot his keys, but my senses told me it was more likely my dear friend Ruth.

"What a pleasant surprise," I said, opening the door with a big smile.

Ruth was also smiling, but didn't hurry in. "I guess you could call it a surprise," she replied, as Bennett Taylor stepped into view.

I stood frozen for quite a while before my manners took over and I invited them in. Both of them were suspiciously quiet, which made me nervous.

"Well, I hope it's good news," I said as an icebreaker.

Bennett looked up from where he had been studying his shoelaces, "It's great to see you again, Hillary. I have to admit that I was a bit disappointed when Ruth's mother told me you were married. I hoped we'd have a chance for another dinner."

"I don't think you're here to talk about that," I said, my impatience getting the best of me.

"I'm putting on some hot water," Ruth said, and she rushed off. "I think we're going to need a nice cup of tea with this conversation."

"It's a curious situation," Bennett finally began, already looking apologetic. "I took a position at my father's law office after graduation—yes, I know it's a copout." He smiled. "But I think my first case is interesting, and a bit serendipitous."

"Do you know what he's talking about, Ruth?"

"No," Bennett said before she could reply. "In fact, you can ask her to leave if you'd like to keep this confidential." He looked at us both and then continued in a very serious tone.

"A few days ago a woman who had just moved to the area hired our firm. She insists that you, Hillary Rubner Emerald, have in your possession an item that belongs to her."

"And which of these things does she say is hers?" I asked, raising my hands.

"She calls it a brass bowl."

I tried to hide my shock as Bennett looked away to open a folder, from which he pulled out a picture. He handed it to me. "This is the evidence she provided, along with the last will and testament of her grandfather. He was a European collector of period pieces, and according to this old police report, sometime between his passing and the settling of his estate, the brass bowl disappeared. The picture clearly shows identifying marks on the bottom of the bowl, so if you show me yours, we can get her off of your back as soon as I return to Kansas City."

"First of all, I don't own a brass bowl," I answered, with more calm than my racing heart felt. "Secondly, I wouldn't give it to you if I did." My rage threatened to overtake me as I pictured Father John holding his precious singing bowl, knowing I would never let it be taken away from him. "Who is your client, Bennett?" I asked, already knowing.

He hesitated, but after thinking it over he seemed to decide it wasn't client privilege. "Adriana Heinrich."

Bennett reached to pick up the picture and began to apologize, "I can see that you're upset, Hillary, and that's not what I came here for."

So much for holding my cards close to my vest, I thought, but I wisely kept my mouth shut.

"She's only a client, Hillary, but I consider you a close friend. I really don't want this to come between us."

I believed his sincerity, but I wanted there to be absolutely no doubt about who his client was. "Have you ever seen her wear leather?"

"She wears nothing but."

Ruth and I were sitting downstairs in front of the fire when George and Will finally got home. They were all smiles until they saw us.

"What's going on?" George asked, slowing to a stop.

Ruth couldn't help but blurt, "Bennett Taylor came to visit tonight."

It got the biggest reaction from Will. "He came to see you here?"

I stood to take Will's hand before he blew a gasket. "I must admit, I can't believe it myself, but yes. Come, sit. It's not at all what you're thinking."

Ruth and I recounted every detail, including an exact description of the marking on the bottom of the bowl. Then I recalled what I could remember about the lady in leather who had appeared in my dreams, and wondered aloud how she had ever tracked the bowl to me.

"Regardless of how she traced the bowl to us, confronting you is a lot easier than dealing with McCollum," Will surmised.

I had to agree he had a point.

"But how on Earth did she find Bennett?" Ruth asked.

None of us could come up with a good answer, and I found that thought unsettling.

We sat in front of the fire until Father John finally arrived home. He usually spent an additional hour with his beloved monks after The Teacher completed his lessons, which was the reason Will had arrived home ahead of him. The four of us looked up as the doorknob turned and continued staring as he walked into the room.

"Okay, what's up," he remarked playfully, as he lowered his lean body into a cross-legged position on the floor. Still high from the energy created from meditation, his smile was unyielding. "Come on, spill it," he said. "I assure you, it can't be as serious as those looks on your faces."

Will leaned forward, searching for words. "John, we had a visitor tonight. The lady in leather who appears in Hillary's dreams is real, and has filed a lawsuit claiming ownership of the brass bowl."

Father John's smile turned to genuine confusion. "I have memories of the Bowl. It sang in our monastery in the Himalayas for centuries. No one ever possessed it but us. At least, not until we had all died trying to protect it." And then it dawned on him. "There were a few decades when it was out of our hands, between the time I hid it in the wagon on the mountain trail and the time it was given to McCollum! Is that it? Is someone claiming it is theirs because of that short period of time?"

"Looks like it on the surface," Will replied calmly. "But nothing is ever as it seems. Adriana Heinrich, the confrontational lady from Hillary's dreams, is fishing for information. So I think for now we should assume that she's interested in the brass bowl for its power, not its wonderful singing voice."

Father John got to his feet and walked into the kitchen. "I'm calling Gilbert and Indira, because I'm the one responsible for its loss the first time around. I need to make sure it doesn't happen again."

He called Gilbert, and we listened to him repeat the events of the evening, after which he instructed him to hide the bowl and to tell absolutely no one its location. "No, not even I should know where it is, no one!" There was a moment of silence before he said, "We will discuss it in the morning, but for now you must keep the bowl safe at all costs."

After hanging up the phone, he turned to us and said, to reassure us as much as himself, "Gilbert and Indira have enough ingenuity to find a hiding place."

It was truly all that could be done, so we all went to bed and spent a restless night lost in our own thoughts.

February 22, 2012

The next time I saw the brass bowl was in McCollum's temple. It was the Dark Moon, the night I was to convince Eugene Atohi's spirit that I was fine and that he should continue his journey.

I quietly pulled Gilbert aside, needing to ask one final question before the ceremony began. "Did you check the bottom of the bowl for the marks I described from the picture?"

"It's funny how I never noticed them before, but yes, I did, and they're the same."

"I knew they would be. Darn it anyway!"

Gilbert raised his uni-brow, "Relax, Hillary. There's nowhere safer than in McCollum's temple, and besides, it's going to be the centerpiece of a wonderful going-away party. I can't wait to hear it sing farewell."

Bells began ringing and trays of billowing incense were lit, as the monks commenced the most hauntingly beautiful chant I had ever heard. The voices of the petite women rumbled and multiplied until you could swear that other voices from beyond our walls had joined them.

"It's the calling," Will said. "The higher realms are calling to Eugene. When the bowl begins to sing, it will be time to say good-bye."

I sat, letting the voices lift me, and as the bowl joined in, I could see the ghostly outline of my Indian guide enter the vessel.

One by one, each person in the temple knelt in front of the bowl, whispered Eugene's name into the palm of their hand, and then gently blew to send him on his flight into the beyond.

"Hillary," I heard someone say as I was helped to my feet. "It's your turn now."

As I knelt in front of the bowl, I could feel the air crackle as the energy swelled. I raised my palm to my lips and found that I had a few things to say before I said goodbye, so I gave myself the time I needed. "I know we struck a bargain, and I understand that I have to send you on your way. But I can't do it before I express my feelings of gratitude. I am profoundly thankful that you found me, for your love was what made me whole again. You've stood by me during my darkest moments, and were inside me during some of my happiest. I am honored to have been the one who gave you your final spark of human life, because I love you, too."

I blinked and let my tears fall freely, for I knew it was foolish to try to hide them from him. "Our bargain has been fulfilled, and now you have to go. Safe journey my dear, dear friend. Always carry me in your heart … for you will always be a part of mine." And then, saying *Eugene Atohi* softly into the palm of my hand, I blew to help his wings take flight.

I slept right where I had sat during the ceremony. Others chanted late into the night while the bowl sang on. I woke at sunrise as Gus cawed outside the temple window. I looked around to find myself among a sea of sleeping bodies. I tried to not wake anyone as I made my way to the temple doors, but failed miserably. I needed to quiet Gus before he woke the entire household. Mom had also heard his familiar call, and after she had gathered a few leftovers from the kitchen for Gus's breakfast, we both bundled up against the cold and walked outside together to find him.

"Gus! Come get your reward for a job well done," Mom shouted with delight. When the huge bird flew down to land in front of us, he didn't seem hungry at all—he seemed agitated. "What's up, Gus?" I asked when Mom finally got him calmed down.

"Maybe he just needs to rest," Mom said. She and I had researched crows enough to know that mystically they were meant to support your intentions, so we both assumed he had helped Eugene on his journey. We thanked him again, left his food in the fork of a tree, and moved inside, out of the cold.

Gilbert and Indira wrapped the brass bowl in a soft cloth and disappeared from the temple. They had become ghosts whenever they were in possession of the bowl. No one ever saw them leave or had the slightest idea where the bowl's hiding place was.

March 8, 2012

Ever since the ceremony, Eugene was often on my mind, and I wondered what a journey into the beyond would be like. I figured if two men as opposite as Alexander the Great and Jesus could agree on something, it was probably the truth. Alexander had said, "As it is above, so it is below," while Jesus stated, "On Earth as it is in heaven."

I figure that both statements referred to the relationship between our earthly selves and the part of us that also resides in the heavenly realms. I'd actually had the pleasure of running into my higher self a time or two in my loftier meditations, so I knew she truly did exist.

I let my mind wander until I was ready to go to bed. It was a full moon tonight, but since I hadn't had any Druid adventures since Eugene had left, I fully expected to have another dreamless night. I rolled over to hug Will goodnight and gave him a big smooch before I arranged my pillows for some well-deserved sleep.

March 8, AD 38

I know that I am not in my beloved Druids' encampment. I force my eyes to adjust to the shadowy light of the full moon and discover I am standing in the center of a city square, amid the remnants of a market that will surely be setting up again at dawn. And then I see the Temple of Jupiter. I am within Roman walls. This can't be happening, I think.

The streets are deserted until one person seems to magically appear out of thin air. He is draped in a toga made of the finest silk, and the ornamental clasp at his shoulder identifies him as a governor of Rome. As he approaches, I move my hand to my side, needing to assess the weaponry I carry.

"Having a problem placing me?" he casually says as he strolls toward me. "To be brutally honest, Hilsbeth, it's a mystery, for we have never met in these physical forms, face to face."

Panicked, I'm frozen to the spot where I stand by a crushing feeling of déjà vu.

The governor circles me slowly as he snarls insults. I can hear the sound of his robes sweeping the ground, while my mind fights for the recognition that will put me on even footing.

"You may know me as the judge and jury, for I can impose capital

punishment at my whim. And yes, I have executed many of your countrymen," he teases in an attempt to provoke me. "Please Hilsbeth, draw your sword. I dare you. For I can order you disemboweled for any action you take against me.

"Think Hilsbeth, think! I command the whole of Rome as far as this disgusting hunk of primitive dirt is concerned! I ordered that inconsequential general to hunt you down! Look at me you stupid twit!"

I might not have made the connection at all if not for his insufferable arrogance—inside the body of this Roman governor was the evil spirit of Adriana Heinrich! They were one in the same. "So this is your relationship to Marcus Flavius! You were the Roman governor in charge of his legion."

He bows deeply in response to my conclusion. "It requires a masculine body to rise to power in Rome, for in this century women are considered breeding stock, and that won't change for ... oh, another millennium or so." Adriana smirks. "And yes, Flavius is completely under my control. They all are, if they hope to reach centurion. No soldier would dare tempt fate while his entire livelihood depends exclusively on keeping me happy."

"Is that why Bennett Taylor is also willing to do your bidding?"

"Yes, there is that karmic connection that's not quite finished. It was simple to find him and even easier to control him. His subconscious has not yet let go of our commander/subordinate relationship. Unfortunately for me, you are still the one he cannot have, and that alone has always had the tendency to make him weak, dividing his loyalties. I've never been able to completely turn him to what you so aptly call the dark side."

"What do you want from me?" I demand. I can feel the weave of my hilt as I wrap my fingers around it—I stand fully armed for battle as Hilsbeth. Hillary is fast asleep.

"We remain in mortal combat, you and I," the governor replies. "Ahead of us dawns a new age, and we will both take bodies again. You will fight for the enlightenment of mankind, while I will come to keep

the status quo." Her aura turns black as her voice thunders in triumph, "I know the weak among humanity are more than willing to join me! Make them fearful and they react with hatred, racism, and bigotry, and I only have to plant the thought! Even the best of them are unaware that they are giving away their power, only to make me stronger."

"We will surprise you, Adriana!" I say with confidence. "You have no idea who you will be facing."

March 8, 2012

A hand was caressing my face in an attempt to calm me. "You're here with me, Hillary. We're in our apartment. Come back, now. Come back."

I clung to him as I opened my eyes, loving the scent of him and soothed to find him next to me.

"You're shaking!" he said.

"Probably because it wasn't one of my normal full moon dreams," I said, offering no further explanation. "I need time alone to get my thoughts straight." I could already see the dawn filtering into our bedroom and knew it wouldn't be long before the Brass Band was sitting in our living room. Will understood when I headed toward the shower without another word. I needed to recall every last detail.

Ruth, George, and Father John arrived within an hour. Gilbert took another fifteen minutes, the same amount of time that it took to get Mom, Dad, and Dr. Edwards hooked up on a conference call. McCollum joined us via computer.

"My worlds are merging," I announced, "and the loose ends are coming together."

The laughter from the moment before dissolved, and the room became totally silent.

"Last night the lady in leather revealed herself as the Roman

Governor in command of Marcus Flavius. That's how she found Bennett." I watched the light bulbs go on in everyone's minds.

"And us," Will said in a voice mixed with understanding and resignation. "The general's karma is tied to yours, Hillary, and Adriana used his love to track you to this location."

The room erupted in multiple simultaneous conversations, but one soft voice was the only one I heard. "Do you think that's why the bowl doesn't sing any more?"

I turned toward Father John's questioning face. "The bowl doesn't sing?"

"No. I've been with it twice since the ceremony, and it feels lifeless."

Dreading the first thought that came to mind, I asked Gilbert, "Do you have access to the bowl?" If the bowl wasn't singing for Father John, something was terribly wrong.

McCollum spoke up. "The monks are gathered in the temple with the bowl as we speak. I can have Indira bring it to you now."

"It's not necessary to bring it," I said. "If you can retrieve it from the temple, you'll be able to answer my question."

Not a word was spoken until McCollum's face reappeared on the screen with Indira and the bowl in tow.

I pulled a piece of paper from my backpack and started drawing as I addressed McCollum. "A lawyer came to see me, claiming that we have a brass bowl that belongs to his client. The lawyer had a photograph that showed a set of identifying marks on the bottom that would prove its ownership. I checked the bottom of our bowl on the night of Eugene Atohi's ceremony."

"Was it marked?" Father John asked.

"I'm afraid so," I replied, as I held my paper up so McCollum could see what I had drawn. "This is a pretty close representation of what should be on the bottom of the bowl in your hands. Can you turn it over and let us know what you see?"

Ruth's hands were covering her eyes as she burrowed her face into George's shoulder. I held my breath as McCollum flipped the bowl over and frowned. "This bowl has no markings."

"No!" Indira shrieked as she nearly climbed over McCollum to look for herself.

"Kate and Terry," McCollum's voice boomed, "Can you hear me?"

"Yes," Dad said.

"Did either of you feel a stranger in the temple the night we set the Indian free?"

"No, there was no one who was uninvited," Mom answered with certainty. "We would have sensed a stranger entering the temple." And because they were our two Druid dreamers, no one doubted them.

"I'm sorry I didn't say anything sooner," McCollum said to the group. "But I've had a nagging feeling that something's been off kilter. So on the night of the black sky, I took it upon myself to ask Hillary's parents to once again be watchful during their meditation for any stranger within the perimeters of our outer walls. I knew they would warn us if anything was amiss. If Kate and Terry didn't feel an intruder, there was not one."

Dad was the first to speak. "Father John," he asked hesitantly. "When the Chinese discovered the location of your monastery and the existence of the bowl, did you get the feeling that you'd been betrayed?"

"Of course! There should have been no rumors. No one should have known about the bowl outside of our enclave."

"If you take time to think about it now," McCollum inquired, "what would your conclusion be?"

Father John face took on a grey pallor, "Are you suggesting that the original betrayer is still among us, and that they are the one who switched the bowl?"

"I am only asking if it could be a possibility."

"Betrayed twice!" I heard Indira say. "What do we do now?"

"You remain silent," Will said, calming the small Tibetan monk "No one beyond the Band and you can know that the substitution ha: been discovered."

I watched Father John crumble as we made him and

Indira promise to say nothing.

CHAPTER
SEVENTEEN

The Band had decided they needed to meet face-to-face as soon as possible to discuss the problem of the missing bowl. Mom and Dad arrived that night, and we expected Dr. Edwards to join us by morning.

Shortly after sunrise, Mom donned her coat and gloves and moved outside, dusted the snow from one of our deck chairs, and sat down to have her morning coffee. I watched her through the window and wondered what had possessed her to sit in the freezing cold; then my question was answered. Gus landed on the chair across from her, and she removed a few morsels of food from her pocket for his breakfast. Then they began to talk.

It was almost an hour before Mom came in, frozen to the bone. Dad took her hands in his. "I wanted to come out and rescue you from the cold, but it looked like something important was going on," he mumbled, as he held her hands close to his mouth so he could warm them with his breath.

"It was! I had my suspicions, but needed to confirm them with Gus before I said anything."

By midday we were getting out of my car at the edge of a wheat field that had long ago gone to seed. Will, my parents, and I walked the

length of the field, flushing out flocks of starlings that rose like ocea
waves into the sky. Gus had followed my car most of the way, bu
refused to come the last quarter mile until we had cleared the field o
unwanted predators.

We turned back when we saw Ruth's car pull up. Meeting then
mid field, we huddled for warmth while waiting for our final tw(
members.

Dr. Edwards and McCollum arrived together. Dressed in darl
clothing and silhouetted against the grey Kansas sky, they made quite i
striking pair. Watching Gus dive from the sky to land on McCollum'
shoulder made the dramatic picture complete.

"So what calls us to this barren field on such a cold day?" Dr
Edwards asked.

"Gus has been very agitated since the night of Eugene'
ceremony," Mom answered without hesitation. "This morning we had i
long talk, and I now believe that he followed the thief that night anc
knows the location of our bowl. Unfortunately, it's not easy to follow i
bird. Therefore, I think this experiment is the best way for Gus to shov
us the direction in which the bowl lies, giving us our next step toward it
recovery."

Gus tilted his head as he listened to each spoken word and seeme(
to be in total agreement. In the ensuing silence, we heard Gus take fligh
as he jumped from McCollum's shoulder and spread his wings to thei
full expanse.

He gained altitude, and because of the sheer distance we were abl
to see across the open landscape, the direction of his flight confirmed fo
all of us that the bowl was to the northwest. And as much as I wished i
weren't so, we knew it was in the hands of Adriana Heinrich.

We didn't make Gus fly all the way to Kansas City, even though it
wouldn't have been a hardship for him. We all covered our ears and

Dad put his fingers to his mouth and let go with an ear splitting whistle that called Gus back to us. Mom stroked his back, telling him that he had done a very good job, but it did little to calm him down. I looked into his eyes and he looked directly back at me. I mentally expressed my appreciation, and he nodded his head in understanding.

We decided to adjourn our meeting to the warmth of Ruth and George's apartment. We knew Gus would arrive home before us, and Buddy would be there to keep him company.

Father John no longer carried himself erect with his chin high. He was bent as he walked into the apartment, looking as if he had aged a decade overnight. As Wangdak, the guardian of the bowl, he had now failed to protect the bowl twice, and it weighed heavy upon him.

Indira entered the apartment with her usual pastel aura, but it was firing hot pink sparks. "I mean, really Gilbert, it's an awfully long journey just to steal a bowl. You're honestly trying to convince me that she kept her vow to incarnate into China, was then adopted by American parent, chose to go to KSU and enroll in your class … and then she accepted Father John's invitation and ended up sitting right in front of the artifact she planned to steal?"

"And that makes her a very cunning individual," McCollum commented. "That's why we have to keep all of this to ourselves, no matter how hard it is."

"I am," Indira said, defending herself. "Every evening I bring the *pretender* out of hiding and take it into meditation and make excuses for its silence. Everyone is trying to manifest their retrieval of memories, but it hasn't been very fruitful since the bowl was swapped. In fact," she added with frustration, "most don't understand why their spiritual progress has slowed." She plopped down on the couch with arms crossed, just daring Gilbert to say a word.

"I think Lee has some very interesting information," McCollum interjected to try to ease the tension. "Why don't we let him have the floor, and maybe some of our questions will be answered."

Dr. Edwards opened his briefcase and removed a stack of paper. "A lot of what I'm going to say will be my own personal conjecture," he began with a smile. "I'll give you a heads-up when I'm wandering off onto one of my own tangents."

We all knew that Dr. Edwards had taken a trip abroad, but had heard nothing about his research until now.

"This part is factual," he joked as he began. "The Bronze Age spans from 3300 to 1300 BC. That was when man first learned to use metal and began forging and casting objects. Taking into account what I already know about our bowl, and without having it carbon dated, I choose to believe that it came into existence around 1300 BC, which means it was made in either Babylonia or Egypt. From this point it's our choice to believe whether it was made by one of the Pharaoh's priests or cast by a humble smithy. Those kind of details we may never know for sure.

"The first mention I found written about a singing bowl was within an ancient Hebrew text. Let me rephrase: It was a diary kept by a woman who lived in Jerusalem three hundred years before Christ. The book is now stored under lock and key, in an environmentally controlled case to retard its deterioration, but I was able to view a transcript.

"She spoke of a mystical vessel that a young shepherd boy found in the desert. It was rumored to generate a fountain of light, which created a protective barrier around the boy and his flock through the night." His blue eyes twinkled as they rolled in his head. "I view this as a myth, which was exaggerated over time, but originates from some form of the real truth. The woman who wrote this account claimed to have heard the story directly from the shepherd's great grandson, who claimed to have once seen the brass bowl."

Father John looked encouraged, "Could it be our bowl?"

"Maybe," Dr. Edwards said. "It appears that the shepherd boy kept the bowl well into old age, only then passing it on to his descendants. Some generations later, that family fell on hard times and sold the brass bowl. From there I lost it for about two centuries. My hypothesis is that it was hidden in a private collection, or that it's owner didn't realize its true value."

It all sounded perfectly plausible to me, so I made myself comfy and just listened quietly. Dr. Edwards gave me a lazy smile, reminding me how much I'd missed seeing him. His natural charisma, broad shoulders, and towering height made him an imposing figure. His engaging personality and gentle manner made him a trusted friend. I smiled back.

"My research completely changed direction when my search for our brass bowl went cold. There was a growing number of references to other mystical objects, and for my own peace of mind, I needed to know if I was on a wild goose chase—just following fables born of imagination that were exaggerated as they were told and retold—or if I would find something of substance at the end of my search.

"I decided to look where I hadn't looked before… I turned to science. I suddenly wanted to know whether an inanimate object such as our brass bowl had the same capability to gain consciousness as an animate object, such as us."

I could tell by the shift in the room that dear Dr. Edwards had touched on a subject that interested everyone.

"I was redirected when I fell into research that dealt with Darwinian evolution, and found research dealing with inorganic matter that could mimic life, and it once and for all changed my mind about the notion of what consciousness really is. They began with the hypothesis that there was some sort of primordial soup or chemical complexity that caused life to originally begin, and suggested that evolution only takes a container, energy, and molecular structure, minus carbon for an artificial life form exist." Dr. Edwards looked amused, "If you think it's improbable, you have to remember that five billion years ago we didn't exist. There was no life on Earth whatsoever. So, if matter is actually evolvable, I believe this is the scientific answer to the mystical abilities that our brass bowl presents.

"For instance," he continued, holding up his hands to hold back the questions. "If our bowl was originally cast for ceremonial purpose in a temple and it was used by a group of very highly evolved holy men or high priestesses who placed their consciousness into the vessel the same way we do ... wouldn't that constant interaction over an extended period of time cause the object to have some sort of energetic life? Take for instance the dowsing rod used for locating water. Is it the person holding the rod or the rod itself that holds the true power?"

"I can see where you are going with this." George said, following Dr. Edwards' train of thought. "If the human is directing their subconscious through an object to create an event, does the inanimate object gain consciousness due to the thoughts being directed through it?"

"Exactly!" Dr. Edwards continued. "Scientists have been exploring the minute, natural patterns of energy and memory fields that suggest that matter has the ability to absorb emotional 'fingerprints,' that channel echoes from the past. This offers the possibility of inanimate life."

This lent more plausibility to what I'd thought since I was a kid. My idea came about one summer when our family took a vacation out west to visit some Indian cliff dwelling. The ancient builders had left behind fingerprints in the mud walls, and I decided that if I placed my fingers into them it was perfectly reasonable that I should be able feel the essence of that person, or at least get a sense of their life. So maybe I wasn't as crazy as I sometimes felt.

Father John asked the first question: "So you're saying, Dr. Edwards, that when a highly evolved soul who lived thousands years ago began using objects to amplify their thoughts in the same manner we use our brass bowl, that we all continue to exist within the object as its own consciousness? That it is human interaction that causes the objects to eventually have manifesting capabilities? And the more highly advanced the spiritualist is who runs their awareness through an object, the more likely this whole phenomenon is to happen?"

"Now you can grasp why I had to begin considering more than just the bowl's physical journey, because its spiritual journey is just as critical." I saw hesitation cross Dr. Edwards' face. "The next documentation of a brass vessel that I was able to locate was from the thirteenth century. It was controlled by a group of powerful and corrupt men." He looked at Father John apologetically. "These men appropriated the brass object for less than honorable reasons, and I'm sad to report that it had become by this time a very dark artifact indeed."

"What brings you to your conclusion?" McCollum asked calmly. "Aren't there other avenues our bowl may have taken than the one you are suggesting?"

"Of course, but this was the path I was led down, so I have to conclude for that reason that it was our bowl."

Closing my eyes, I listened to Dr. Edwards' synopsis. "You've got to understand that this was a period in time where there was much to be gained. The Ottoman Empire had sole access to the Black Sea, making Istanbul the center of trade between Europe and Asia. A well-placed entrepreneur would accumulate not only affluence, but also immense wealth that could sustain a family for generation. There were fortunes to be made, and who better to take their share than this group of immoral and unethical families."

Father John wanted to argue for the virtue of his brass bowl, but paused to allow McCollum to speak.

"Let me put everyone's mind at ease. If indeed an artifact can gain awareness, it would also accumulate karma. Therefore, it also has the ability to uplift itself from whatever depths it may have fallen to."

Father John seemed to relax, so Dr. Edwards continued. "Shortly after that, the legends completely ceased. The bowl was probably stolen or traded, making its way into Tibet, where our monks would have buried it deep in a cave so it could do no more harm. And following McCollum's train of thought, after being bathed in the monastery's life for hundreds of years, it became the object we know today."

When the topic was opened up for discussion, new hypotheses were emotionally debated. At the peak of the debate, I watched Dr. Edwards withdraw and quietly take a seat next to Ruth, nimbly hooking his foot around a package he had tucked under the table. It was the first time I had noticed the nondescript bundle, but I was definitely paying attention now.

"I was able to make a stop for you, Ruth," he whispered, as he pulled a thick, leather bond manuscript from its crumpled newsprint wrapper. It had rusted hardware and a small padlock to make sure the book remained closed. I wondered if this was to protect the book or the reader. "I came across an old gypsy in Hungary, and she was very anxious to trade this book for what cash I had in my pockets." He smiled conspiratorially.

Conversations ceased, and we all warily eyed what now lay in Ruth's lap. Dr. Edwards placed another book on top of it. "She indicated that this might be an instructional booklet, but she wasn't completely convincing." The smaller book was certainly an ancient text. The ink was faded on its worn cover, and the title was handwritten in some obscure primitive language. "I hope it furnishes you with answers, but I encourage you to take a great deal of care. I was instructed NEVER to open the book when the sun was not shining, and always in the presence of a holy object."

Ruth looked thrilled, but George gingerly took both books off her lap and secured them in his personal lock box.

After an uneventful morning meditation, I decided to make breakfast for Will and my folks. We had scheduled another meeting with McCollum in two hours, to continue the discussion on the recovery of our brass bowl, and I had not come up with one single good idea that could help. I was hopeful that Mom might do better, because she was out on the deck talking to Gus and Buddy.

"Do you think she's getting some good information?" Will asked, putting his arms around me.

"I hope so, because I've got nothing!"

"Me, too," Will replied, surprising me.

"Can't you just become The Teacher and find the bowl?"

"I wish it was that easy! The Teacher doesn't really exist in this realm, only in the higher ones. And finding the bowl is purely *our* human journey, and he won't interfere."

"I guess I'd never thought of it in that way, but it's too bad. He'd make an incredible detective."

Will laughed and pulled me closer. "I don't think we have to worry. Your mom seems to have it well in hand."

"It isn't that I actually have conversation with Gus or Buddy," Mom replied to McCollum's question once we were all seated. "It's that images appear in my mind."

"Remarkable," McCollum said, and I watched Mom fight to remove a huge smile from her face.

"Even though Gus knows where the bowl is being hidden," she continued, "I have no way of determining the exact location myself. But one thing that Gus has made quite clear to me"—Mom looked remorseful—"is that Eugene Atohi didn't leave the bowl before it's theft. I'm sure he thought he had time."

McCollum bowed his head and closed his eyes.

"That might not be so bad," George interjected. "Maybe he can give us the bowl's location! After all, we do have the spirit he guides sitting in our midst."

"That we do," McCollum answered, regaining his composure.

148

"The moon phase that Eugene used for contact you in your dreams is only days away. Maybe it will work just as easily for you to contact him. You may use my temple and all of the boys if need be. Everything I have is at your disposal. Or maybe you'd like to contact Eugene from the comfort of your home. The choice is yours."

Oh great, was all that came to mind. Will must have known what I was thinking, because he covered my hand with his.

Gilbert raised his hand and McCollum acknowledged him. "Yes, my boy, what is it?"

"If you would like to consider a second option, I think I have a way to catch our thief." Reaching into the front pocket of his backpack, he retrieved an assortment of photos. He then fanned them out in front of him and began to explain, "I set up a camera to take periodic shots of my classroom when the lights first appeared, to see if I could isolate what was happening. It never worked very well." He shrugged. "In fact, once the Brass Band agreed to help me, I had forgotten about the photos completely." He thumbed through the pictures, looking for one in particular as he spoke. "It occurred to me that at the time of our experiment we were only concentrating on one anomaly, but what if there was a second? What if our thief carried a different signature ... a darker one!"

Gilbert pointed to the picture that he had shuffled to the top. "I think this is what we've been missing!"

We all leaned in, squinting to try to see what he was talking about, and sure enough, there it was, a barely visible dark spot.

"That's our thief!" Gilbert said triumphantly. "My plan to catch this person may seem elaborate, but I've been over it with Father John and Indira, and we think it is foolproof!"

George was already smiling. He loved springing a good trap!

CHAPTER
EIGHTEEN

March 8, 2012

I waited for the turmoil inside me to subside as Will took his place beside me. I would search for my spirit guide alone, leaving Will to sit with my body.

We sat on the floor with our backs against our bed and waited for the full moon to rise, knowing that this was the time Eugene Atohi and I did our best work together. I began to feel Will's hum circulate through me, and knew it was time for me to start my journey. I closed my eyes and thought only of my Indian guide's voice and the last words he'd spoken to me.

"Now, dear spirit, we have one more thing we can accomplish together. Close your eyes, Hillary."

The same panic ran through me now, as I wondered if I were capable of this journey. The darkness behind my eyelids went from looking like the static on a TV screen to an absolute jet black, and I knew the journey had begun. I pushed away my self-doubt and set all my insecurities aside. I closed my mind to the everyday sounds of our apartment and only let the voice of my Eugene Atohi into my consciousness.

"Pull yourself inward until you are contained entirely within your third eye. Concentrate all that you are into a point of light and use that as your power. Open your mind to what you want, and use your light to

make it so."

I found the power he spoke of and anchored myself within it. When I opened my eyes, I sat across from him.

"Thank the Great Spirit that you have come!"

I tried to talk and found it difficult to form words. It was taking all of my concentration to control the light body I was in. "Very good to see you, Eugene … I expected you to be far beyond this world by now," I managed to convey.

"I also expected to be gone, but I find that I am trapped. One moment I was floating in the ecstasy on your breath, hypnotized by the voice of the singing bowl. Then suddenly I realized I was unable to extract myself from it."

I could hear Eugene's voice growing weak. "Hillary, I am drowning in this darkness."

"The bowl was stolen from the temple on the night of your ceremony. We're trying to kinda … well … there's no nice way to put it. When we find out where it is, we're going to steal the bowl back!" I was finding it easier to convey my thoughts, but my anxiety was growing as I began to grasp what a terrible situation my friend was in. "We need to recover the bowl before it takes on its new owner's negativity."

"It's already in the process! My light is nearly out!"

"Tell me what to do to help you. You're my spirit guide. Guide me!"

That got a little laugh.

"First, tell me how you found me?" Eugene Atohi began.

"I cleared my mind and concentrated only on you."

"Perfect! Now, concentrate on something that will help you find out where we are," he said, as I too noticed his light diming.

"The address! I need to see the address!"

"Okay Hillary, clear your mind. Set aside everything else. Draw all that you are into the pinpoint of your third eye and …"

Eugene's voice disappeared, and I was no longer with him, but standing—correction—*floating* in a very well appointed home. It took me a few moments to figure out how to move around in this new, gravity-free form. I began doing something similar to a breaststroke and hoped no other ethereal bodies were in the room watching my struggle. I awkwardly maneuvered from place to place, feeling more like a frog than a light being. It made me wonder if this was how ghosts were created, as spirits that just decided to carry on once their bodies had dropped away.

Closing my virtual eyes, I once again focused all my intentions upon finding the address, my latest idea being that I needed to move outside to view the numbers on the house. I felt a small jerk forward and opened my eyes to find I was still no closer to my destination. Then there was unquestionably noise at the front door! Someone was here!

Wondering if I would be invisible or not, I kicked my feet frantically, trying to move out of sight. I was relieved when the mail flap on the front door opened and a stack of mostly bills landed on the floor below me. BINGO!

Swimming my way down to floor level, I looked at one of the letters as …

"Sun's up, Hillary! Come back to me," Will whispered.

In that last moment before returning to Will's arms, I looked at the letter, burning that address into my mind: 39401 West Fortune Avenue, KC, MO.

I reached for the paper on my nightstand and quickly scratched down the address before sticking it in my pocket and turning my attention to something much more important. "Eugene needs our help! He's drowning in the bowl. The monks must know how to stop it!"

Indira pleaded with us to let her begin the phone tree to engage the help of all the monks she absolutely knew were not involved in the bowl's theft. "They can help!" she implored. But it wasn't the time to reveal our hand. Without knowing exactly who the thief was, we were forced to keep all of the monks uninvolved.

That left only the boys to wage the battle against the dark energy that kept our Indian friend trapped. As one young man would come out of meditation, another would enter. They reported a mighty etheric fight in progress. The evil was growing in the bowl almost as fast as they could fill it with light. Until the tide was turned and Eugene was free, no one was willing to remove themselves from the equation for very long. I found a corner where I could sit down, and closed my eyes to join the skirmish.

March 10, 2012

It came fast, a black behind my eyelids so pure that there was no question that I had left my body. The first sound I heard was Eugene's voice. "Thank you, Spirit Lady. The light that the chanting has created is allowing me to wiggle free. I'm glad to have this last moment with you so I can say goodbye, for I will not remain for even one moment once I am unrestrained."

I opened my eyes to see my spirit guide in full regalia, and it was spellbinding to look upon his true face for the very first time. He was everything I could have imagined. His dark brown eyes shown bright from behind his ochre war paint, his lashes long and black. His skin was a flawless brown, surrounded by a headdress of eagle feathers. It was a picture that would remain etched in my mind's eye for all of my days.

"I am ready to meet the Great Spirit," he said in reaction to my smile. "Until we meet again, know that your life's calling is here on Earth, and you're worthy of the position that you will rise to! Do not

question," he said, as the final strands were released and he became the light.

I sat for a while, wondering what the rest of that statement might have been if he'd had time to finish: Don't question if I am enough ... Don't question that I have the strength ... Don't question my path? I was willing to go on and on, when it struck me: Eugene Atohi had finished his statement ... so I shut down my mind and stopped questioning.

I had stayed for a few extra minutes so I could be alone with my thoughts, when I was interrupted by the sound of someone turning the closet doorknob. I flailed my arms to try to hide; it had completely slipped my mind that I was still in Heinrich's home. Taking control, I slowed my breathing and floated to the ceiling as the door opened.

Adriana's flawless hand, with long nails painted blood red, reached for the bowl. She paused only for a spilt second before continuing her conversation with her guest.

"I suggest something ought to be done sooner than later." Jack Black's voice cracked the air like a whip.

"We have plenty of time now that we have the bowl. I can all ready feel its energy. Can't you?" Her voice was slippery as an eel. "It was naive of them to think McCollum's house was impenetrable. They haven't even noticed that a switch was made. My spy studies with the monks in McCollum's house, and within spitting distance of his precious boys. Nothing could be more perfect! She's informed me that they chant with the imposter every night, while we use the real one to grow our power! They don't have a clue how fast they are losing ground!"

I could see the dark shadow that now existed within the bowl.

"Let's watch the news and see how our side is doing," she said, and laughed as she shoved the bowl back into the closet. "Our mass of unaware on-air minions are embedding fear in the minds of everyone who listens. Spreading bad news twenty-four hours a day and giving mankind a feeling of hopelessness! Isn't it splendid? People don't even realize they are being brainwashed."

I jerked back into my body, still holding my breath. McCollum was at the front of the room, congratulating everyone on freeing Eugene Atohi. I stood up among a sea of seated bodies. *Do not question!* I heard in my mind and put all of my uncertainties aside.

"Hillary, I see that you have rejoined us!" McCollum said, and instead of shrinking under his gaze, I straightened my back and answered.

"Yes," I said, as I pulled the paper from my pocket that I had scribbled on this morning. "And I know where the bowl is and who is using it!"

McCollum motioned me to the front and I took my place beside him. I felt confident and unshakable, and whether that feeling remained with me in the future or not made no difference, because in that moment I was the mystic warrior through and through!

We arranged for a group of seventeen boys to be in the temple twenty-four hours a day to meditate with our precious brass bowl. They were to hold the darkness at bay just enough that it would not be noticed by Heinrich.

Gilbert was working to identify the individual who was the dark spot on the original photographs he had taken when the flashes had begun in his classroom. He had divided the auditorium into zones and assigned a monk to sit in the center of each.

"We're testing to make sure we haven't missed a student who is on the same path as us by giving them another opportunity," Gilbert lied. "The Brass Band will be watching from the front to see if there are any new lights among you.

I knew he felt terrible about lying, but once we were able to find which zone was missing a twinkling aura, we would know who the traitor was. Father John took his seat just as the auditorium lights went down.

We were armed with a blank drawing of the auditorium and were prepared to X-out every quadrant with a light, thereby identifying our thief.

A few minutes after Gilbert began his lecture, I turned to Ruth. "Do you see anything?"

"No, I don't see a thing. Maybe once they find their beacon, their signal goes out."

We sat and watched for the entire ninety minutes. Father John got up from his seat and began to move around the room. "Did you see that?" I asked Ruth as the lights came up. I think I saw something, and I think Gilbert saw it, too."

As the bell rang and everyone rushed toward the doors, Gilbert took his only chance. "Hold on a minute! If there is someone who would like to meditate with the man standing at the side door, please join me after class!" Gilbert kept shouting even though no one was listening. "The tall gentleman with the bald head and the stud earring, he is an amazing man. Someone on the right side of the auditorium needs to listen to me!" The room emptied and we were left alone, looking at one another.

Indira patted Gilbert on the back. "We'll find another way, Gilbert. Now that we know that that particular aspect to our auras no longer functions in the same way, we'll take a closer look at your pictures."

The other monks were already on their way to their next classes, and we were ready to leave when we heard a lone voice say, "Whom do I speak with?" And when we turned, there stood one lone Asian student. "I feel you were speaking to me."

Father John stepped forward to shake the man's hand.

"I slip into the back of the classroom on the days when I am able to get away from work," he said looking up into Father John's eyes. "Today I felt it was important that I attend. I think you must be the reason."

I shifted so I could view the man against a dark background, and took a good look at his aura. It flashed and then flashed again until it slowly turned off. Like the others, I supposed he didn't have a need for it now that he had found his destination.

The man's name was Dorje, and he was very different than the others who had been drawn to Father John. He was more my Dad's age, and had immigrated to the States as an adult. Dorje just smiled at us, not particularly surprised that his journey had taken an unexpected turn.

CHAPTER
NINTEEN

Ruth and I took a quick trip to Kansas City. We felt a talk with Bennett was in order. We decided to meet at the club, and it was just as I remembered it—elegant and filled to the brim with the up and coming. I had an uncomfortable feeling that I was being watched, and sure enough, I was. Turning, I came face to face with an attractive and all-grown-up, Bennett Taylor. I couldn't help but smile.

"Still happily married?

"Still am."

"Just thought I'd check," he said, before turning to Ruth. "And how about you, Ruth? Still happily in love?"

"Absolutely!"

He kissed us both on the cheek before we sat down, and I got the felling he might be a little lonely. "How about you, Bennett? Anyone special?"

"I had a couple of dates with one of your least favorite people," he admitted, and personally, I was glad that he had brought up the subject of Adriana Heinrich himself. "I have nothing against older women, especially a gorgeous one in leather, but she didn't seem to want to have a relationship. She wanted to own me … heart and soul."

I wanted to help him understand why he felt the way he did about her, but figured he'd think I was out of my mind. Besides, we'd never talked about anything spiritual before, and now probably wasn't the time to break the news to him that his girlfriend used to be his commanding officer.

"I'm just looking for a relationship that's a little more give and take," he finished. "Kind of like the ones you two have."

"Well, Bennett, we're glad you aren't head over heels over Ms. Heinrich, because she's what we're here to talk about!" Ruth was off and running before Bennett had a chance to gather his thoughts, which he clearly wanted to do. "Has she said anything more about the artifact she sent you to talk to us about?"

"Funny thing—once I told her you didn't have it, she fired our firm and we've never talked about it again."

"No wonder," Ruth mumbled under her breath.

"She did ask me quite a few questions about you, Hillary, but I never gave her any details … as if I know any!" He laughed. "Generally, all I know is that you married a guy who is absolutely nothing like me, who you and Ruth had met at a party at some big estate just off campus."

"You told her all of that?" Ruth asked.

"I suppose I did. It's nothing that I thought was confidential," he insisted. "I'm sure she could find it all online if she wanted to. If you type my name into a search engine, you can find out anything: my address, age, and underwear size."

Ruth and I both knew from our own experience that nothing about Will, George, or McCollum's house would show up online. But if someone were given the approximate location of McCollum's house, it would be easy enough to find by methodically expanding a perimeter around the campus.

"Do you have plans to see Adriana again?" I asked casually.

"Maybe, if she wants to take another pass at me before she moves."

"Moves," Ruth gasped. "When's that happening?"

"Why do you care?" Bennett's curiosity was piqued.

I'd never seen Ruth so speechless. The silence went on until I just decided to tell him the truth. "She's not who you think she is."

"An overbearing, malicious, and unpleasant person who is difficult to have an honest conversation with? That lady?"

"Well, yes," Ruth sputtered.

"I might have fallen in lust with her, but I got a pretty good glimpse of her ugly side. It began when she realized I actually care about the two of you." Bennett blushed before continuing, "She's a hypocrite. I'm not sure what her game is, but in no way does she live up to the moral standards she claims. I suppose she was just giving me what I wanted so I'd fall for her hard and fast. And it worked. I'm still licking my wounds."

When I looked into his eyes, my heart broke for him. "I am so sorry, Bennett."

"Oh, I'm fine. I was really just in love with an illusion."

I felt a twinge of guilt when I recalled how I had manipulated him in the lifetime we spent as Hilsbeth and Marcus Flavius, and even then, he had comforted me in my last moments of life. My eyes began to water, and I wanted to cry for all that had gone between us that he would never know. "Falling in love with an illusion might be the cruelest trick of all," I replied, knowing that I had once been that exact thing to him.

"I sincerely feel bad for you, Bennett," Ruth said, picking up her childhood friend's hand. "But here comes the insensitive part. We need a favor."

Smiling, he answered, "I'd do anything for my two best girls."

Now it was my turn to blush, because I remembered the huge crush I'd had on him last year. I also vividly recalled the nights Hilsbeth spent with the great Roman general Marcus Flavius in the dream world, and those thoughts made my heart race. I was lost in my memories when I was brought back to reality by Ruth's confession.

"I hate to admit that I lied to you, but we didn't want that evil lady to know we had the brass bowl. In fact, we weren't sure how she found out we had it until we discovered one of our friends had double-crossed us and was in cahoots with her." Bennett's eyes lit with intrigue. "Anyway, just to be blunt, she stole it from us and we need to steal it back. The brass bowl has belonged to a group of Tibetan monks for hundreds, if not thousands of years. In no way is it hers."

He grinned. "Tell me what you want me to do, Ruth and I'll tell you if I'm capable."

"One more date. Convince her to go out with you one more time before she leaves."

I wasn't sure what he was going to say. He was wearing his broken heart right there on his coat sleeve.

"The bowl is a family member to these Tibetan monks. I promise it is the right thing to do," Ruth implored. "One more date. We'll just need her out of her house for one hour."

He replied with the simple gesture of squeezing Ruth's hand, "Does it matter when?"

March 12, 2012

We had two days to prepare for Bennett's date with Adriana Heinrich. He was meeting her for a drink after work on Friday to say goodbye. Her scheduled departure date was Sunday.

My dilemma was the conflict between thinking I was one of the good guys and committing a crime. But it wasn't McCollum's.

"Don't worry, my dear," McCollum grinned with reassurance. "By morning, I will know who among us will benefit by recovering the brass bowl. This undertaking will do no damage to their spiritual trajectory; instead, this act will be a balancing of karma for things that have taken place between the involved individuals in the past."

"It really works that way?" I asked, confused by what I believed to be the moral ramifications.

"Human judgments are not the judgments of the Universe. I will commune with my higher being and find the one who will burn off negative karma by the act of returning a beloved family member back into the arms of the ones who bring it peace and happiness."

Ruth and I didn't feel that was any worse than what we had asked Bennett to do, so we agreed and got to our feet to leave McCollum's quarters.

"Hillary, your part is far from done," McCollum said, stopping me dead in my tracks. "I am familiar with your belief that an object can communicate its history to you, so you must spend tonight with the bowl that is in our possession and find out how it came to be in our temple."

"But I haven't actually succeeded at it!"

"I have the utmost confidence in you, Dear One. And during your time with the bowl, please reassure whatever consciousness it may have gained that we seek not to send it into harm, but to have it hold a place of light within the darkness. The bowl, even as a stand-in, has been the center of phenomenal ceremony for the last few weeks, and has also been loved. It may be gathering a power of its own.

"Ruth, you must serve in the same capacity for Hillary as George does for Will," McCollum instructed. "Tonight, in the event that Hillary has to leave her physical body behind, you must be its protector until her safe return."

"Of course," she replied. "I'd be honored."

Indira delivered the bowl to the temple, and after leaving it directly under the single light that illuminated the room, she quickly left. Ruth found a place to sit in the shadows while I walked over to stare at what I considered to be just a regular brass bowl. I repositioned it on the first step that led up to McCollum's chair and made myself comfortable on the floor in front of it. I placed my hands on my knees and opened them, palms up. Unsure what to do next, I quieted my mind and let all my thoughts melt away. I let my heart lead and mentally embraced the object, concentrating only upon what it had to tell me. Time passed, and I neither heard nor felt anything. But steeped in the confidence McCollum had in me, I continued to sit patiently, silently coaxing the bowl to tell me its secrets.

Unwavering, I waited and waited, my physical hands open. It may have been hours before I thought I felt something for the briefest of moments. It was an uncomfortable twitchy sensation, but I was thankful that something was happening. I settled my energy back into my body and waited for what might happen next. I was bewildered as I watched a set of hands, as transparent as ghosts, appear on the bowl and instantly began to dissolve. I reached for them, not sure what else there was to do. As my hands overlaid the ones on the bowl I instantly felt the jittery feeling return. It was very specific, and I knew if I felt it again, it would be because I was in the vicinity of our thief.

The spell lifted, and I found myself sitting dumbfounded in front of the bowl. I was beyond excited that my experiment had worked, and felt an intense need to express my gratitude to the *imposter*. "Thank you for allowing me to see how you came to be in our midst," I said. "I appreciate your faith in me and your knowledge that I will use this information wisely." Not knowing whether it had truly gained any awareness while in the company of the monks, I just kept talking so I could fulfill my promise to McCollum. "You are now marked on the bottom to match a very powerful brother of yours, the one who occupied this temple before you. That bowl will now return to its rightful place, and in this endeavor, you must play an important part. You are now of the light, but must reside in darkness."

I heard an almost inaudible whimper, and knew it had originated from the bowl in front of me. Touched by the depths of its sadness, I made a desperate promise that I would keep for the rest of my life. "No matter where you travel, I will visit you. I will never leave you alone to be consumed by the dark. But if you find yourself there, meditate as you have seen us do, and know you are not alone." I couldn't help but weep for what was to come for this fledgling that had not yet had a chance to fly. I whispered, "You have served a great purpose," and felt Ruth's hands lying gently on my shoulders.

March 13, 2012

The four of us had made arrangements to spend the night at the Witherspoons', knowing we'd need a place to stay in K.C. after we had swapped the bowls. We pulled up to the estate around noon, and after a nice lunch with Ruth's parents we unpacked and began our wait. By five o'clock Ruth, Will, and I were beyond anxious for Ruth's cell phone to ring.

Mom and Dad were sitting in a car one block away from Adriana's house, trying to look like a couple of lovers under a blanket in the back seat, although they were actually a couple of Druid dreamers deep in meditation. They were getting used to the feeling of the neighborhood, so they would be able to warn us if anything were to go awry.

McCollum had surprised everyone by picking George as the person to recover the bowl. While living as a Roman governor, Adriana had insisted that the Druids must die a slow and torturous death to ensure that no others would follow in their footsteps, and George's death was the worst of all. He was left crippled and slowly bleeding to death, with his Achilles tendons severed, and the Roman butcher watched as he held Ruth's deceased body, fighting to keep the flies and scavengers at bay until his last breath.

Bennett finally called Ruth and told her that he would pick up Adriana at six and try to keep her occupied until eight. That gave us two hours to get in and out.

Our plan worked perfectly. Dad called us when Adriana left the house. Bennett had managed to place a piece of tape on the locking mechanism, so the door was open when George emerged from the shadows and turned the knob.

"Will, I think we have a problem," were the first words we heard when George called. "She's already packed. This place is nothing but boxes."

"Hold tight, George. We're on it."

Ruth and Will looked at me, and my mind began to race. "I can try, but I'm not sure if I can find it now that Eugene is no longer in it."

"Sure you can," Will said. "I'll help you." And with that, he took my hands, and his life force rushed through me. I closed my eyes, trying to quiet my mind, which kept seeing images of Adriana and Bennett returning early. *Okay, Hillary*, I said to myself, *let the thoughts melt away and pull yourself inward until you exist only as a point of light.* Everything went pitch black, and I knew I was free of my body. I envisioned the singing bowl that Father John had held so affectionately, and instantly found myself inside a cardboard box. It was dark and musty, and filled to the brim with crinkled newspaper and bubble wrap.

With no other option available to see if I had landed in the correct location, I humbly said, "Hello my friend." I waited in the darkness until it become aware of my presence. My heart opened as I heard the bowl's response. It began to sing with the joy I thought was reserved for only Father John.

I heard George laugh. "Keep it singing. Locating you should be easy."

I watched as George lifted our bowl from the box and replaced it with the imposter, who was now a new friend.

I stayed to talk, so it would know what was happening. "The switch has been made and you are no longer in the hands of the Tibetan monks. You will now exist alone, much like you did before you came to our temple. But we are in this together, you and me, and I will visit as often as I can. Call to me if you are in need." I pictured my physical body so that I could make my journey back to it. As I left the box, I heard a small sob and knew for sure that this bowl was also becoming conscious.

March 14, 2012

We arrived home midday Saturday and weren't surprised to find Indira, Gilbert, and Father John sitting in the living room when we opened our apartment door. Father John looked as if he hadn't slept in days.

George had the honor of placing the bowl safely back into Father John's loving hands. We all laughed, as the bowl became absolutely giddy.

"You're going to have to figure out a way to control it!" George stated flatly. "The monks will notice its behavior and wonder what's up. You don't want to let the traitor know that the authentic bowl is back."

The bowl stifled its song as if it understood what we were talking about. "We'll work on it, but for tonight we celebrate," Father John insisted, and sat down with the bowl in front of him and began to chant. Indira joined him, and before long we were all chanting with the joy of making music together again.

The rhythmic chanting released me from my body and I reeled wildly, looking for a familiar place to land.

I hear the roar of a motorcycle engine and suck in a deep breath, hoping that I am in my light body and that Adriana Heinrich, the lady in leather, doesn't feel my presence.

"And what makes you think that I need to know about this?" Adriana's voice says calmly, although the tension in it is palpable.

"We think they are up to something," Jackson Black insists,

glancing at the young girl sitting awkwardly beside him for confirmation. "My ability to wish myself into Hillary's proximity is fading."

"Did you actually think that she wasn't going to grow beyond your mediocre skills? You are a buffoon! If you want to keep up with Mrs. Hillary Rubner Emerald, you can have your new little friend train you in some of their higher practices," she sneers, as she beholds the Chinese girl Jackson has obviously fallen for.

Black places his heavy arm possessively around her narrow shoulders, his flesh damp with perspiration. "You can do what you want with your precious brass bowl, Adriana, because it will never make you equal to the energy coming from McCollum's place."

"I don't care about McCollum or his boys," she says, as her anger increases to a crescendo. "I can feel the negativity growing in the world! Mass murders, horrendous natural disasters, corrupt politicians—all paralyzing this country. Suicide bombers are willing to kill indiscriminately in the name of God." She laughs. "How will the light ever be victorious when people continually kill in the name of their saviors? History teaches mankind absolutely nothing!"

"What should we do now?" the brown-eyed girl asks, shrugging her shoulders under the weight of Black's meaty arm.

"Wreak havoc! Keep the monks off balance. I don't really care!"

"What are you talking about?" she yells, suddenly becoming hysterical. "I helped you. I betrayed everyone for you! You owe me!"

"I owe you nothing," Adriana growls, and I can feel the heat of her breath blow though me from my hiding place in the shadows. I watch as even egotistical Jackson Black begins moving away. "If I need you, I will call you. Otherwise, don't let your shadows cross my path."

Adriana sniffs the air as if she has caught the scent of something. I immediately pull all of my energy inward and concentrate my mind on the first hiding place that comes to mind.

It takes a moment for my eyes to adjust to the confined area, and as the second brass bowl begins to become aware of my presence, I hurriedly warn it to be silent before it can make a sound. "Shhhh. We can't be found together, but if you like we can sit and meditate before I'm called back to my body."

When I finally roused myself from meditation I found that I was alone in the living room with a blanket Will had tucked around me for warmth. I could tell by the cool temperature in the room that everyone else had gone off to bed quite a while ago. I could hear Dad's soft snoring muffled by the closed guest room door. My nose was freezing, and the thought of Will's warm body made me eager to join him under the covers of our bed.

I slept like a baby once I was tucked in beside my heater of a husband. My sleep was so sound that I didn't notice he had gotten up until I heard him talking with my folks in the living room.

"Where did you disappear to last night?" Dad asked when I opened the bedroom door. "Did you fly somewhere over the rainbow?"

"Ha ha," I said, mocking his lame attempt at a Kansas joke. "Actually, I didn't end up anywhere as pleasant as Oz, and I would have loved a pair of ruby slippers to help me get home again."

I worked my way around the room, hugging Mom and Dad first and ending with Will, as I told them about the previous night's travels. "I spent my evening hiding in the shadows, lord knows where," I added under my breath, "listening to a conversation between three of our least favorite people, Adriana Heinrich, Jackson Black, and our little disloyal monk."

That got everyone's attention. "You know who she is?" Will asked.

"Yes, I do, but I'm hugely disappointed because now I won't get a chance to use my mystical detective skills."

"You've been working on the case without us," Dad teased. He still had bedhead, so Mom was running her fingers through his hair to try to make it lie down.

"Well, kinda!" I said with a shrug. "I spent a night in the temple with the imposter before George switched the bowls back. McCollum had asked me to see if it had any information about our thief's identity. So I did what I used to do as a kid. I opened my hands and sat with the bowl, waiting patiently for it to talk to me, and *abracadabra*! For once, it worked like a charm."

My parents, being great parents, had always made a big deal out of everything I'd ever done, whether successfully or not. I suppose it was to encourage me, but I think this time they were truly impressed that my old habit had finally accomplished something.

"That night in the temple, I actually got a psychic feeling of our thief," I said. "I was going to walk among the monks and identify the culprit by mystical means, but yes"—disappointment now dripped from every word—"last night I saw her face."

My parents weren't the least bit consoling. "That's great! Isn't it?"

"I suppose so, but I was looking forward to testing my childhood technique," I said.

"And just taking your light body to the same location as the thief and looking into her face isn't amazing enough?" Dad asked. "I think astral travel would be incredible!" I had to admit he was right.

"I've known since childhood that the *hands open* thing should work, and finally, after all my years of waiting for something to happen, I was going to be able to use it to solve the mystery of the stolen bowl."

"It still can happen," Will said, giving me a wink with his dreamy blue eyes. "Tomorrow we'll go to McCollum's early and you can sit just inside the temple door with your eyes closed. When the thief enters you can identify her first by feel and then by sight."

I adored that Will was totally serious about his idea. Soon a smile began to creep across my face, too. "Okay, but don't make a big deal about it. If it doesn't work, I don't want everyone to know how juvenile I've been about this."

"Okay, only us," Mom said putting out her hand. The rest of us placed our hands on top of hers to complete the pact. "Only us!"

March 16, 2012

Will and I sat in meditation just inside the temple door. I had raised my shawl over my head so that it fell over my face, and sat with my head bowed. It was Will who alerted me to the fact that people were beginning to arrive. I focused my energy into my opened hands and waited.

I recognized some people by the shuffle of their slippers and others by the heaviness of their footsteps. Jimmy's steps were so light that I would have missed them completely if he hadn't stopped in front of me. In that instant I wanted to call off my experiment so I could get the hug I knew he had in store for me. That was when I felt it—a jittery, nervous energy that I knew belonged to our thief. I pulled my shawl away from my face and opened my eyes. Jimmy interpreted my unveiling as an invitation to launch himself into my lap, so I opened my arms as I looked just past his little head to confirm that my intuition was correct. I recognized the figure as the one I had seen with Jackson Black, and with relief, I buried my face in the baby soft scent of Jimmy's fine hair.

"Have you established the identity of our thief?" McCollum asked as we exited the temple.

"Yes I did, but how did you know?" I asked, looking sideways at

Will to see if he had spilled the beans.

"It is my job to know!" McCollum replied. "I was the sole member of the Druids given the task to remain conscious. It has now been two thousand years, and although this body grows old, I have retained all of what was asked of me.

"If you knew what I was doing tonight, do you also know the identify of the thief?"

His expression was tender as he acknowledged my surprise. "I have been in search of my enlightenment for tens of thousands of years, and while your soul is a bit younger in comparison"—he smiled at my surprise—"I have to be very mindful not to interfere with the journeys of others, for the journey you have just taken has taught you much."

I could feel that my mouth had fallen open, so I closed it and continued to stare at him.

"There are three reasons I did not interfere," he said, holding one finger up. "You would not have learned that even as a child you were aware of the wonderful power within you and kept believing in it no matter the odds." Then a second finger appeared, "Your power to transport your light body effortlessly from place to place would have been delayed by years, maybe lifetimes, if not for the immediate need to help your Spirit Guide. And the third might be the most important one of all," McCollum said placing his hand upon his chest. "The unexpected occurrence of watching your heart open to what most saw as an inanimate object and giving that bowl *a vision* of itself. That is an immense power to possess indeed, my Dear One."

I paused a moment to take in the fact that McCollum was proud of me. It felt incredibly wonderful. "Do you see everything we do?" I asked, calling to mind things that I didn't want anyone to know about me.

"Not the way you are thinking," he grinned. "I am only interested in the advancement of your being, not personal, day-to-day events."

I sighed with relief and went back to our original subject. "Now that we know who our thief is, what should we do?"

"I never let my *knowing* take the place of someone else's growth," McCollum assured me. "I trust that the Brass Band will arrive at the perfect conclusion. Please let me know when you have come up with a plan."

I nodded my head. "You'll be the first to know!" And I knew I was speaking very literally.

CHAPTER TWENTY

March 18, 2012

Wanting desperately to find an answer to the conundrum of how to confront our thief, I walked across campus and went to the location where I could always find them. I began focusing on my question as I pushed open the library door and made my way up to the glass-floored room. I tapped my fingers to discharge static electricity and began my search by closing my eyes as I ran my fingers along the edge of the shelves. I walked slowly back and forth, confident I would encounter the book that held my answer. Responding to that special feeling, my hand stopped and I pulled a book from the shelf. I wasn't at all surprised when I let it fall open and began to read the words of one of the greatest proponents of non-violence who had ever lived, Mahatma Gandhi.

> *Non-violence is the greatest force at the disposal of mankind. It is mightier than the mightiest weapon of destruction devised by the ingenuity of man.*

I read on until I found a statement that was irrefutable and seemed like it could be my answer.

> *Power is of two kinds. One is obtained by the fear of punishment and*

> *the other by the act of love. Power based on love is a thousand times more effective and permanent than the one derived from fear of punishment.*

Closing the book, I sat down at the reference table to think about what I had just read. Knowing love was the path I had to take in calling our thief to task, I had absolutely no idea how these words pertained to my situation.

I pushed the library door open and stepped out into the cool afternoon air. Chilled, I stopped to unzip my backpack and pull out the jacket I carried for that very reason.

"Well, look who we have here!"

Turning to face Jackson Black, I momentarily closed my eyes, hoping that he would disappear, but no such luck!

"Aren't you going to say hello?" He grinned smugly.

"No, I'm going to say, go away!" I turned to leave, but Black seized my arm. It was physically painful, and frightened me to the bone. I could feel his brashness, and knew he was growing bolder.

"Let go of me," I demanded. There were plenty of people around us who were on their way to class, and a few of them began to slow down to watch. "Now, Black!" I jerked my arm as hard as I could and felt his fingers dig into my arm even harder.

"Let go," a gentle voice said, so softly that I hardly heard it. "I think the lady asked you politely. Now, I also ask you. Let go of her, sir."

The person coming to my defense was not a buff football player, but the small Asian man whom I had last seen twinkling in Gilbert's classroom.

"Go away, old man," Black admonished, paying no attention to

174

the monk. Time slowed as I saw the crowd gather. Black's grip was tightening, and no one else from the surrounding group was stepping forward to help.

"This is your last warning," Dorje calmly stated as he stepped to my side.

I saw the monk's aura expanding as my antagonist responded with a laugh. That was Black's first mistake. Jackson's second error in judgment was entering Dorje's personal space. I'd heard of the art of turning a person's own motion against them, but this monk was a master. As Jackson moved forward, the old gentleman gracefully moved past him and with an almost indiscernible motion pushed Black to the ground.

Infuriated, Black got to his feet and charged us. The more force Black used, the more damage he did to himself. I was in awe as I watched Jackson Black retreat in defeat and disappear into the crowd.

"May I walk you home, Hillary?" Dorje asked, offering me his arm.

"I would be honored!" I exclaimed, and we walked away amid an uproar of applause.

Ruth was sitting on my front porch trying to warm herself in a sunbeam when Dorje and I arrived home. She seemed agitated, and I wondered what was wrong.

"Hi Hillary," she said, standing and shoving her hands deep into her pockets for warmth. "Hi ..."

"Dorje," I finished for her, because I knew she wouldn't remember his name.

"Do you ... have time to talk?" Ruth stammered. "I ... I really need to talk! He can come too," she added, waving her hand. "Maybe he'll know something about what, well, you'll find out."

"Come on in before you catch a cold, Ruth." It was an overcast and damp day that begged for a dry apartment. I unlocked the door and hurried a shivering Ruth inside. Dorje silently followed. "Both of you, have a seat and I'll make something warm to drink."

"I've been researching the gift that Mom gave me," Ruth began, turning to Dorje to fill him in. "This relic has been passed down through the females in my family, and as far as I know, most of them treated it like a keepsake, like it was a sting of pearls or great grandma's old wedding ring. Well, I've been looking into it, and it seems like anything but!"

"May I see the artifact that you speak of?" Dorje asked politely.

"Sure, I brought it with me." She walked over to her ten-gallon purse and dove in to retrieve it. She continued talking as she searched, "Since it has come through the centuries to me, I want to make use of it."

Walking back with the box in her hand, she offered it to Dorje. "I've been looking online for things that are similar, and the things I find either don't give me enough information to come to a solid conclusion or scare the crap out of me."

The monk peered into the box with great interest.

"Do you know what it is?" Ruth implored.

"Yes, I believe I do," he replied.

 Tell me what you think," Ruth whimpered.

"May I?" he asked, motioning to the object.

With Ruth's permission, Dorje gently lifted the object from the box, turning it over and over in his hands. Ruth and I sat calmly—or at least I did—waiting for him to speak.

"Do you know much of your female lineage? Do you know of their beliefs?"

"Yes!" Ruth perked up considerably. "Yes, we're Catholic. I attended a private girls' school, as did my mother! My grandmother was

176

the first born of immigrants from Hungary. Her father moved to the US so he could seek his fortune, you know … the American dream.”

“Do you know much of his wife, your great grandmother?” Dorje inquired.

“No, my recollection of any stories about her are a little cloudy. She’s the one no one really talked about.”

“Then I am confident your great grandmother is the last female in your family who actually used this for its intended purpose, and I believe that your great grandfather encouraged her to embrace the Catholic faith after finding out what she really was.”

“What was she?” Ruth asked, holding her breath. She was a bit hesitant, and very excited.

“A witch,” he said without judgment.

I didn’t know if Ruth was going to faint or jump for joy when she finally came out of her stupor. For a long time it seemed as if she’d turned to stone, never to move again. First there was a weird motion she made with her mouth, kind of fish like. I think she was formulating questions as they madly ran though her mind. Finally she picked her simplest thought and fashioned a sentence.

“My great grandmother was a witch?”

Smiling, he simply said, “Do you have a flair for magic, Ruth?”

Ruth shook her head, no.

“She can definitely develop it,” I insisted, amused that Ruth was speechless. “It makes sense. After all, she came to the Druids for training.”

Ruth’s mouth was working, but still no words were coming out of it.

“It’s a ward,” Dorje whispered.

This revelation aroused feelings of anticipation inside me. Finally Ruth would have the answers that she’d been looking for.

“It’s the physical embodiment of power,” Dorje said. He placed the object back in its box and moved it away from Ruth’s bewildered stare, “You need to ask your mother if she has any psychic abilities, because regardless of her religion, these abilities usually run in families. Your ancestral powers would be passed down to you through your mother's bloodline," he added, looking at Ruth thoughtfully. "Of course, you have also brought the accumulation of accomplishments from your past incarnation forward as well. I call those *soulular* gifts. But in this case we are talking about your *cellular* gifts, the ones that have been passed to you through your genetics, the memories that are in the cells of your body." He gave Ruth a kind smile and stated, "This ward should awaken those memories for you."

Ruth made a dismissive noise. "In either case, I got nothin'!"

"You don't give yourself enough credit, Ruth, I said, trying to encourage her. "I think you should find out more about your great grandmother. Maybe in the process you'll find out more about the other women in your family." I knew there was more to this than met the eye.

Well, this was going to take another trip to Kansas City, and Will and George weren't very thrilled about us driving alone. Wednesday was the quickening full moon, and there was going to be an etheric opening that night. Will was planning on getting his final three boys into the flow of The River of Knowledge. It would be a very auspicious time for McCollum's household, and of course George would be needed to look after their physical bodies while Will led the boys into the ethers.

The pull that I once felt during the full moon had waned since my encounter with my spirit guide, Eugene Atohi, but Will still worried about me being away from him on those nights. But regardless of how Will and George felt, I was supporting Ruth in her search for information, and we were going to strike while the iron was hot.

I heard George in the living room asking Ruth to be careful; I also heard some assorted kissing sounds. I put my last piece of clothing in my overnight bag and zipped it shut.

Will had been very concerned ever since I'd told him of our plans to leave right away, but he knew better than to try to change my stubborn mind. Ruth had been my wingman for two thousand years; now it was my turn to stand by her. So we loaded up the car, and since Will was already at McCollum's in preparation for the full moon event, I left a love note on the table telling him that I'd be back in two days.

I hardly gave the Witherspoons' gate a second look. I'd been through it so many times that the big mansion had just become the place where Ruth's folks lived. Ruth had not told her mom that we were coming for a visit. She was convinced that the questions she had about her great grandmother would be answered more honestly if her mother had no advance warning. Ruth wanted to watch her mom's expressions and decide for herself how much her mom really knew about the ancient wooden knot.

By the time we got our bags out of the car and up to our rooms, Mrs. Witherspoon had lunch on the table. Ruth's dad, as she had expected, was away on a business trip, leaving just the three of us, plus staff.

"So, what brings you girls to Kansas City?" Mrs. Witherspoon asked. "It must be something special for you to miss classes."

I knew this was Ruth's opening, and hoped she would take it. I saw her shift in her chair, straighten her shoulders, and then launch straight into the fray.

"Mom, I have a few questions about the artifact you gave me," she stated with the utmost calm. "I've been researching it and found some interesting information."

"Yesssss ... I thought you might," she replied, looking slightly sheepish. "I had a few questions myself when I first took it into my possession."

We sat quietly, but Ruth's mom was going to take some prodding.

"When did you first get it?"

"Well Ruth," she said, trying to retrieve the memory, "I think it must have been when I was about nineteen or so. Once I gave birth to a health baby girl, your great grandmother insisted on coming for a visit. She said see needed to see you, to look into your eyes … and boy, did she ever look into your eyes. She seemed very pleased that you had inherited her green eyes."

I noticed that Ruth's mom was rubbing her hands together, and the more I watched, the more I began to see a pattern.

"Mrs. Witherspoon," I began, but she interrupted.

"Please, call me Joyce. No need to be formal."

"Okay Joyce, can I ask you the significance of what you are doing with your hands?"

She placed them under her thighs to get them to stop moving. "You must have brought that"—she seemed at a loss for words—"the thing in the box, you must have it with you."

"Yes," Ruth replied, taking it out of her pocket and placing it on the table.

"I've never told you about your great grandmother because most of what I've heard are secondhand stories, and you know how I feel about gossip. From the time I was very young, too young for adults to think I was listening, I would hear things whispered at family holidays or a few words when my grandfather had too much to drink, nothing very conclusive."

"Just talk to me, Mom, tell me what you think," Ruth coaxed.

It took about fifteen minutes—and a bit of brandy in her coffee— to persuade Joyce that we could be trusted with the family's dirty little secret, but finally she loosened up.

"Your great grandfather was a extremely religious man. Many were in the early 1900s. He didn't drink alcohol, nor did he smoke or use foul language, but most of all he didn't approve of the occult. He saw it as sin against God, a tool of Satan." She added with an undertone, "He claimed his heart had been stolen. He loved the mysterious gypsy girl before she had even looked up to meet his eyes."

"I gathered over the years," she continued, enjoying her coffee more and more, "that it all began one night when a gypsy caravan opened up shop outside of the Hungarian village that your great granddad lived in. The news of a particularly striking young fortuneteller spread like wildfire. Your great aunts liked to sarcastically say that it was because of her ability to cast spells, but regardless, one night Fred—your great grandfather—and his friends couldn't resist their curiosity any longer and slipped out of town and into the wanderers' camp to see what their fortunes held. Well, Lola—the beautiful gypsy girl—and Fred fell in love, and you know how foolish young love can be. Lola promised, whether she was truly convinced or not, that she could be happy converting to Catholicism. Fred began reading the Bible to her every evening, and after their marriage, he quickly moved her as far away from her gypsy roots as he possibly could by emigrating to the United States. I think"—Joyce was almost squirming in her seat—"that you can only pretend for so long."

"Pretend she was happy?" Ruth asked.

"No, they were very happy and in love right up until the day Fred passed. I mean you can't just change your faith to make another happy. Lord knows she tried, but the night she came to me and we sat on the porch with you in my arms, she just couldn't pretend anymore. She hadn't given that artifact to her own daughter for fear that her husband would discover that she had not fully left her occult beliefs behind. She said that I should pass it along to its rightful owner—who she made very clear was you—and that I would know when that time was right."

Almost apologetically, she continued with Ruth's hand now in hers, "Oh, honey, have I made a mistake? I don't want to burden you with that old thing."

"It's no burden, Mom," Ruth soothed. "Lola meant for me to have it. You did good!"

"Oh, I'm not sure. I had to lock that thing away because it gave me nightmares."

"Nightmares about what?" I broke in. It had to be asked. Maybe it wasn't my place, but I had to know.

"Dancing, full moons, birds. My hands would move, making this strange drawing in the air. I would wake your father. Oh, I don't even want to think about it!"

"Then let's not," Ruth said with a huge smile, changing the subject. "Let's go to the Plaza and shop! There is that wonderful little boutique that you like. We can have a vanilla latte and gab the day away."

That seemed to ease the tension and put a smile back on Mrs. Witherspoon's face. "Go get your purse, Mom. Hillary and I will pull the car around to the front of the house."

With a few minutes to talk confidentially, Ruth said, "I knew it! I've been reading, and it says that the power runs in families, like in yours. It was just ignored for a few generations in mine. I wish I could have met Lola."

I put my hand on Ruth's arm to warn her of her mother's approach. No need to get her upset again.

The mood lightened immensely once we began to shop. Ruth and her mom were experts, and moved from shop to shop with the ease of butterflies pollinating spring flowers, leaving money here and there and taking flight to the next boutique. By the time we stopped for lunch, Mrs. Witherspoon had begun to enjoy her reminiscences of Lola and Fred's enduring love affair.

CHAPTER
TWENTY-ONE

March 21, 2012

Ruth and I were back in Manhattan by the time the full moon rose, and because neither Will nor George would be home that night, we decided Ruth should stay in her old bedroom in my apartment. It would be just like old times.

"I found something online," I told Ruth. "Look at this," I said pushing my laptop toward her. "It says most witches keep their abilities to themselves or within their coven."

"Wait just a minute," Ruth said puffing out her chest. "Are you calling me a witch?"

"Yes, I thought we agreed on that?"

"That word conjures up such ugly images for me, warts and bad fashion."

I laughed as I continued reading. "*Witches are humans who have a certain flair for magic and psychic abilities.* That's you all over, Ruth, but listen to this." She began to speak, but I shushed her so I could finish. "*'When you cast a spell repeatedly within a 48-hour period, you become weak'*—but this is the part about your artifact—*'A witch uses an object to amplify her power, such as an amulet or a ward.'* How about that? Dorje was right!"

Vicki Renfro

"Okay, I'll go with calling it a ward, but I'm done with this stuff online. There's just too much to sift through. I think I'll go to our answer man, Gilbert. He'll know where I should start."

"Call him! It's still early," I encouraged her. "Let's open Pandora's box."

"Answer man ... I like that handle," Gilbert laughed as he stepped into the apartment. "What can I do for you ladies tonight?"

Ruth told him the story about her great grandma, Lola, and how the ward had come down through the females in the family and was now hers. "So, how do I use it, Gilbert?"

"Okay, let's start at the beginning," Gilbert said thoughtfully. "I, for one, am happy to finally have the answer to a question that has baffled me since the first gathering of the Druids."

Ruth and I waited silently for the big reveal!

"Have you ever looked around our gatherings, looked into each face and everyone's eyes?"

I began to grin, knowing what Gilbert was going to say.

"You differ from the rest of us in one very obvious way. You have green eyes, Ruth."

I could see her going around our circle in her mind and checking the color of everyone's eyes, and when she came to the same conclusion, she said, "I can't believe I never noticed. How come you never said anything, Hillary?"

"I noticed, but never considered it important. I guess it is."

"Green eyes are those of healers. So let's start there," Gilbert decided.

He looked very confortable sitting on my couch. It brought to mind all the times he had sat in that exact spot to answer my

184

questions. Things had changed since Will and Indira had come into our lives, and I truly missed him.

"You're missing the mark, Gilbert." Ruth said. "The sight of blood makes me faint. I've never wanted to be a doctor or nurse. I don't even take vitamins."

"As a mystic," he scoffed, "You wouldn't work with the things of this world. You'd use the energetic world. Hold out your hands, Ruth."

Gilbert held his hands just above hers. "Hillary, feel this." I moved my hands into position and felt the heat radiating from hers.

"Ruth, you can use this energy for healing or for whatever you choose," said the answer man, "and the cool thing is that your ward is here to help you. Take time to know what the gifts are within you, and then discover how this artifact can aid you."

It was very late by the time we were finished talking, so I tossed a pillow and blanket to Gilbert and informed Ruth that her old bed had clean sheets and that I was going to bed.

"Call if you need me! Sometimes dreams on the full moon really suck." They laughed, but I knew that tonight I would miss having Will with me.

I lay in bed, amused by the conversation I heard through my bedroom door. Ruth was annoyed by the idea that she was a witch, finding the idea unpleasant. "How come I just can't be a Druid like the rest of you?"

Gilbert tried to relieve her anxiety by explaining that it was her choice. She had the ability to become a crucial warrior in the uplifting of the planet, and she could call herself the Original Supernatural Goddess if she liked. "What you call yourself is not important; it is the purity of your heart that matters."

When the apartment became silent, I found I couldn't sleep, so I focused my energy to my third eye and let all of the day's anxiety fall away. I took a deep breath, focused on the second bowl, and floated away to visit my friend.

March 21, 2012

I find myself next to the second bowl, in the closet, where it is collecting dust. I wonder if Adriana Heinrich no longer holds this bowl in high esteem. I remain motionless for a while, settling into my new surroundings, when I hear it—the soft rhythmic vibration of the bowl as its spirit begins to wake. "Hello my friend," I whisper, making a quick mental check to assure myself that we are alone. "I'm glad to find you well."

I move my spirit into the brass bowl and became aware of the many things that exist within it. I can feel the strands of thought that Father John and his monks have placed within it, and also the qualities of Will, George, Ruth, and the other members of the Brass Band. I am enjoying the experience, when I become aware of something that makes me feel ill. Fixing my mind on it, I follow the thought to its point of origin at the edge of the bowl.

"I'm gathering followers, and I will build a world from the misery they create," Black whispers into my ear. "Look around you Hillary. This is my dream."

I open my eyes to peer into Black's world and, I am severely distressed. Sorrow and discontent are the status quo in his realm, and man's connection to self has been lost.

"What have you done, Jackson?"

I hear a scream and turn to look ... but I know instinctively that it's not of this world.

Jumping to my feet the moment I was back in my body, I ran to Ruth's room. She was upright in Gilbert's arms, sobbing.

"Ruth, tell me what you saw," was all I needed to say to prompt her. She had done this for me many times, and now it was her turn to recall her dream before it faded away.

"George and I were on our way to Coritani. We were to meet with a chieftain in order to assemble an army, but we had stopped for the night. We were sleeping just off the road, hidden under the vegetation, when we woke to the sound of horses."

I watched as Ruth's brow knitted and her hands balled into fists, "He was a big man, and George was caught off guard. There was nothing he could do when I was dragged away into the undergrowth by the others ... well ..." she just couldn't bring herself to talk about the abuse she'd suffered. "George was screaming my name until they finally dumped me in a pile next to him." She looked up at me, trying hard to hold herself together. "George was bleeding, Hillary! Bad!"

"Oh, honey, you don't have to—"

"I've seen you do this a million times, Hillary. Just let me finish before the dream slips away."

I sat on the edge of the bed and led her back to where she had left off, Gilbert took her hand, "And what did you do then, Ruth?"

"My hands were moving, drawing a pattern in the air." She sat up a little straighter. "I could see my chi as my hand repeated the same shape, one on top of the last, over and over again. I used the last of my strength to build a barrier between the Roman barbarians and us. I knew neither George nor I would live much longer, and I wanted those last moments to be ours.

"The Roman butcher's voice continually taunted us. He was incredibly angry, incensed by the fact that he could not physically reach us. *'Your heads will soon be ornaments on the end of a stick,'* he said." Ruth gagged a little. "He intended to cut our heads off and display them as a warning to anyone who might think of following The Great Hilsbeth."

Ruth was beginning to shake visibly from the sheer horror of what she had experienced. I was worried, but Gilbert was steady, so we let her go on.

"The amazing thing was that my barrier held! I died in George's arms, and I'm sure he followed me shortly after." Ruth took one last breath before breaking down. "IT HELD!" Between enormous shuddering sobs, Ruth added, "The pattern I was drawing in the air is the same design as my ward."

I held onto Ruth and began to weep with her. It wasn't long before Gilbert followed suit.

I heard the front door swing open and saw George enter the room. No one said a word. We didn't have to. George had heard Ruth's cries while sitting in meditation in McCollum's temple, and had come home to save her because this time he could. Taking Ruth into his arms, he picked her up as if she were an infant, cradling her head against his shoulder. He placed her hand on his beating heart to prove to her that he still lived, and carried her out of our apartment, letting the door close silently behind him.

"McCollum called me back from the ethers, straightaway," Will informed Gilbert and me as he closed the front door about twenty minutes later. "McCollum does not fault George for leaving because the pull on his heart must have been extraordinarily strong. I know how it must have torn him apart to leave our bodies unprotected, but there was no power on Earth that could have kept him from Ruth! This is the anniversary, you know? And unlike two thousand years ago, this time he's whole."

That statement stunned me, and I began to understand why Ruth had had that particular dream tonight, during the etheric opening of the full moon.

"Thanks for being here, Gilbert." Will was sincerely thankful that Ruth and I weren't alone, and since none of us were going to be able to sleep now, I made tea.

Ruth bounced back as well as anyone could have expected, helped by the fact that McCollum had released George from all his duties so he could spend his time with her. I knew that being told of your death in a past life was vastly different than the shock of actually reliving it. The intense emotions cause such a flow of adrenalin in your body that you're trashed for days.

When she became steadier and decided to take action, Ruth went out and obtained all sizes and varieties of crystals: rose quartz, amethyst, ajoite, and aragonite. Knowing we'd have plenty of time to talk when she was ready, I just watched her from my window as she buried them at each corner of our property. She had also become much more serious during our evening mediations, and in a lot of ways, I saw myself in her. After a glimpse of the power she'd once commanded, she wanted it back.

March 22, 2012, equinox

With the light and dark perfectly balanced at the equator and the light gaining in the northern hemisphere, I thought this equinox could be an especially useful time for Ruth and me to develop control our own light, the chi energy that exists in all of us. Ruth was beyond determined to learn to use her life force to create a protective barrier like she had seen herself make in her dream, and I had a longing to master my chi as well.

Vicki Renfro

We both were immersed in silent concentration as we began our first chi-gong movements, and as time passed, I felt a calm drift over me.

"I know this is helping my stress levels," I said, as we both moved with incredible slowness so we could get the biggest bang for our buck.

Ruth ignored me as she persisted tirelessly, unmoved by my sudden chatty mood.

"In the old days, you would have been breaking into a tap dance by now," I said. "Your sense of humor is dissolving."

"Stop kidding me, Hillary. I have a long way to go before I'm able to build that impenetrable wall of energy, and I know it will come in handy someday." She moved her hands in the shape of her ward and looked at me, pleased with herself. "At least I have that part down."

We continued to find time every day, and with practice, practice, and more practice, our chi began to move in our bodies. And although mastery was still somewhat beyond my reach, Ruth was beginning to bloom into a confident woman!

April 22, 2012, Dark Moon

Ruth had arranged a meeting with George, Will, and me in McCollum's temple at 11:00 p.m. The late hour would ensure that all of the boys would be fast asleep.

I knew Ruth was nervous because this was going to be her big debut. Tonight she would stand in front of the ones she trusted most in an attempt to reconnect with the gift that she knew she once owned.

"Who really knows if something's going to work until you try," Ruth mumbled as she instructed George to lower the lights, and she stepped to the center of the room. I saw that she was wearing her ward on a leather band around her neck, and appreciated that she was using it, in combination with the energy of McCollum's temple to amplify her own abilities. Saying a little prayer and centering herself, Ruth raised her hands.

Tonight, her personality had changed from flamboyant to apprehensive, so I added a prayer of my own in hopes that this evening would be a huge windfall for her. George and Will devoted all their attention to what Ruth had in store for them, leaving her no other option than to begin.

Turning, she began drawing the silhouette of her ward in the air. She had discovered a Wiccan spell in that big, fat book Dr. Edwards had given her, and she spoke it, over and over, as she moved, placing one pattern over another. I held my breath, wanting with all of my heart for this to work.

I motioned Will to step forward to the first X that Ruth had placed on the floor. The air crackled with electricity, and for the briefest of moments, I thought I could actually see the design of the ward suspended in front of her. Ruth continued with more zeal as I motioned Will to move forward to the second X. I watched Will's face as he moved in Ruth's direction, and knew that he felt it.

"Well," Ruth said, as she finished and dropped her exhausted arms to her sides. "Did you feel the air in the air get thicker? Did it feel like an invisible wall?

I could tell by Will's expression that he totally agreed with her assessment, but Ruth needed to hear the words.

"Ruth!" George thundered, drawing her attention away from Will. "I am so proud of you!" He wanted nothing more than to run to her, but the he couldn't get traction because of the strength of her protection spell. He moved like he was slogging through deep water. We all laughed until finally he popped through to the other side of her incantation, and with unexpected emotion tenderly picked Ruth up and held her to his chest. It was romantic until I heard Ruth whimper.

"I can't breathe, sweetie! Put me down, put me down," Ruth squeaked.

He set her back on her feet and ran his fingers gently through her hair. "I had no idea," an awestruck George said. "You are a powerful woman!"

Will and I left—this needed to be a private moment.

Ruth became even more driven by her success in the temple, and with dogged determination continued to build an etheric security field around the perimeter of our apartments. I wasn't sure what her end game was, but I slept easier knowing that no uninvited guest would be visiting.

May 6, 2012

Another full moon brought the Brass Band together again, and we sat to meditate before exchanging stories about what we had been doing.

Indira had convinced Father John to keep the brass bowl with him at Ruth and George's apartment, so it would have an opportunity to sing freely without its true identity being discovered. The bowl had obeyed the request to remain silent when in the presence of the monks, so tonight, as we filled it with our deepest desires for the world, it sang with abandon.

Mom had placed a perfectly timed dinner in the oven, and by the time we all emerged from meditation, the aroma of it persuaded all of us that we were starving. As we seated ourselves around the table, the conversations about what we'd been up to began in earnest.

Mom and Dad expressed their feelings of loss since Father John no longer came to the farm to meditate. Gilbert declared his love for Indira, and although we were not surprised, we were all very happy for him. Dr. Edwards did surprise us by inviting Will to be part of a new study on channeling, pay included, which got an enthusiastic yes from both Will and me. Ruth proudly informed the group of her Wiccan ancestry, and of her developing powers. I told stories about my friendship with the second bowl, and also suggested that we should set a date to talk about the thief who had caused this whole mess in the first place—but that was overshadowed by the joy of us all being together again and the fact that the thief seemed to have disappeared.

Father John interjected information about the advances the Tibetan monks were making now that they had settled into their new quarters in McCollum's carriage house. That only left George.

At first he blushed. Then he stammered. Finally he just came out with it. "I already have permission from Ruth's father, and I've wondered what would be the best way. Well, I decided this was it." Turning to Ruth and going down on one knee, George pulled a small box from his pocket and opened it. "Ruth Witherspoon, would you do me the incredible honor of becoming my wife?"

Ruth's lip began to wobble and her eyes watered. Gilbert began to say something and Ruth shushed him. "Just give me a minute to bathe in this! I want to remember it forever!"

George grinned, looking at no one but her.

"Yes! The answer is yes!"

First came setting the date. We looked at the waxing and waning moon cycles, but knew she'd have to pick her date by when her selected event center would be available. Mrs. Witherspoon had hired a wedding planner, and with only six months to go, I knew my mom had the most difficult task of all: she had to teach George how to dance.

"What are you going to do about the guest list?" I asked. "Are you going to mix pagan and Catholic?"

"Heck, yes! I'm going to mix mystic boys and my grandparents, McCollum and my high school friends, and my drama classmates with the young and wealthy of Kansas City! It's my day, and everyone will be there to witness my *happily ever after!*"

"Big wedding, then?"

"Giant," Ruth gloated.

"What about George's parents?" That made her stop and think.

"George has a family … wow, George has a family and I'm going to meet them," she said with wonder. "I need to ask George about his guest list."

Eventually our lives began to settle back into normality after the initial excitement of the engagement wore off. Other than Ruth's weekly call with her mother to talk about the wedding plans, we settled back into our daily routine of chi-gong and school.

"Do you have any interest in spending time with me in Topeka?" Will asked, once we had realized how much time we'd be apart due to Will's new job with Dr. Edwards.

"Would I be able to spend any time with you during the days, or only after you got home from work in the evenings?"

"I'm not sure about anything beyond the fact that I'll be staying at Dr. Edwards' home, and that I'll miss having you curled up next to me at night."

"Does his guest room have a king-size bed?" I asked, wrapping my arms around him and moving closer.

"You'd turn me down because of the size of Lee's guest bed?" he replied giving me a wicked look.

"No, I'm going to turn you down because of my job."

I occupied my long hours without Will by going within and visiting the second bowl. I felt a need to follow up on that *dark Jackson Black thing* from my last visit. It seemed obvious that they were trying to tap into the higher powers they were convinced the bowl possessed. For all I knew, the second bowl might also be capable of manifesting for them.

It was neither a full or dark moon, so I felt confortable leaving my body to astral travel a bit. I closed my eyes and shook off the day, set my worldly thoughts aside, and pulled my energy inward until it only existed at my third eye. Concentrating on the bowl, I willed myself to move from my body to join the bowl—wherever it was now that the leather-clad lady had moved.

To my surprise, I found myself standing in the shadows behind a sizable circle of dreadfully dark people. They were an angry, disenfranchised, and downright negative group of souls, but to my enormous relief, no one had noticed my entrance. I tried to define the emotions I felt crawling on my skin. They ran the gamut of loneliness, desperation, envy, remorse, loathing, and revenge, and all were united by the magnetic power of something dark. Then I heard her voice and thought, *Yes, what sad, lonely guy wouldn't be drawn to this exquisite woman and her sultry influence?* She had convinced them that she truly cared.

"We are gathered to create what we desire for ourselves, mankind be damned," she declared with no preamble. "I will never leave your side—never," Adriana whispered, as she walked from man to man, running her fingers though their hair, causing their souls to surrender. "I will nurture you, ensure your growth, and be your special friend."

I watched the devotees who surrounded her and saw their eyes roll back in their heads as they listened to her hypnotic voice. She was spellbinding in her movements and seductive in her touch.

"I have acquired a relic with amazing powers. This artifact has found its way to me, for I have always been its rightful owner. It loves and serves me alone."

There was an audible *ahhhh* as her admirers became even more enthralled.

"The brass bowl that I hold in my hands can make a poor shepherd a king or a slave into a master, and if you obey me, I will give this all to you." She bent to set the bowl in the center of the circle, swaying her hips to hold everyone's attention.

My heart broke for my brass friend, and I felt its confusion. So, in an effort to bring comfort, I focused my energy and relocated myself into bowl before any attention moved from Adriana Heinrich's rear end to the vessel she held in her hands.

"Shhhhhhhhh,"I mentally told the bowl before it could make a peep at my arrival. "We both have to remain quiet!" I felt the consciousness of the bowl move close to me. "We must resist what they place into you tonight. Let's fill the bowl to the brim with the love we feel for each other," I suggested. "Then their thoughts won't be able to enter you and will dissipate into nothing."

"You seem to have found your strength," I heard a voice say inside me, and smiled at my Indian spirit guide's return.

"Sometimes I forget it is actually a strength," I answered, thankful for the reminder. *"I'm glad you came."*

196

"I watch you always, and I thought, under these circumstances, you could use a little help. That's quite a group of nasty toadies out there, and even though most of them have guides who are of the light, I'm afraid no amount of grace will change the current trajectory this group is on. Ms. Heinrich has a very strong hold on their souls."

I snapped to alert as a particular voice in the room gripped my attention. "Do you hear that?"

The bowl moaned inwardly. "His thoughts are especially repulsive, and cause me pain," the bowl conveyed, "and he's been here a lot lately."

"It's the one who was referred to as the Butcher of the Druids," Eugene said, as I connected Black's face to the voice. "He carries an obsession for you, Spirit Lady. His preoccupation comes from his Roman incarnation, and his fascination with possessing you places you in great danger. He has a perverted desire to have what the Great Marcus Flavius desired and couldn't. This psychosis is the demon that drives him in this lifetime."

I was silent, paralyzed by the image of what came to mind. "Don't manifest any of this!" I spoke to the bowl. The light began to diminish, and I was afraid. The darkness from the circle was almost suffocating.

Sucking air into my lungs in a frantic attempt to regain my body, I woke in my bed … alone. Falling limp on my pillows, I sent a mental message to Will, telling him how much I missed him, and in return I felt a feeling of warmth wrap around me. Rolling over in an effort to go back to sleep, I sighed a goodbye to Eugene. Then I heard a ruckus at my front door.

I heard the door open, and I heard a voice say, "Don't worry! It's only me, Hillary!" This was followed by a slam and the weight of someone sitting down on my bed.

"George hitched a ride to Topeka with Will, and I've decided to spend my time placing a protection field on everything I value using my ward."

I watched her as her hands moved in a precise motion around me. "Thanks, Ruth!" I said, in true appreciation for what she was doing for me. "You're just what I need right now." I swung my legs over the edge of the bed and pulled my t-shirt back into place. "Want some hot chocolate?"

"Yeah, I can't sleep. How about you?"

I smiled easily, not stating the obvious. "Come on, Ruth, tell me what has you spooked."

Evidently, she had been more frightened by the realization of who Jackson Black was in our past life than I had expected her to be. Actually, I had mistakenly believed that she had long ago figured out that he was the dreaded Druid executioner.

"What's he doing in the same town as us? He cut off my head in that lifetime. Yes, only one among hundreds, but still, he's here with us, again!"

"I think your newly discovered powers will protect us," I soothed. "I mean, doesn't it seem like perfect timing to you?"

"I guess so," she said as she began to calm down.

I knew I should tell her about my latest experience with Black and Adriana Heinrich, and that they were now working in partnership, but decided it could wait.

"I didn't know George was going with Will," I said, changing the subject to something brighter. I could see Ruth's shoulders relax as her mind switched to George. A smile crept across her face, and the dread of Jackson Black disappeared.

"George loves spending time with Will, and it was a perfect opportunity for him. I think McCollum may have gone, too."

"Wow! I can understand Dr. Edwards' interest in doing research on the connection between Will and The Teacher, but getting a peek into McCollum's head too must be an incredible bonus." We both laughed and fell into wedding talk. It was always the best subject to cheer Ruth up—it was so totally human.

A few hours before sunrise, I tucked a blanket around a snoozing Ruth and went back to bed. We had talked until she fell asleep on the couch, and I saw no reason to wake her up.

When Will and George arrived home on Friday evening, they found Ruth still living in my apartment. Ruth didn't apologize for being a little freaked out about Black, and when I finally admitted to my knowledge of the group Black and Heinrich were assembling, George and Will were a bit freaked, too.

"I think we need to inform the Brass Band, and inform McCollum that he needs to take precautions," Will said.

George agreed, and decided there was no reason to delay informing McCollum.

Things had become less formal since the advent of the Brass Band. McCollum was easier for me to talk to, and the high level of energy in the house had become commonplace. Will knocked on his door and McCollum invited all of us into his quarters.

"Something important brings you to me today, so let's get to the point," McCollum said, and to my surprise everyone looked at me.

"Well, last Wednesday night," I began, "I had an opportunity talk with Eugene." Everyone nodded, but didn't say a thing, so I continued. "When the subject of Jackson Black came up, he called him *the butcher of the Druids*, and said he was obsessed with me, that he was a danger to me, and it's the demon that drives him." Everyone else in the room was dead serious.

McCollum turned to Ruth. "How are your protection spells

coming along? Are you able to gather the light in a strong enough concentration to form a defense?"

Ruth sat up straight, loving the well-deserved attention. "I've been practicing, and I believe my abilities to protect us are growing, but to tell the truth, nothing has been tested."

"What do you feel would be an adequate experiment?" McCollum inquired.

"I guess I need to weave a protection barrier in a public location and then wait to see who can penetrate it, but I'm not sure how to do that."

"I think Hillary can help us with that." McCollum said. Turning to me, he continued. "If you could return to the bowl in Ms. Heinrich's possession and eavesdrop to determine a public location where Black frequents, we can send Ruth there prior to his arrival." To reassure Will and George, who were both now on high alert, he added, "We will make sure neither of your beloveds are in any danger. After all, it's only an experiment, one that can be called off at any time."

After talking for the better part of an hour, we determined that my spirit would attend Heinrich's weekly meeting on the following Wednesday night. That would be when we'd begin to put our plan into motion.

May 16, 2012

Will and I made our way down to Ruth and George's apartment on the following Wednesday evening, and were joined there by Gilbert and Dr. Edwards. Dr. Edwards had decided that this was a worthy experiment to include in his research, and was very interested in taking an active part. Will had earlier concluded that we should also include the original brass bowl as part of our group in order to magnify what we wished to accomplish tonight. Gilbert had kindly borrowed it for the evening and placed it in the center of the room.

My husband wanted me to have every safeguard possible as I entered Ms. Heinrich's home, and because Will was unwilling to let my soul travel into the viper's nest unaccompanied, he would relinquish his body to The Teacher so I would have someone to watch over me.

I closed my eyes at nine o'clock sharp and began to gather myself into a single point of light, and within moments, I found myself in the company of my friend.

"Have you remained strong?" I asked, expanding myself within the bowl that was still tucked away in the closet.

"I have been holding onto the light until you returned," I heard within me.

"I've brought a friend. His name is The Teacher."

The bowl lit with laughter! "The Teacher will never fit inside me. His energy is much too expansive."

Shhhhhhhh, I softly reminded the bowl. "The Teacher is here to watch over us from above."

We waited quietly for the inevitable, filling the bowl with a sense of peace, comforted knowing that the Brass Band sat watch over Will's body and mine. My consciousness felt a nudge, bringing me back to awareness, as the bowl was lifted from its closet shelf and placed in the center of the meeting. I made myself small and tried to relax so I could listen more carefully. With The Teacher close by, I knew I was safe.

"Welcome," I hear a sultry voice announce as the seduction of her audience begins. "Tonight we will again use my magic bowl to magnify our will. We want the world to bend to our desires, and we will create that with the power of our minds."

Her arrogance is remarkably reminiscent of the life she spent as a Roman governor. Then she had ordered the destruction of the whole Druid civilization with no remorse. The thought makes my skin crawl, so I force my attention back to the present and finding a location that will work to test Ruth's abilities. The moment happens when Black suggests that they gather on campus to create a disturbance at the same place I had first seen him the previous year. Pleased to receive the information I'd come for, I am free to spend the rest of my time helping the bowl with its ability to remain at peace, so that it might resist the thoughts that it is sure to bombarded with once I'm gone.

I'm jarred back to consciousness when I feel Adriana's hands on the bowl. She rubs it sensually as she speaks to a particular person in the room. Curious, I move to where I can watch. Her counterpart is a newly tattooed young lady with short, spikey hair. Her soul is stained by anger and blackened by vengeance, but at the same time I can feel a deep burden of despair buried beneath. It is a confusing mixture, considering the intense set of her jaw.

"Thank you for your loyalty," Adriana says with indifference. "I speak not only of the loyalty you have shown in this lifetime by once again bringing me the brass bowl, but of the many lifetimes you have served me."

"I betrayed my monastery for you," the girl says, glaring at her. "And you killed them all."

"I had to," Adriana answers, inserting a bit of sentiment into her voice. "I had to determine the bowl's location."

"And they took that location with them to their deaths," she spat back. Beneath her make-up and tough exterior, I recognize her as our thief, and my heart breaks for her. The burden of her betrayal was more than her soul was able to carry, and she is suffocating under the weight.

"I could have stolen it for you then, like I did this time. Your brutality was uncalled for."

The bowl shifted, and once again we were in the silence of the closet. I knew my delay in returning will cause The Brass Band immense anxiety, so I say goodbye and hear the bowl moan its farewell as I once again find myself back in my living room.

Will and I opened our eyes simultaneously, reassuring one another that we were okay.

"We found a location for your test, Ruth," I said, looking at Will. "Go ahead and tell them."

"Hillary, I wasn't the one with you. I have no idea what took place."

"I sometimes forget that your not actually around when you give your body to The Teacher, that you are meditating in a different dimension until you are called back to your body. But I appreciate that you let him come with me tonight," I said, realizing that I was also the only one in the room who had witnessed the conversation between the thief and the evil lady.

"So, what's the location?" Ruth asked, eager to put together a plan.

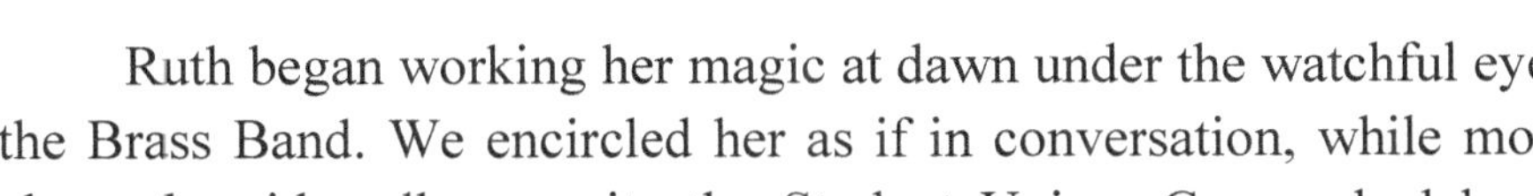

Ruth began working her magic at dawn under the watchful eyes of the Brass Band. We encircled her as if in conversation, while moving along the sidewalk opposite the Student Union. George had brought along a piece of chalk to mark the perimeter of Ruth's test area, so we would know exactly where the protection began and ended. Then we got a cup of coffee and waited for the show to begin.

We heard the noise before we saw their approach. They were obnoxious, and we watched as the students began to move away from them. They seemed to know whom to push to get a reaction, and before long the verbal fighting began. Then Black's head snapped toward me as if yanked by a string. He smiled, and I stood to meet his challenge. It was the best way to move him toward our chalked-off area.

Ruth was the first who saw me get to my feet, followed by Will. I knew he wanted to stop me. I could see him stiffen, but he stayed in his seat. I walked toward the first chalk mark on the sidewalk, and Black's eyes followed me. Once I was away from the protection of my group of friends, Black began to come toward me. I placed myself on the furthest chalk mark and turned to face him.

"Are you finding me irresistible?" he said, taunting me.

I said nothing.

"I see why you chose me over your inadequate lapdog of a husband. I have what you crave." He motioned toward his anatomy.

He reached for me, and as I took a step back, I heard the shifting of chairs against concrete as the Brass Band prepared to come to my rescue.

Black stopped. "Don't move away from me," he ordered.

"I'll do as I please," I replied, baiting him and taking another step backward. "What's wrong? Are you afraid of a little *light*?"

He was infuriated. "Me afraid of you?" he oozed. "You know you want me, so come and see what you've been missing." He moved his hips in invitation, as his cronies urged him on.

I openly laughed. "I will never do anything but loathe you."

"I will control you," he vowed, rage coloring his face. "Your movements, your mind, your affections." His lurid attempt to impress his buddies was faltering.

"No, I control you," I said, pointing a defiant finger at him as I prayed that Ruth's line would hold.

He began to close the space between us. I could see the doubt momentarily cross his face as he hit the mark. But he seamlessly used his bravado to cover his inability to move any closer. "You're not worth my time today. I have other plans for this fine morning, but soon … soon your desire for me will consume you, and on that day you will come begging." He turned to laugh with his lackeys, feeling like he had won.

I just couldn't help myself. "Coward! You afraid of a little girl?"

His eyes filled with fury as he hit Ruth's first barrier one more time. I whispered, "You are a fool to think I would ever consider you worth a second thought." I knew I had pushed him too far when I heard him growl, and watched him push through the first mark.

I turned my back to him and walked to the second chalk line, then turned to face him. "Come on Black. Come get me."

I knew the Brass Band was on their feet moving toward me, Will in the lead. I motioned for them to stop and watched Jackson hit the second mark. His nose flattened as if he had run into a glass door—and then began to bleed. He looked at me with disdain as he fished for a ratty Kleenex his had in his pocket to stop the bleeding. Our eyes met, dark to light. There was no mistaking that a battle had been waged— and it was our side one, the dark side zilch.

CHAPTER
TWENTY-TWO

We remained at the Union to gather more information on Ruth's barriers, and we discovered that her abilities were stronger than in our wildest imaginings. We watched some students walk through the chalk marks unobstructed, while others had a totally different experience. Not seeming to notice the impediment consciously, they would just slightly redirect their paths to move around it. We hypothesized that a person of pure heart could penetrate the barrier, but all we knew for sure was that the effectiveness diminished with time.

"Great job, Ruth," Will said. "But it has to last longer. It needs to last at least eight hours to protect us while we sleep."

"I'm sure I can do that with practice," Ruth answered confidently.

"We need you to do it now," George told her, "beginning when we get home. I think Hillary just made herself an enemy." He took her hand. "I'll help in any way I can."

"Me, too," I added. My cockiness diminished as my guilt about causing trouble for the Brass Band increased.

"Let's head home so I can get to work." Ruth was determined to build a wall that a bulldozer couldn't penetrate!

Ruth already had a routine of using the design of her ward to lay an etheric barrier around the perimeter of our house. She had been doing that for a few months, but we didn't know if her repetition would make it stronger. Her new habit was to begin her rounds the moment she completed her morning meditation, and I had begun to notice that Buddy always left at the same time she did.

"George," I whispered, as I watched his eyelids flutter when he returned from meditation. "What's up with Buddy and Ruth?"

"I've been watching them myself," he answered softly, "and I believe that Buddy must have joined our group to help her. He has a keen interest in what she's doing and sometimes seems to be assisting her in picking locations. I figure every witch needs her raven … Ruth's is just a tad smaller.

We watched Ruth through the front window, busily working her magic, and it wasn't long before George joked about whether or not we'd be able to get through her barrier ourselves. "What if we've had a particularly bad day with less than uplifting thoughts?"

We had a good laugh, but the more I thought about it the more I wondered if maybe George could be right.

It took a few days, but eventually I was able to convince Will that I would be safe walking to my classes and work alone. "No one will hurt me there. Not only am I protected by just being in public, but I also have my own chi. I've been practicing, and I can feel the energy building in my hands." I took the stance of a super hero to try to make him laugh. "Lighten up, sweetie. I need to live my life, or Black has already won!"

I watched as Will's posture changed, and he finally relented, because as much as he wanted to protect me, he knew I was right. So, he kissed me goodbye and I headed off to my first class.

I enjoyed school because it helped me keep a hold on my sanity. Everything in the study of mathematics was absolutely black and white.

No grey, pinks, or indigo, just complex formulas that had the same answer time after time. Everything about mathematics was so orderly and in its place, whereas nothing else in my life ever seemed to be. It made me regret that this term would soon be coming to an end.

With Ruth's big day only four months away, she finally convinced her parents to open up their home for her most special guests. "It's really the perfect place," Ruth assured them. The people who mean the most to me can stay on our grounds. McCollum and the Brass Band can spend the night in the guesthouse, and the boys can set up tents near the tennis courts." Dorje had informed Ruth that he could arrange lodging for the girls at a nearby Buddhist facility, and with Indira and I staying in the house with Ruth as her bridal party, we'd all be taken care of.

Ruth's mom was in heaven, planning the reception and the after-party festivities. Between Ruth's guest list and her parents, it was shaping up to be the party of the decade! And even though the wedding was going to miss the equinox by a day, it was still a good omen for the newlyweds due to the nights becoming longer.

I actually thought the most amazing thing about the wedding was that the dresses Ruth had picked out for Indira and me weren't typical never-to-be-worn-again bridesmaids' fashion. They were sophisticated and elegant, and she had arranged for a seamstress to alter them to fit us perfectly.

Everything was flawless, other than Ruth's nerves about meeting George's parents. I had never seen Ruth so anxious since ... well, I guess never.

"They will love you," George reassured her over and over. "If anyone should be nervous, it should be me. I haven't seen them in twelve years."

I had a hard time imagining what that would be like, but at the same time I was intrigued to see what his parents were like. Will's and my wedding had been so private, with only the Brass Band in attendance, that I didn't have the chance to meet Will's parents and wondered if I ever would.

I made a habit of spending my Wednesday evenings hanging out with the second bowl, watching the group become more and more frustrated with their inability to manifest Adriana Heinrich's master plan. By June the bowl was no longer removed from the closet, and it became a convenient meeting place for me and my spirit guide.

Will's job in Topeka was providing a nice income, and the scientific research on the channeling phenomena was valuable for Dr. Edwards' research, but I found myself becoming lonely now that my classes had ended, and Ruth spent most of her time with George.

I had a romantic candlelit dinner on the table when Will arrived home on Friday evening. I wanted him to know how much I loved and missed him, and I intended to spend as much time in his arms as humanly possible.

When the sun once again peeked above the horizon line, I slid out of bed to join Will as he prepared for morning meditation. "I've been thinking, and I have come up with a new idea," I informed Will as I settled in beside him.

"And what's that?" he asked, as I felt his hum fill me. I had missed it so much that my eyes began to water. He watched my unbridled emotions well up inside me and wrapped me in his arms. "Whatever it is, Hillary, things will be okay."

I sniffled and reached for a tissue. "I want to go with you next week. I don't want to be here alone," I admitted. "It's summer and they don't need me at work."

"That's great news! Why the tears?"

"I was just unprepared for the loneliness." I cuddled up as close as I could get and used his life force to carry me away.

I did all of our laundry and was packed by the time Will returned from McCollum's. I also had the dishes done, the apartment cleaned, and the car gassed up. I was delighted that Will was looking forward to our trip as much as I was.

Our drive only took ninety minutes, and Dr. Edwards seemed pleased when we arrived. He had a lovely home near the Washburn campus, so during the days while Will and Lee were at work, I was planning on spending my time at the campus library doing some research of my own.

Waking up to Will's smile on Monday morning went a long way toward curing my loneliness. The sun was shining, and I could smell the coffee brewing, so I let my nose guide me while Will hopped in the shower. I found Dr. Edwards sitting in a sunbeam reading the morning paper.

"Cream and sugar are on the table," he said. "The mugs are on the counter by the coffee maker."

Once I had my coffee mixed to my liking, I took a seat at the table with mug in hand and said, "I have to ask: do you have a favorite room at the Washburn library?"

"Unfortunately, there's not a glass-floored room," he answered, looking at me over the frames of his reading glasses. He knew exactly what I was asking. "But I do have a favorite route across campus. Let me draw you a map."

He pulled out a piece of paper a placed an "X" where a bench was situated, "I suggest you take a break when you reach this location. This bench overlooks an open area. The flowers are in bloom and smell magnificent. You'll like the energy in that spot."

Before the conversation could go any further, Will entered the room still tucking his shirttail into his khakis. He had begun growing his hair longer, but it was at that unmanageable stage—not quite long enough to pull back and too long to style.

After a quick breakfast of toast and eggs, we said goodbye and I watched him and Lee drive away.

May 26, 2012

Dr. Edwards was correct about the flowers. They were so fragrant from where I sat on the bench that I was sure that was why he had suggested I stop at this particular location. I set my backpack to one side and leaned back to take in the scent and soak in the sunshine.

A warm breeze brushed my face, bringing me back to this world. I hesitantly opened my eyes, surprised that I had momentarily drifted off. But I was even more surprised by the scene in front of me. There, amid the singing birds and the brilliant blossoms was a young man moving slowly in the practice of tai chi. Spontaneously, passing students were beginning to stop, laying their belongings aside to join in. I watched until it was just too much to resist. I stood and walked to a space where I could observe and follow the movements of the leader.

My body moved awkwardly, but I knew this practice would be a good way for me to gain mastery over my chi, so I pushed on. As the session came to an end and the participants began to drift away, I asked one of them, "Does this happen every day?"

Smiling back at me over his shoulder, he answered, "Every day at nine, twelve, and three."

Walking back to where I had left my pack, I wondered whether I would be able to memorize the routine in the few days I had left in Topeka.

I arrived home to find Dr. Edwards busily cooking dinner, with Will as his lovely assistant. He asked, as I entered the room, "Did you enjoy the bench?"

"Yes, I returned three times! Thanks for your suggestion."

Will looked at me quizzically, but the subject changed to their research project and the secret between Lee and me remained.

Over the next week I found myself falling in love with the Washburn campus. The people were friendly and the grounds easy to navigate. I made sure to be at the bench three times a day, and by the time Will and I headed home the following weekend, the routine was firmly planted within my memory bank.

CHAPTER
TWENTY-THREE

June 4, 2012

I felt edgy when the full moon began to light our apartment. We were in the comfort of our own bed and Will was fast asleep beside me, but for some reason I was waiting for the other shoe to drop. I began repeating my mantra to calm myself, and in the next moment, I found myself pulled to the location of the second brass bowl.

"Shhhh," I hurriedly whispered when I realized where I was. "We don't want to wake the evil queen." I swiftly tried to adjust my eyes to the darkness, hearing the bowl begin to sing for joy at my return. "Hush," I warned in a panic.

As my eyes began to see through the darkness, I saw the shadows cast by the full moon and a sky sporting an array of stars. We were outside, and the bowl was unceremoniously covered with last night's garbage.

"Oh, my god!" I gasp. "You're free." I looked around and surmised we were in the alley behind Adriana Heinrich's house. Laughing, I said, "Contain yourself! I don't want you to be discovered before I can get back to my physical body and come to retrieve you." I heard only one more squeak before there was only silence. "Where is this place anyway?" I asked, looking around for a hint. Until now I hadn't worried about where the evil one's new crypt was. I moved to the curb to look around. *"This can't be!"* I thought, realizing where I was.

"Will, get up!" I said as I shook him awake. "We've got to get dressed."

Will rolled out of bed and without question put on his jeans.

"The second bowl is free! It's in a trash can and we have to get there before the garbage truck does."

"Where is it?" Will asked, as he scooped up the car keys and we locked the door behind us.

"Behind Adriana Heinrich's house ... across from Washburn campus!" We hit the road, knowing that every minute counted. I dialed Dr. Edwards' cell as soon as we pulled away from the curb.

A very groggy voice answered. "Hello."

I began to explain exactly what we needed him to do when he interrupted, "I'm not at home, Hillary. I'm at McCollum's."

The realization made me want to cry. It was almost dawn and we were still an hour away.

We entered Topeka as the city was coming to life. The streetlights were turning off, and unfortunately for us, the city workers had starting their shifts. It was all I could do to sit still when I noticed that the trashcans along College Avenue had already been emptied.

"Hang a left down the next alley, Will." I held my breath.

Our tires caught in the deep ruts, causing us to move slowly along the fence that kept us hidden from the waking neighborhood. I couldn't take it any longer and hopped out of the car, combing through the trash cans as Will drove beside me. My heart soared when I saw the reflection of something shiny in the sunlight. I ran toward it and there it was, sitting with a banana skin draped over it and filled with yesterday's coffee grounds. This was the first time in a year that the bowl and I had met in this dimension. I motioned for Will to stop the car and I picked my friend up, cherishing the feel of the cold metal between my hands. It didn't recognize me in my physical form and remained very quiet. I hugged it to my chest and hurried back to the car, pausing only momentarily to brush away the debris. Feeling a rush of relief, we turned toward home.

I knew the bowl was frightened, so I closed my eyes and went to it in the energetic form it was more familiar with. "Both forms are me," I explained. "We are taking you home." The bowl broke into song and didn't stop until I quelled it outside of our apartment.

June 5, 2012

I called each of the Brass Band members and arranged a meeting for the following weekend. Everyone arrived by evening, and although I had managed to keep the news of the second bowl's recovery a secret, I could not keep the huge smile from my face.

Everyone was curious about my animated mood, because I was barely able to contain myself. Kindly, Mom put off serving the Vern's donuts I had picked up until after I made my big announcement. I stood and tapped my fork on a water glass, indicating that I needed silence.

"Once upon a time, we named ourselves for a magical brass bowl that had become a beloved member of our family. And even though we discovered that we were only meant to be temporary caretakers of that magnificent artifact, losing our namesake left an empty spot in my heart."

"Here, here," George echoed my sentiment as he took a swig of tea.

"Before the undercover retrieval of our beloved bowl, we had a second bowl, an imposter that sat at the center of many sacred ceremonies in McCollum's temple. We were asked to use *that* bowl as if it were our real artifact in hopes of discovering who had stolen our beloved one. Eventually, all was resolved and the bowls were once again swapped, and we returned our namesake to the Tibetan monks."

I stopped to take a deep breath and finished. "Once again, leaving the Brass Band empty handed."

"Here, here," George toasted, beginning to enjoy himself and making Ruth laugh.

"During our time with the counterfeit bowl, I made it promise. The night it was placed into Adriana Heinrich's evil hands, I pledged to always remain its friend because I had begun to feel a consciousness building within it." I listened as the room became suddenly silent. Will set a plain cardboard box in front of me and I brushed away a tear as I continued. "Adriana gained no power from the counterfeit bowl in her possession. Not because it was powerless, but because its loyalty lies with us."

The box began to sing with anticipation and I had to laugh. "This bowl is the one that truly belongs to the Brass Band, and it is no charlatan." I reached into the box and placed it on the table. "Meet the newest member of the Brass Band, who must always remain our secret to ensure its safety."

Everyone was thrilled that our vacant spot was now going to be filled with a brass bowl that was truly ours. We moved the bowl to the ceremonial center and automatically took our places on the floor, forming a circle around it. One by one, everyone fell into a deep meditative state, pouring their love into *our* brass bowl.

Everyone, but me. I sat just watching the bowl. Listening to the small, happy noises of joy it made as it was filled with positive thoughts, which it sent shooting in all directions for mankind to hold on to as the window of enlightenment opened a little wider.

Will and George eventually constructed an insulated box for our bowl because of its inability to remain quiet. We loved its beautiful song, but we needed its existence to remain undisclosed. But the bowl spent very little time tucked away in its soundproof box. Ruth always practiced her protection techniques in its company, and I liked to set it at my feet as I nimbly performed my Tai Chi routine around it.

Our nightly meditations regained a joy that I hadn't noticed was missing. Each of us recognized a new awareness of the power that was growing within us as individuals, making the Brass Band even more formidable. We used the bowl to augment our original technique of sending everyone in the world the very same things we wished to manifest for ourselves: love, compassion, and healing for all things broken.

June 10, 2012

I had just gotten home from the library when Ruth came for a visit. She powered through the front door and plopped down on the couch, exhaling with exasperation.

"Hard day?" I asked, taking in her exaggerated movements.

"Ya gotta keep a sense of humor, is all I have to say," she answered, hauling herself to her feet and marching to the kitchen to put on some hot water. "I just left grocery store, and was obeying all of the traffic laws, I might add." She placed two mugs on the table. "And a lady drove up behind me, laid on her horn, and then flipped me off! I'm telling you, Hillary, people are getting nutty out there." She laughed. "The tension is getting higher and higher as the energy cranks up as the window for enlightenment opens. It's like we're being shoved through a funnel, and until we break free at the other end, people are being stretched to their limits."

I nodded, knowing exactly what Ruth was talking about and was thankful that I had found a place inside myself where I could go to find peace.

"I guess for some people it's hard to see a way through the gradue," she continued on a roll. "Especially if you don't understand that your thoughts are what's creating the crap in the first place. All I can say is, ya gotta pray that we all get through this safely."

The kettle whistled, and she disappeared into the kitchen.

"Are you sure you didn't run a stop sign or cut the lady off?" I teased.

She gave me *the eye,* the one that dared me to question her, which only made me laugh harder. "You mark my words, Hillary, things are heating up out there. I bet McCollum would agree with me!"

"Oh, we don't have to ask McCollum. I absolutely agree with you, Ruth," I said, as I submerged my teabag into the depths of my cup. "And I suppose it's just going to get worse until we all find a way to lighten up."

"You know what does it for me? Reading a good bridal magazine," Ruth chuckled, pulling a folder from her purse. "I've been clipping pictures of my favorite things and thought you could have a look. George is okay with anything, so I'd really like you to give me a real opinion. Besides, as my maid of honor, it's mandatory that you help me."

"Okay, show me your stuff," I snorted, rolling my eyes. But in truth, I was genuinely interested.

She spread out an array of magazine clippings that showed color schemes and bouquet designs, but she hadn't decided anything for sure. Then she placed a picture of the design for her wedding gown, white and covered with intricate lace and pearls, on the top of the pile.

"I know what you're thinking, Hillary. How can I be planning such a flamboyant wedding when I am marrying such a private person? Well, I'm making up for the lives in which we were too poor to have a wedding. But most of all, Hillary, it's to make up for the life we died filthy and covered with each other's blood."

I knew very well which life she was talking about. "That's a good enough reason for me," I responded, with a lump in my throat.

"And it's a good enough reason for George, too." She delved back into her pile of paper in an attempt to change the subject before her tears overflowed. Rummaging around, she continued to talk. "I think he's even getting used to the idea of declaring his love for me in front of every person I've known since kindergarten." She slid a sleek black and white photo across the table. "Look at what I've picked out for him and Will to wear. They'll be the two most handsome men in the room."

I looked at the pictures and had to agree.

"Can I talk you into a walk in the sunshine?" I asked, with the slightest hint of a plea in my voice. I could hear the birds chirping outside the window, and everything in me was being pulled to join them. "A little vitamin D will do us both some good."

Ruth swept her samples back into the folder and shoved them into her oversized bag. "That's a good idea. I need to decide if I'm going to try to drop a size before the wedding or attend as my voluptuous self," she said as she ran her hands over her hips.

The park was quiet. In fact, we were the only people there, which was surprising for such a spectacular afternoon. We were on the sidewalk that circled the perimeter, so Ruth picked up our lazy pace to see if speed walking was an exercise she was willing to take up. She began pumping her arms and asking me questions.

"Have you ever thought about contacting Will's parents?"

"I thought about it when I was pregnant. I would have liked for them to know they had a grandchild, but other than that, no. It's like Will no longer has a connection to them," I answered honestly. "Are you asking because you're still nervous about meeting George's parents?"

"Yes," she admitted, dropping her arms to her sides as she tried to catch her breath. "I suppose I need to have a heart-to-heart with George about his side of the family. For all I know, he might even have siblings, aunts, and uncles … cousins!"

That idea caught me off guard because it had never occurred to me that Will might have a brother or sister.

Vicki Renfro

"You ladies should have an escort. The police keep circling this park looking for a shady character whom they claim is very dangerous."

My skin crawled when I recognized the voice. I felt Ruth grab at my arm as I stretched myself to my full height and turned around. "Go away, Black. We don't want your company," I asserted, as we changed our direction to head home. All my memories of him, past and present, flashed through my mind. I saw images of him covered in Druid blood and I was terrified, but I vowed not to let him see my fear. "Leave before I call the cops myself," I threatened, as I pulled my cell from my pocket.

"Well, isn't that a coward's way out," he spat, grabbing my arm and twisting it.

I pulled away, feeling my feet slide into a familiar pattern as my arms moved automatically in a motion to evoke my chi. I knew Tai Chi could be a lethal defense, and I was willing to do anything to defend Ruth. My palms became hot and my movements fluid.

Black looked into my eyes and took a step back. "Well, well, a pacifist no longer," he said, sizing me up.

I remained silent as I felt my fingertips begin to tingle.

I didn't hear the patrol car arrive or its doors slam shut as the officers approached. The police had Black spread-eagled on the ground before my tunnel vision dissipated and I relaxed my stance. Ruth shook me, "It's okay, Hillary."

We held onto each other as we watched Black being manhandled, fighting and kicking all the way to the patrol car.

"They'll never keep us apart, Hillary," he yelled over his shoulder as they stuffed him into the back seat, but I was praying this would be the last time I'd ever lay eyes on him.

June 12, 2012

My sleep was restless, leaving no doubt in Will's mind as to what my nightmares were about. He had also stared into the eyes of the

220

monster we knew in this lifetime as Jackson Black, and even though I had blessed myself before I fell asleep, I just couldn't erase the fear that evil man evoked in me.

Ruth and I had discovered that there had been a number of complaints filed against Black, from stalking to sexual assault, and we weren't surprised by any of it. Knowing that he was in jail and awaiting trial should have eased our anxiety, but it didn't.

Ruth insisted that we join her and George for comfort food once we had arrived home from witnessing Black's arrest, "to put all of the ugliness behind us." Will agreed that it was a good idea. "No need to let the creep invade our psyches," Ruth asserted whole-heartedly … but he had effectively worked his way into mine.

We joked about comfort food being the same no matter where you were raised, so I wasn't surprised to see plates stacked high with grilled-cheese sandwiches with a side of tomato soup.

"George could have gone with mac and cheese or meatloaf," Ruth teased, as she tried to ease my mind. "But he knew what was most likely to put a smile on his girl's face."

I smiled at Ruth's attempt to make everything normal again.

"Don't worry, Hillary," she said. "You would have kicked his butt if the cops hadn't shown up. I was completely safe with you!"

We concluded that we were glad to have seen the last of Jack Black. With all of the charges stacked up against him, he would be doing years of jail time. Will took my hand and I held on tight, closing my eyes for a moment to give thanks for the people who surrounded me.

"Okay," Ruth said with a huge smile, "Now for the pièce de résistance." Once she had all of our attention, she presented the bag she had hidden behind her back. "Ta-dah."

She was right! We spent the next hour gorging ourselves on hot Vern's glazed donuts.

It was interesting to see how fascinated Ruth had become with growing herbs. In every corner of the kitchen or small beam of light that shone into their apartment, there was a pot with a new little sprout of something growing in it.

"So Ruth, are you going to start mixing up potions and medicines?" I asked.

"No," she laughed. "George is growing culinary herbs. I have to wild-craft mine. My herbs grow stronger if they live along a riverbank than they ever would in a garden. The other day I found the phone number for a medicinal herb instructor pinned to the bulletin board at the bookstore and I gave him a call. He takes groups on walks through the countryside to find and identify plants. My first walk is next week. I can't wait to figure all of this stuff out!"

I suggested that she pick my dad's brain, too. "He knows a lot about plants and has a few special places on the farm where he lets bear root grow. The strong smell is enough to make your eyes water, but it can sure knock down a cold. He'd love to take you on his own walk sometime."

It was around midnight when Will and I excused ourselves and climbed the stairs to our apartment. Cuddling into bed, I asked—no, *begged* Will to let me go to Topeka with him again. "It would be fun, and I want to spend more time practicing my tai chi at Washburn. I'm on the brink of something really great here. Please, please, please."

Will didn't usually break my heart, but this was an exception.

"We won't be in Topeka next week. We're meeting another research group in Kansas City. I'm really sorry, Hillary. I know what it's like to be on the edge of a breakthrough," he answered, brushing my hair from my face. "Maybe you should try going inward and ask the universe to bring you a teacher here. I mean, there must be someone in town."

"I'm glad your work is getting more exciting, sweetie," I said, trying not to show my disappointment. "I love you." I kissed him goodnight and pulled the covers up around me. I knew, since Will had made the suggestion that I ask the universe to help me find a teacher who lived nearby, that I should. So as I entered the first hazy stage of sleep I took his advice and I closed my eyes and began.

"Hello Eugene," I said, "it's Hillary. It's been a while since we've talked, and a lot has happened, but I guess you know all of that. I knew that he saw everything from his vantage point and that he would hear my plea. "I have a favor to ask, and instead of asking the random universe, I thought I'd narrow it down to you. I'm on the brink of something big! I've made great advances in moving my chi, but I need to have a teacher to make that last leap. If indeed there is a teacher nearby, can you send him to me? I promise to keep my eyes wide open. I miss you.

I took one last breath before falling asleep.

CHAPTER
TWENTY-FOUR

June 18, 2012

I woke in time to send Will off with a good breakfast and a promise from him to call me before he went to bed. In preparation for my day, I took a shower, and when I went out on the deck to let my hair dry in the sunshine I heard a squawk from Gus, who was perched on the lawn chair next to me.

"Well, Gus, it's a big day. I've got to get out there and give myself the opportunity to run into my new tai chi teacher, because I don't think it's likely that he'll come knocking at my door."

Gus answered with an inquisitive look.

"I'll walk over to campus and meet you on the bench outside the library. You can keep me company while I look for my miracle." I pulled my hair into a ponytail, put on my flip-flops, and locked the front door behind me.

I watched Gus fly from tree to tree, waiting for me to catch up with him. Finally he took to the sky, and when I reached the bench, there he sat. "Wish I could fly," I said, taking a seat beside him and getting out my water bottle. "That would make this tai chi stuff moot." The campus was quiet except for the few people pointing at me and Gus. I just smiled and put out my arm for Gus to sit on. It always amazed people to see his wingspan.

Once he was balanced on my arm and had hopped up onto my shoulder, we settled in. "No telling exactly what we're waiting for," I explained to Gus. "Or how long it might take. We might just be looking for an opportunity that will lead me along a path to my desired end." I scanned the area looking for possibilities. "I promised Eugene Atohi I'd keep my eyes peeled."

"Eyes peeled for whom?" a soft voice asked from behind me. Gus chattered happily as he jumped to the back of the bench, and I turned to identify the owner of the enchanting voice.

"Well, what a nice surprise," I said. It was Dorje. "It's been much too long. How are you and your monk companions doing these days?" I moved to one side, motioning him to take a seat.

"We've been staying pretty busy with the uplifting of earth and all," he joked. "How about you?"

"Will's working with Dr. Edwards in Kansas City," I answered.

"Is that why you have your bird out for a walk?"

I couldn't help but feel delight at his gentle nature. "Yes, Gus is very good company," I chuckled, "but I still miss going to work with Will in Topeka. I found the most awesome tai chi group, and I miss practicing with them, but …" I trailed off as the old gentleman gracefully stood and began to move with a rhythm that was mesmerizing.

"Is this what you do?" he asked, sweeping his arms upward as his feet stepped to make a fluid turn.

I just sat with my mouth open, listening to him speak as he nimbly continued. "I was sitting in meditation this morning when I heard a very clear voice say, 'You need some fresh air. A walk through campus would be the perfect thing.' I never ignore those voices." He giggled. "They always guide me on the most wonderful adventures. Did you have a voice tell you the same thing?"

"I was the one asking," I admitted, as I watched him neatly finish with a graceful bow.

"And what were you asking for, Hillary?"

Vicki Renfro

"For a tai chi teacher."

"How about a fifth Gold Stripe Grandmaster?" he asked as he agilely stuck a pose. "I would love to have one last student."

I got up and stood next to him. He slowly began his routine from the beginning, and I followed his movements while he spoke of the infinitesimal nuances that create a master.

Thank you, I whispered to Eugene Atohi.

Gus watched us, not making a sound.

"You've learned very well," Dorje said. "Would you like to meet with me again?"

"Yes, I would love that."

"Tai chi is a practice that we monks execute at the close of the day. Please join us. We begin as the sun sets."

Gus began to squawk, and my heart skipped a beat when I heard the reverberation of a motorcycle engine echoing off the library wall. I turned to see the lady in leather dismounting her bike and walking toward me.

"Look at you," she said. "Dancing with the old man."

I could feel my body temperature rise—along with my apprehension.

"I see you remember who I am," she said. She smirked as she circled me and Dorje. "Do you recall my prediction? The one about your husband's death?"

Paralyzed by the thought of life without Will, I was unable to speak, but Dorje spoke for me.

He stepped forward and bowed. "You know little of what true destiny is."

She burst into laughter. "You hide and watch old man. My prediction will come to pass."

"Everyone has the ability to change the destiny that was meant for

226

them," he replied serenely. "When the seed of life is planted, its outcome is not predetermined. Its growth depends not only on the environment, but on how well it is nurtured. The ground may be fertile and produce abundant life, or the seed may perish in the dust of carelessness." His eyes met hers. "So dear lady, what destiny are you creating for yourself? Because that is the only one you truely control. Are you living an authentic life of love and compassion, or are you—"

She interupted with vehemence. "Take a good look at me, old man. I have it all—wealth, beauty, and power. My destiny is alive, and more vibrant than than what you call life. Can't you feel it?"

"Even one who is malicious at heart may avoid the karmic result by a shift at the soul level," Dorje replied compassionately. "But I can see your path is a complicated one."

"I may be a lot of things," Adriana replied evenly. "Greedy, yes. But I am not evil. I've seen evil, and it goes by the name of Jackson Black. In fact, I believe him to be insane."

"The manipulation of such an individual is a very dangerous endeavor. You should think very carefully about what you are doing."

"And who are you to judge me and what I do?" she replied squarely.

"It is only a stranger's observation," he whispered, bowing in conclusion.

She was pissed, but refused to show it. To a casual onlooker, they could have been two friends talking, but to me it was apparent that they were in full combat.

Adriana turned and glided back to her bike, and with a terrifying roar of the motor, drove away.

"You know she's the one who arranged for the theft of your brass bowl?" I mused softly after the noise had disappeared.

"That does not surprise me," he said, smiling up at me. "And you know that Will is the master of his *own* destiny?"

"Yes, but sometimes my fear blurs the truth. My mind goes right to the worst scenario before I can gain control. But I'll learn with time, because I know control of the mind is a formidable power." I smiled back at him, following my smile with a bow.

"May I escort you home, Hillary?"

"There is nothing I would like more," I admitted. We walked in comfortable silence as Gus flew ahead of us—but not too far; he stayed close enough to keep us in sight.

"I once had a bird," Dorje said. "Nothing as magnificent as your friend, but incredible just the same. He came to me with a broken wing and was never again able to take flight. It was heartbreaking not to be able to help such a being return to the sky. But you, Hilsbeth," he said without doubt, "I can make soar."

I was slightly embarrassed and a little proud. "You really think so?"

"I know so. This practice is not new to you. The knowledge and ability exist within you because you have perfected the use of your chi in many previous lifetimes and used it with precise accuracy. You have used it as protection, and when forced, you have used it as a weapon."

"My monks," he continued with an understanding smile, "have no need to move beyond the flow of energy it provides. It assists them in their joining with the higher planes, the I AM, which is in and of itself, a great accomplishment. But to have you as my student will enable me to stretch myself even further, and that I look forward to."

"Thank you, Dorje," was all I could come up with, so I just let him talk.

"It will be wonderful to have you attend our evening practices. You know that Gilbert also attends?"

I actually hadn't known that.

"He and Indira have rekindled a very old bond. The love between them brings an additional dimension into our ashram that would not exist without them." Pausing, he asked, "Do you know how much Gilbert misses you? He understands that your life has changed since your marriage, but still the yearning for your company exists within him. So my becoming your tai chi master will be good for many, on many levels." His eyes twinkled. "When next you speak with your guide, please convey my gratitude for facilitating the crossing of our

228

paths."

"I'll do that," I said, and I knew that was a promise I would be keeping very soon.

"Also Hillary, I want you to heed Adriana Heinrich's words about Jackson Black's madness. Gilbert has told me the Druid stories, and the part Black played in the murders of your people. He is not a man to take lightly, for there is much unresolved karma between him and your Brass Band. Please, be watchful."

I'd never thought of it as unresolved karma, but I could now see it clearly, and a shutter went through me. "He's in jail" was my reply, but Dorje saw my fear.

"We will complete your training and then you will be a formidable match for any foe who believes they can defeat you."

I sighed with relief and let all thoughts of Jack Black and Adriana Heinrich fall away before I knocked on the lower apartment door. When it opened, I asked George if Dorje and I could come in.

"Of course," George said. He was more than happy to see both of us. "To what do we owe this pleasure?" Ruth entered the room, sparkling with the joy she naturally exuded.

After a round of bear hugs and an offer of refreshment, I was finally able to answer George's question. "I'd like to introduce Dorje to Buddy. Is he here?

Dorje's face lit with amusement as George whistled and Buddy took flight. Landing on George's outstretched finger, he made the introductions. "Buddy, I'd like to introduce you to Dorje, a monk who has traveled halfway around the world to join us in this lifetime. Dorje, this is our friend, Buddy, who has revealed himself to be Ruth's spellbinding assistant, and an integral part of our paths unwinding."

We watch Dorje's eyes flicker with a light of knowing. "Yes, he is an essential part of your story, isn't he," Dorje said, as he put out his finger and Buddy flew to him. "Someday Buddy and I will discuss it, but for now, I would just like to enjoy his company."

When I returned to my empty apartment, missing Will with all of my heart, I figured I had all the time in the world to go on a little trip of my own. I dropped down on the floor in my normal spot. Then, obeying a spontaneous impulse, I slid silently over to where Will typically sat. With my legs crossed and my meditation shawl pulled tightly around my shoulders, I began with a quick affirmation:

> *Dear God and Goddess, Guides that watch over me and the great power within. Bless me as I make this journey toward self-awareness and into union with my divine self. Surround me with white light and guide me to greater knowledge. So be it, it is done.*

I moved all my attention to my third eye, and as the thoughts about the outside world entered my mind, I blessed them, one by one, and let them drop away. Eventually there was only me and my mantra. I released my earthly body, only holding onto the image of the brass bowl that sat on the mantel, one floor down in Ruth's apartment. I heard the song begin, and I smiled inwardly as I said hello to my friend. "It's nice to meet this way, just me and you," I said in that space between breaths and the place where everything exists. I felt the vibration of the bowl as it answered, yes. I asked it, "May I sit with you while I call to my spirit guide?" Again the answer was yes, so I began.

"I call to the spirit guide who always looks over me, the one who has healed my soul and will be with me for all time." I knew I had other guides I wasn't conscious of, so I made my declaration as clear as possible. "Eugene Atohi, please accept my deepest gratitude and appreciation for my new tai chi master, Dorje." I had to laugh as I added, "You sure made quick work of my request."

"There is no time within the dimension from which I come," I heard a voice reply. "There is only the present."

"Well, arranging the meeting between Dorje and me was sheer

genius!"

I heard a chuckle. "I am all knowing from the place where I now stand. I have moved far beyond the physical form; therefore, it was my pleasure to facilitate the opportunity for you to find your heart's desire. I am thankful that you had the wisdom to look for it."

I floated, held aloft by the vibration of the bowl and the wonder of once again merging with the energies of the universe. It was hours before I felt my consciousness being pulled toward my body. Dusk had fallen, and it wasn't long before I knew what had called me back. Somewhere in the fading sun, my phone was ringing. I fumbled for a light switch and frantically reached for my backpack. It was Will. "Hi sweetie," I said, "I miss you."

The loving voice on the other end sighed, "I love you, too."

"Are you and Lee finished for the day?"

"Yes, and from what I have heard from others, I was a spectacular success. Too bad The Teacher attended all of the session instead of me, because I think it is a subject that I would have found very interesting. Dr. Edwards says he will fill me in on the details over dinner." Will sounded exhausted. "How was your day, my sweet, beautiful wife?"

The sentiment warmed my heart and went a long way toward momentarily easing my loneliness. I knew Will felt bad about my not being able to hang out on the Washburn campus, so I didn't waste any time in telling him about my good fortune. "I have a new tai chi teacher, a fifth gold-stripe grandmaster!"

"That was fast," he said. "Instant manifistation is a profound power." He knew that there was also a dangerous side. "Now, you *must* master your thoughts. *All of them!"*

Even though I knew he was right, I wasn't in the mood to discuss another disipline I had to learn, so I changed the subject. "I asked my spirit guide to help in the search for my new teacher."

"And whom did Eugene send to you?" He chuckled.

"Dorje. Who would have guessed? I've been invited to the monks' evening practices, so thanks for waking me up. Without your call, I would have missed my first class." I looked at the clock and said, "Got to go, sweetie. Tell Dr. Edwards hello for me and call me tomorrow!" I heard an, *I love you* from the other end of the phone before Will hung up, and then I was moving at full speed toward the carriage house.

I pulled up the cobblestone drive, past the exterior wall, and parked in front of McCollum's newly renovated carriage house. It made a perfect home for a large group of reincarnated Tibetan monks, but as I past through the front door, I heard the familiar echo of my own footsteps on the stone floor. I couldn't help but reminisce about my first meeting with Will on this very spot. I looked up and saw the very same elaborately beamed ceiling, aged to the color of rich mahogany, and the walls that still carried the chisel marks made by the workmen who'd built this place a hundred years ago. That Spring Fling party for four was the best thing that had ever happened to me, and now, looking back, it couldn't have been more perfectly planned. George and Will's request has slipped by an inattentive clerk, and only two invitations had been sent out—the recipients being Ruth and me. I was still recalling that first evening when I ran headlong into a smiling Gilbert.

"We've been expecting you," he said. "I've saved you a place." And as always, Gilbert had save me a primo spot, front and center. I scooted past a few monks who were still in meditation and sat on the rug that was saving my spot. Gilbert just beamed.

I looked into that sweet, cherubic face that I had neglected for months, and only saw love in return. It was as if no time had passed. He was still the same square-shaped boulder with arms and legs that I had met so long ago at the intermural fields, but now he possessed a peacefulness that pleased me beyond belief. His eyes were alive with a twinkle that I knew had been lit by the beautiful Indira, who sat motionless in meditation on the other side of him. I smiled back.

A bell rang as Dorje gracefully took his place at the front of the room. Moments later our bodies were in motion, and the entire room moved in perfect unison. It was magic. As my arms glided and my hands reached toward the zenith of the motion, I imagined my chi arching in a brilliant light that streaked upward. I extended as I completed each movement and felt my life force circulating around my body.

At the completion of practice, I was both exhausted and exhilarated. Everyone began to talk and move toward the kitchen for a cup of evening chai tea, but I remained in the place where I stood. Left alone in the room, I began to move in slow motion, repeating the exercise we had just finished. My mind turned off and I just let it happen, feeling the imaginary patterns of light my hands made as they moved.

When I had finished, I gathered my belongings to leave and headed toward the front door. Walking, half in a trance, I noticed no one.

"Wow. Hils, who would have known? That was beautiful!" my dear friend Gilbert said with wonder. "The light just danced."

"What do you mean?" I asked with astonishment. "You could see it? I thought it was my imagination."

"We all saw it," Dorje answered, and with a smile, he said, "You were soaring!"

I decided to stay and join Dorje and Father John in the room just outside their sleeping quarters. Father John had moved in with his Buddhist clan when the carriage house construction was completed and he and Dorje had become roommates, since they were the only males in this household.

We made ourselves comfortable, and hearing the door open behind me, I turned to see Gilbert and Indira entering with a large tray of refreshments.

Father John was the first to speak. "I talk to your parents at least once a week, Hillary and they never mentioned a thing."

Gilbert quickly joined in with a few questions of his own, which caused Dorje to put his hands up to hold back the inquisitive tide. "I too, had no idea how advanced Hillary's talents were, but it shouldn't come as a surprise to any of us. Once you take into consideration that all of us carry our gifts forward, lifetime to lifetime. Of course it stands to reason that she would master in this lifetime what she had mastered before. All ability can be quickly revealed again, once given the proper amount of attention."

"I'll say," Gilbert added under his breath, smiling at me.

Indira passed around a platter of fruit and sweets while everyone else in the room continued talking. I took a couple of pastries while Indira poured me a cup of fragrant tea. I actually had nothing to add to this conversation, and found I was satisfied with Dorje's explanation.

"I think our first official guests in our new home should be the Brass Band," Dorje suggested. "Where better to reveal your reclaimed talents than among the ones who know you best? 'The light show,' as it has been dubbed tonight, is a colossal accomplishment, but I must tell you, Hillary, you will achieve much more. Your next step is to learn control, balancing that light, the energy, on the tips of your fingers and toes. Let it dance in a circle, never leave your aura unless you intend it to. This will enable you to conserve your energy."

I listened intently, absent-mindedly letting my tea grow cold. "You said I bring this gift forward from previous incarnations?"

"Yes, yes," Dorje chirped. "That's why you were known as *the mystic warrior* when you lived as a Druid. Your control over your life force was so refined that you were invincible on the battlefield. You were able to repel a foe with a motion of your hand or allow an assailant to move within range to face his inevitable death."

I felt horror-struck by the casual talk about my ability to kill so effortlessly. It must have shown on my face.

"It was a far different and more dangerous time that we are talking about, Hillary," Dorje said, consoling me. "Your clan's survival depended upon your leadership, and your ability to defend them. There is no dishonor in defending the ones you love. If it makes you feel better to know, Hillary, each of us has killed many times in the thousands of lifetimes we have lived upon this planet. It is inevitable." He reached across the table to pat my hand in reassurance.

"Well, that's a mystery solved," Gilbert said, as he sat his empty teacup down with a thud. "I always felt there were a lot of blanks in our Druid story. I mean, Hils, you've given each of us detailed accounts of the powers we possessed. You gave us the ability to see ourselves clearly as an intricate part of an amazing community. I guess you just couldn't see yourself. So I say, *you go girl!*"

"Thanks guys," I said. "I appreciate your support." I gave Gilbert a sideways smile. I could feel the truth in everything that had been said.

"Now," Dorje said, "before we adjourn for the evening, we must talk about a practice schedule. You are welcome to attend any of our evening practices—yoga, meditation, chanting—but you must be prepared to stay to work with me for at least one hour after our friends have finished."

"That's very generous, Dorje," I said. "Thank you very much; I am genuinely honored. But I do have one other burning question before I head home."

"What's that?" Father John answered. "Ask us anything you like."

"Is your brass bowl here?"

"Oh, yes," Indira quickly answered, "and its true identity no longer has to be hidden because our crook has disappeared. We never disclosed her identity, but she must have suspected that she had been discovered."

"We do still keep its storage place a secret among the people in this room," Father John added, as he opened the hidden drawer in the table between us.

I instinctively reached for the bowl as he drew it out, and wasn't insulted when it didn't sing for me. "It's wonderful knowing that it's home again," I told Indira.

"We've heard stories about the brass bowl that the thieves put in its place. Are they true?" she asked.

Now it was my turn to grin. "Yes, all of them. The bowl first began its process of awakening while residing on the altar in McCollum's temple. So, when George made the second switch, I promised the bowl that I would never leave it alone with Adriana Heinrich. I just couldn't do that to it. It broke my heart to think of it with that evil woman, so I pledged to visit as often as I could. We got to be friends. It was our lucky day when Adriana decided it was worthless and threw it in the trash. Luckily, Will and I retrieved it from where it had been deep-sixed before the morning trash pick-up. We consider it the ninth member of the Brass Band."

"It sings for us like this one sings for you," Gilbert added. "It really loves Hillary the most, but it's coming around to accepting all of us."

I was touched by his comment, even though I wasn't sure if the bowl could actually love. I gave the bowl I was holding back to Indira, and she tucked it safely into its hiding place.

"Do you ever wonder how the thief feels about betraying you?" I asked casually.

Father John was curious. "Why would you ask us that?" His eyes were gentle, and I knew he wasn't angry.

"Because I saw her with Jackson Black," I said, and her emotions were a mass of contradictions. I felt sorry for her. I've been reading a little Gandhi, and he says, 'love is the ultimate weapon.' I think in this lifetime, I would like to use that power."

June 19, 2012

I answered the phone on the first ring. "Will, how are you?"

"The question is, how are you? Did you make it to your class last night?"

"I did, and I have an open invitation to attend more. When will you be home?"

"Is tomorrow soon enough?" he teased.

"No, but it will do," I said, jumping for joy inside. "I can't wait to tell you everything! Oh, by the way, Gilbert and Father John say hello."

"Are you cutting this call short?" Will asked with a chuckle.

"Yes, I don't want to spill the beans. Just hurry home. I love you, Will.

"I love you, too."

It was after dark when Dr. Edwards dropped Will off at our front door. I met him with a kiss that definitely said I was glad to see him. He smiled as he dropped his bags on the living room floor and followed me to the bedroom. I wouldn't be telling him my news tonight!

June 21, 2012

"I never sleep this well when I'm away from home," Will said, as he reached over to kiss me good morning.

"I never sleep this well when you're away, either," I sighed. Having him next to me filled me with a contentment that was very hard to explain. I felt safe and I felt whole.

"Do you want to take a shower and tell me your news over eggs and toast, or do you want to tell me now?" he asked, lifting himself up onto one elbow to gaze at me with his amazing blue eyes.

"I'll tell you the important part now and the other over breakfast," I said. I took a breath to prepare myself emotionally. He remained quiet, waiting for me to begin my tale.

"When I was having the dreams about our past lives together, I was in awe of how powerful each of you were," I began with a shrug. "McCollum and Dr. Edwards were shape shifters, Mom and Dad were dreamers, Gilbert could control nature, George was a great warrior,

Ruth was always fuzzy until recently, and you were The Teacher, and the most important person in my life." He kissed my hands as I continued. "As for me, McCollum told me that I was a *mystic warrior*, but I never knew what that meant. Earlier this week, I found out."

"Hillary, that's wonderful!"

"I know! I finally feel like I have an identity!"

He rolled onto his back and I snuggled in, resting my head on his shoulder. "And what did you find out about yourself?"

"My chi was my power … and Will, I've found it again."

We dressed and headed to a local café. I twined my fingers between his as we walked and talked. I filled Will in on the details of my week, knowing that on some level he was already aware of all of it. Either way, he was proud of me and I was a little surprised by just how much that mattered.

After a short discussion, I got out my cell phone and dialed Ruth's number to invite her and George to join us. It meant putting off breakfast for an additional thirty minutes, but I saw it as quality time I could spend with the man I loved.

Will filled me in on the experiments he had participated in for Dr. Edward's research. Locked in a remote room with a panel of observers, Will was asked to channel The Teacher and complete a list of tasks. Mainly, it consisted of reading symbols from cards that were located in a different facility some three miles away.

"Of course we scored 100 percent correct," Will said, and he chuckled. "But scientists are born skeptics, and they were convinced that one of the people in the room with me was giving me some kind of weird signal, or that I was reading someone's mind. So, to eliminate all of those possibilities, I was left alone in the room for the second round of tests, just me, a pencil, and a pad of yellow legal paper."

"Another perfect score?" I smiled.

"Yes. Dr. Edwards got a kick out of the other researchers' insistence that it must be a trick of some sort. Then they did a complete physical poke-and-prod to determine whether The Teacher had the ability to control my vital signs, which I really found interesting."

The Teacher was able to slow Will's vital signs down to the point at which they were undetectable, just like the Yogis in India can do.

"Didn't have the slightest idea he could do that," Will commented. "Dr. Edwards gave me all of the daily test results every night over a gourmet meal. Besides those dinners, the trip for me was pretty much a blank."

I raised my eyebrows in question.

"Beyond the drive to Kansas City and the drive home," he reflected easily, "I was never the one occupying my body.

We were still scanning the menu and talking about Will's trip when Ruth and George arrived at the restaurant.

"How's the research going?" George asked with a roguish smile. "Think I should accompany you on your next trip? I can give them all the details about The Teacher over the last … say"—he paused to gather his thoughts—"oh, I'd say for at least the last two dozen centuries."

"Dr. Edwards and I would love your company, George. I'm sure the other researchers would find you to be a very interesting specimen. But without scientific proof, they would consider all of what you said to be invalid, even if it was extremely entertaining."

We finished breakfast with little being said about the wedding, because Ruth's first herbal walk was foremost in her mind. She had learned that in any given area there are eight indigenous plants that can heal any ailment.

I loved her enthusiasm—as the Brass Band grows older, having a healer in our midst may prove to be valuable.

CHAPTER
TWENTY-FIVE

July 26, 2012

Ruth discovered a book that explained the meaning of flowers, and was putting together a wedding bouquet that would ensure happiness.

"Hillary, what do you think of this combination of colors?

I looked at the pictures Ruth had cut from a gardening magazine and tried to imagine them in a wedding bouquet while I listened to Ruth's explanation of their meanings.

"Chrysanthemums would not be my first choice, but the white ones mean truth and the red mean sharing. A marriage will never survive without those two ingredients. I'll add red rhododendron for passionate love and one single yellow tulip to represent how hopelessly in love I am with George." She took a breath and looked up at me for my opinion, but before I could answer, she added in a flurry, "For the greenery, I can't decide between holly for domestic happiness or ivy for fidelity."

"I think red is your color, Ruth, and white and yellow will be beautiful accents. For the greenery, I'd pick holly because George loves you so much that his fidelity will never be in question."

She smiled as she put an X through the word *ivy* on her list and moved on to the next subject. Her mom had picked out a number of venues in Kansas City that she thought would work for Ruth's dream wedding, but had left the final decision up to her daughter.

"You only get married once," Ruth explained. "Or in our case, once each life or two. George has filled me in on the details of some of our past nuptials, and even though they were primitive, they have all had a smattering of style." She laughed out loud. "Okay, that's an extreme exaggeration. Most were held in less than desirable locations, although historically they were pretty typical. Grime and lice were the norm back then. But I'm telling you, Hillary, this wedding is going to make up for every flea-infested lodge and bug-infested barn we've ever been wed or hand-fasted in. And for our honeymoon, all I can say is, the mattress won't be lumpy."

I laughed with her, remembering our Druid lifetime together. *Primitive* would have been a kind description of our village by today's standards. I had come to really appreciate the modern improvements like flushing toilets, soap, and modern medicine.

"George says to do whatever I want. He'll be at the altar waiting for me no matter the size of the crowd. And I mean to have a throng of people there to witness our vows." She opened her planner and revealed a list of possible locations. "McCollum will be presiding over the wedding." She was positively bubbly. "So, no church, just a place that is large enough for the wedding guests and the reception afterwards." Looking up, she asked if I'd be up for a KC trip to check out her short list.

"Of course. Let's just go on the days that Will's away."

"Next week it is!" she said, stuffing her list back into the manila folder. "We'll leave Monday morning."

My mind and feet were in serious need of help by the time we'd finished our whirlwind tour of possible Kansas City wedding venues. I was exhausted by the endless sales pitches and hard marble floors, which caused the Witherspoons' sunroom to be the perfect place to stretch out my legs and close my eyes. With the blinds drawn to block the mid-July heat and a slight breeze from the ceiling fan, I was in paradise.

Ruth hadn't said which place she liked the best, but I could tell. She seemed drawn to a sprawling property by the name of Rockwell Manor, but its austere feeling made me uncomfortable. I spent my time there self-consciously checking my reflection in the floor-to-ceiling mirrors, smoothing the wrinkles out of my clothes, and feeling outclassed.

The lady who greeted us wore a tailored Pierre Cardin suit with Prada heels—not that I would have recognized them as such, but Ruth gushed over them.

She showed us a set of banquet rooms that definitely weren't the type with movable prefab walls. No, these were marble and mortar, with decorative pillars that held up an enormous span of elegantly painted ceilings. One end had full-length windows that opened onto a magnificent garden where the wedding ceremony could be held, weather permitting. Or it could be held in the pavilion, which could seat hundreds of people. I think the thing that sold it were the onsite cottages that could house her out-of-town guests, if necessary.

Ruth expected the fall colors to be beautiful, and knowing how happy it made her made me happy, too.

"What do you think?" she asked, pulling the Rockwell Manner brochure out of her purse. "This one?"

"I think it fits you to a tee," I answered, and meant it. "I'd call and reserve it before some *other* filthy rich family rents it first," I teased.

"Mom's going to love this wedding as much as me, showing off her little girl and her little girl's big handsome hunk of a future husband to her friends is her fantasy, too. They won't know what hit 'em!"

We had a good laugh when we seriously thought about what having McCollum there might do to the unsuspecting guests, and decided that along with their first helping of Shakipat would come a huge dose of great happiness and peace. Now, with only two short months to pull

242

together all the details, the planning would begin in earnest.

Will and George acted interested in the details, but they were glad I was taking the brunt of it. Ruth made a *donation* to Father John and the Buddhist monks, even though they had volunteered their services for free. She wanted her wedding march to be the beautiful chanting of Tibetan monks, rather than the typical, bland organ music. McCollum's boys also wanted to be involved, so Ruth decided the more chanters the merrier.

An orchestra would play for the wedding reception, which left Mom busily teaching George the waltz and foxtrot. He was going to knock Ruth's socks off!

The only thing that George had asked was to be in charge of picking the music for their first dance. He insisted on keeping his choice a secret, which both pleased and frustrated Ruth to no end.

"You can dress me and instruct me on the finer points of etiquette, but you will never pry the name of the song from these lips," he teased.

I continued my private tai chi lessons with Dorje as often as possible, and by a wonderful coincidence, my lessons happened to be scheduled at the same time of evening when the monks were practicing the music they would be performing at Ruth and George's wedding. The low reverberations made it both poignant and lovely. I knew the vibration of their voices improved my movements, and imagined their chanting would also lift the level of Ruth and George's vows to include the gods and angels.

Once my routine was complete I turned to leave … and spotted my biggest fan sitting exactly where he always sat to watch me.

"You're an inspiration, Hils," he said, standing to meet me.

"Thanks, Gilbert," I answered, taking a closer look at him. "I do believe you've been primping. I like it!"

"Thanks," He rubbed his newly plucked eyebrows. "I never really cared before Indira"—he blushed—"whether I had one great, hairy eyebrow or two. But now I want her to look into my face and see a man who loves her dearly looking back, not the disheveled professor I'd let myself become."

I thought I was going to cry! "That's the sweetest thing I've ever heard."

Indira eased in behind him and took his hand. "Would you like to join us for evening chai?"

I said yes, thrilled to see how much she loved Gilbert in return. I watched as they walked away; my short, boulder-shaped friend with his arm around his beautiful Asian Goddess.

August 15, 2012

I was maid of honor, and Ruth's sister and Indira were bridesmaids. Will was best man, and Gilbert and Dr. Edwards were George's groomsmen. I knew the guys were going to look incredible in basic black tuxedos because in a moment of pure inspiration, Ruth had decided on a white and black wedding to symbolize the yin and yang of existence. I thought there could be nothing more appropriate.

And just as appropriately, they would spend the dark moon in McCollum's temple in a private ceremony, and in the light of the full moon they would be wed before multitudes.

Aug 25, 2012

Ruth arranged a special KC trip for the ladies in the bridal party. We were to meet with a fashion designer to look at fabric samples and the drawings that Ruth had put together herself.

I was touched by the time Ruth had spent sketching individualized ideas to match each of our personalities, and no matter what the designer settled on, our dresses were to incorporate the essence of Ruth's original idea. For me the fashion designer had picked a raw, white silk that hung perfectly to accentuate my height and slim hips. She recommended that I highlight my hair and apply a spray-on tan to accent the dress and my blue eyes. By the end of the afternoon I'd agreed to every suggestion. I figured if Will was going to look remarkably handsome, I would try to do the same for him. Besides, Ruth had invited all of her country club friends, and I still remembered how I felt when they scrutinized me. Interesting how my awakening hadn't softened some memories at all.

Once we were finished with the last details of our dresses, we witnessed the final fitting for Ruth's wedding gown. She walked out of the dressing room and onto the pedestal that sat in the center of the room. I took in every detail while the tailor pinned the hem. She was lovely. I mean, knock-me-down gorgeous.

It was classic, yet sexy. There were a multitude of white pearls threaded along the intricate lace on the bodice. The skirt fell so gracefully that she seemed to be floating as it flowed behind her. Ruth's poise was remarkable as she stood in her matching heels and veil.

"Oh my God, Ruth, you look incredible!

Ruth's sister just smiled because she had seen the dress before, but Indira had much the same reaction that I'd had. "Oh my god, George is going to be overwhelmed!"

"That's the plan," she said, and she blushed. "I'm expecting each of you to keep my secret."

We all gave our solemn promise not to disclose her dress deign to another living soul.

We stayed at Ruth's folks that night, and Indira was surprised by their wealth. It wasn't something that was well known back at college. I just patted her on the back and said nothing.

Breakfast was served in the formal dining room just as the morning sun lit the fresh-cut flowers that adorned the center of the table. We started with coffee, moving slowly through the pastries, fruit, and main course. Mrs. Witherspoon could really orchestrate a meal. The staff served us expertly. Indira's eyes twinkled at the experience, and I enjoyed having a chance to get to know her better.

The ride home was nothing out of the ordinary until we spotted our men sitting at the kitchen table. Ruth had arranged appointments for George and his groomsmen, and had insisted that they actually go the stylist she had picked out for them. They looked incredible. Will looked roguishly handsome, and George absolutely striking, but I beamed at the metamorphosis Gilbert had undergone. Rather than making a big deal of it, I just gave him a minuscule thumbs up and softly whispered, "smokin' hot," as I walked past him. He had a hard time concealing his delight.

Knowing how much I enjoyed my peaceful moments communing with *our* brass bowl, my dear husband suggested we meditate before everyone headed home. The bowl sang when we placed it in the center of our circle, and when I finally re-opened my eyes after meditation, I found I had stayed with my brass friend far longer than everyone else. I sat alone in our living room with a blanket tenderly tucked around me. I smiled, knowing that Will had done it because he loved me.

CHAPTER TWENTY-SIX

Dark Moon, September 16, 2012

The temple was particularly dark. McCollum had decided that the only light would come from seven candles around the perimeter of the room, which represented the seekers and their search for truth. Everyone sat quietly in our traditional black robes, letting the temple bask in the softness of nightfall. When McCollum entered the room, clad totally in black and accompanied by his golden aura, he stood in his own light as the eighth candle. The temple was silent in anticipation, for tonight was a very special occasion. This would be the true marriage between George and Ruth, the ceremony that recognized their bond through all eternity.

McCollum turned to face the altar that had been placed in front of the window and left open to the starlit sky. He began to pray softly, and he invited all the unseen guests to join us. He moved as if in an intimate dance, lighting incense and bowing in all four directions, as he requested the company of the Gods and Goddesses, Guides and Beings of Light, Angels, and Nature's Spirits. Lastly he invited the ancestors who had come before us.

I opened my palms and closed my eyes so I could breathe in the changes occurring in the room as McCollum's summoning came to pass. I could feel the movement of the air as the multitudes of spirits joined us. An evening breeze brushed my face as the temple doors were opened, and everyone turned to watch as Ruth and George entered. I heard a few whispers and giggles, and I had to smile myself when I noticed Buddy atop George's shoulder. They were positively brilliant in their white clothing, both beaming uncontrollably. They joined McCollum at the altar and the Dark Moon ceremony began.

"Everyone who has joined us tonight is blessed by the witnessing of this very rare occurrence in life," McCollum began, as he marked both the bride and groom with a dot of vermilion powder on their third eye. "For pure love is a powerful phenomenon indeed. May it light our paths toward understanding, allow compassion and forgiveness within our hearts, and remove all that holds us back from becoming.

"This location—between the eyes and raised a bit—is said to be a gate that leads to the inter realms." McCollum's hand once again dipped into the vermilion, and with a graceful movement placed a crimson dot on top of Buddy's head. "Tonight we come together to witness the joining of two souls who are on a fantastic journey. It has always been destined and is now fulfilled. The two arrows who have been loosed toward the same target will more quickly reveal the miracles of inward realms." McCollum smiled. "But tonight we must speak about the journey of the heart."

Just hearing the words gave me a luminous feeling in my chest. Will took my hand in his, and I felt my heart chakra open a little more. My body warmed to the hum I knew was my husband's life force, and I found myself relaxing into it. I felt like I loved the whole world … almost. I wondered if the one exception, Jackson Black, would stop my enlightenment, or if one day I would evolve enough to also see the god, which must also exist in him, too. I smiled to myself and laid my head on Will's shoulder, leaving those thoughts for another day.

"I have witnessed your union in many of your lifetimes," McCollum stated, placing a gemstone in George's palm before joining his hand with Ruth's. "I have seen the children you have birthed, and watched both of you grow old, but never have I seen the two halves of your same soul merge so completely as in this lifetime. It takes the ability to love one's self to enable soul mates to love each other, for when you look into the eyes of your beloved, you are looking into your own. It is your *acceptance of self* that allows this total merging of your hearts. The green flame within you has been lit, and love will rule your lives from this moment forward. May your life together leave a path so lit by love that others will find it easy to follow."

George turned to kiss Ruth, and as their heart chakras met, I knew the world would never be the same again … it was going to be much, much better. And in the last moment of silence before the chanting began, I heard McCollum whisper to Ruth, "Your great grandmother is very proud you! She's in the front row crying tears of joy, for as you embark on this path of discovery you will carry a piece of her with you."

You'd think that chanting would be a solemn thing, and it can be, but tonight was not such an occasion. Tonight was a time for dancing and singing and celebrating, because another light was lit on planet Earth, and this light was a bonfire, drawing us another step closer to opening the window for human enlightenment.

CHAPTER TWENTY-SEVEN

September 20, 2012

Ruth wanted her friends to accompany her on a fun-filled extravaganza around Kansas City, which made it more than a typical bachelorette party. The evening was beyond what any of us could afford with the exception of Ruth, so Ruth found her joy in being able to provide an evening among the privileged of KC for all of us.

Dressed in our finery, we gathered on the elevator to make our decent from our very posh rooms out onto the Kansas City Plaza. The discussion about where to have dinner had been a very complicated and amusing conversation. It had moved from filet mignon to seafood, ending with vegetarian. Ruth and I were relieved that the monks hadn't insisted on vegan!

I watched people around us watching us. We were an unusual group, being that all but the two of us were monks, albeit beautiful female Asian monks. We turned heads everywhere we went, and I found myself wondering if it was because of our Shakti or the group's absolute femininity. And even though many a man's eyes followed our group around restaurants and bars, nary a one approached us.

I was a bit tipsy when I arrived back at my room from my two glasses of wine. I knew I should meditate during such a beautiful crescent moon, but instead I flopped across the bed and fell fast asleep.

Shiva moon, 2012
I was roused by the sound of a motorcycle engine incessantly revving near my head.

"Wake up Hillary Rubner Emerald," an angry voice insisted as the roar of the motorcycle got even louder.

"Okay, okay," I answered covering my ears. "I'm up!" I watched as Adriana Heinrich swung her long leg over the bike and walked toward me, stopping a mere three feet from my face.

He killed me," she said as I met her eyes, and I had the strangest feeling of déjà vu.

"Who?" I asked, knowing I had asked this very same question on the first night we met. But that night I was Hilsbeth, and protected by my fallen soldiers. Tonight I was alone.

"He did, but his greatest trophy is going to be your husband, Will."

The same struggle was beginning within me when I felt a hand on my shoulder and turned to face McCollum.

"Come with me, Dear One. This place is not for you. You cannot help her and you mustn't be drawn into the realm for which she is destined." He drew me near, wrapping me in his cloak, and led me toward a light, where we both sat down, side by side. "Tonight is the fifth night since the dark moon. The crescent moon that hangs in the sky tonight symbolizes creation from what has passed before. It is the Shiva moon, named for the most powerful god of all, the destroyer and creator."

I grew calm once I was in the light, but as I listened to McCollum's words I couldn't shake the confusion of his presence in my dream. He must have understood what I was feeling by my expression, because his next words were an explanation.

"Tonight Adriana Heinrich passed from her body under violent circumstances. I am here to make sure no harm comes to you."

"Dead??" I asked, bewildered. "How? She said 'he' killed her. Who is he?"

"I will find you when the sun once again has taken the sky, my dear. We can speak then. For now, you must return to your body and leave this place behind." He gently placed his hand over my eyes, closing them. "Sleep well."

September 22, 2012

I woke to a knock at the door. I felt well rested, but slightly muddled. "Who is it?" I asked, as I rummaged through my luggage for my robe.

"It's me," Will answered, "and McCollum."

I opened the door to two very serious faces. "I'm sorry, did I oversleep?" I asked, looking around the room for a clock.

"No, you haven't missed anything." Will's intensity softened as he came into the room and kissed me on the cheek. "We just wanted to talk to you before you heard from someone else."

I ran my fingers though my hair and used a rubber band from the end table to tie it into a ponytail. I took a seat, and a ghost of a memory crossed my mind. McCollum stepped forward and my dream came rushing back. "Oh my god! She's really dead!"

"Yes," McCollum stated with no preamble. "They found her body last night in Chicago. It's become apparent that she has a group there like to the one she organized in Kansas. It's also clear that she found no protection from the darkness that she spent her life nurturing. The police are now looking for Jackson Black." McCollum placed his hand on mine. "He was released on parole while awaiting trial, but once he is captured he will never again be free. There were many witnesses, so there is no doubt of his guilt."

"I remember now! She was in my dream!"

"Yes, she was," McCollum's gentle voice calmly answered.

"She told me he wants to harm Will!"

"I have searched our past lifetimes," McCollum continued, unruffled, "and have found no karmic relationship between Will and Jackson Black. I believe there was no reason for her statement beyond your distress."

Will sat beside me, unflustered. "Jackson Black is three states away, and the police feel sure that they will apprehend him within the next twenty-four hours. There is no need to worry about me. George will have my back."

My mind raced the entire time I showered, but as I wrapped a towel around my hair and began laying out my clothes, my thoughts eased. I had breakfast plans with Ruth on this last day before she became Mrs. George Elliot, and I didn't want anything to ruin our special time. I heard a knock at the door and I swung it open ... after looking out the peephole.

"Wow, Hillary, are you freaked out? I came right up once I heard!"

"No Ruth, not at all," I lied.

"Come on, Hillary. The truth," Ruth nudged.

"Okay, it was freaky having her come to me of all people. I mean ... she was dead! Wouldn't you think she'd have someone better to haunt than me? I just hope she's decided to move on."

"George isn't worried at all, but still ... murdered by Jackson Black! He's more depraved than I imagined," Ruth shuddered.

"The only good thing is that Black will spend the rest of his life in prison, and we'll never have to worry about him again. So, my best and dearest friend," I said with a smile, "how do you want to spend your last hours as a single woman?"

"Lets spend some quiet time, just you and me, hidden away at the club. We can reminisce and no one will find us there."

We sat at our favorite table, the one by the pool that overlooked the golf course. We opened the umbrella and ordered wine spritzers. For a while we just sat quietly, enjoying each other's company.

"Our lives have sure changed," Ruth said wistfully.

"Do you ever wonder what would have happened if one of us had turned around and gone back to the dorm before we reached Will and George's Spring Fling party?"

"I suppose destiny would have created another path for our meeting," Ruth answered with conviction. "I'm glad it happened the way it did. It sure has made life exciting!"

"More exciting than when you were in Kansas City with me?" a voice asked as a pair of huge arms wrapped around Ruth. "Was my love just not enough for you?" Clint teased, giving her a big wet kiss on the cheek.

"It's a little too late for you to be declaring your love for me! If I only had known, George wouldn't have stood a chance. But now the wedding plans have been made," Ruth shrugged as she turned to face him.

"Well, if it can't be me, George is the one I'd pick for you. He seems like a real stand-up guy."

"Yes," Ruth answered dreamily. "I have to agree with you. George has enchanted me, and I don't think I'll ever be free of his spell. He's absolutely the most wonderful guy I've ever met."

"Well, now my feelings are really hurt," another voice chimed in. "I thought I was the most wonderful guy you'd ever met." I grinned as I watched Bennett go down on one knee and take Ruth's hand. "Tell me it's not true, Ruth. Don't tell me that you're taking yourself off the market forever!"

Ruth was blushing and giddy with laughter, and I loved seeing two of her oldest friends flirting with her. She gushed with pleasure.

"You both have forever missed your chance to join me in marital bliss, because soon George and I will be barricaded in our honeymoon suite for at least a week."

"Are you going somewhere warm?"

"Doesn't matter," Ruth chimed. "We'll be inside." And we all just gazed at her irresistible smile. "You're both coming tomorrow?"

"Wouldn't miss it for the world," Bennett said as he rose to his feet. "We'll be the two men crying on the bride's side of the aisle. Tell George he's a lucky guy for both of us."

"I plan on telling him that every day for the rest of his life!"

Clint bent to kiss Ruth goodbye, and for a long moment Bennett's eye locked with mine. I saw both Bennett and Marcus Flavius, and knew that they both had a place in my heart. Bennett only looked confused as he gave me a sad smile and turned to leave with Clint.

The childhood reminiscing began in earnest once we were alone, and over the next few hours I leaned considerably more about my best friend. Like so many of the people I had met recently, Ruth felt like a stranger in her own family. This is not to say she didn't love them, because she did. She just had never formed the kind of deep bonds with them that I had formed with my parents. She had always thought this was because she had spent so much time away at boarding school, but after much surmising, we concluded that Ruth's soul connection wasn't to her parents but through them. Her past-life ties were to her great grandmother, not her immediate family. It was interesting that her closest childhood relationships were with Clint and Bennett, which made us both wonder how Clint fit into the picture. We talked and hypothesized, but knew we wouldn't come up with the answer today.

"Let's go shopping," Ruth finally said. "I found a place online that I'd like to go."

Vicki Renfro

I was up for anything, so we paid the bill and Ruth had her car pulled around to the curb.

I was surprised when I noticed we weren't on a street full of designer boutiques. Instead, Ruth was driving in a neighborhood of small, brick bungalow homes that had been turned into commercial space, with most occupants using the back rooms as their living quarters. An array of colorfully hand-painted signs were attached to everything from fences to power poles, and they advertised a range of occult practices, from fortune telling to star charts. Ruth pulled to the curb in front of a house with no sign at all and sporadic weeds growing in an unkempt yard.

I stood with Ruth on the porch while she searched an indigo-colored doorframe for an identifying mark. Once she was satisfied that we were at the correct location, we entered an even more disheveled interior. The room was lined with dust-covered bookcases and cracked glass counters full of small, unidentifiable jars, animal bones, and feathers.

A tiny bell had rung as we entered, so we just stood waiting until the proprietor joined us. She had a very interesting taste in fashion. Standing well over six feet, she was adorned with layers of colorful clothing, scarfs, and bangles. She looked like a supersized gypsy.

She thoroughly inspected us from head to toe, and once we were completely intimidated, her red lips parted into a big, toothy grin. "You must be Ruth?"

"Yes, I am." Ruth stepped forward and extended her hand heartily. "I've read so much about you online, and am pleased beyond words that you could see me on such short notice. It's very nice to meet you, Nadya."

As we were gathered up and ushered into a back room, I was wondering just what my dear friend Ruth had gotten us into.

256

"Please sit," Nadya insisted, as she began lighting candles and using one of her million scarfs to shine her crystal ball. "Who are you interested in contacting today?"

"My great grandmother, Lola."

"Did you bring something that belonged to her?" the medium asked. "Something she had a strong connection to that can guide me to her?"

Ruth nodded her head and pulled the artifact's box from her jacket pocket. When she removed the lid, the sight of the ward made Nadya's eyes twinkle.

"Oh my! I have considerable in common with your great grandmother. I look forward to making her acquaintance."

Ruth placed the lid back on the box and set it in the center of the table. I felt my right hand being taken by Nadya's man-sized one. It was hot to the touch, in contrast to Ruth's, which was chilled to the bone.

There was the pungent smell of bad incense in the room, and I worried about protecting Ruth as Nadya slipped into a trance and began to speak in muffled voices. There were many at first of these voices, which made me worry that our medium might be schizophrenic, but none seemed overly interested or willing to stay. Then there was only one. Nadya's sleepy brown eyes slowly opened, and she looked at both of us before settling on Ruth. She began speaking to her tenderly, and I felt my body relax.

"Hello, my exquisite child. You are of my flesh and of my heart. I have watched you every day of your life and know you well. So now, in our short time together, ask me what you please so you may also know me."

Ruth's hand tightened on mine, and when she said nothing, her great grandmother simply smiled and continued, not wanting to waste a single moment of their precious time together.

"I was born to a splendid family in the year 1895." There was a sparkle in her voice that made me like her immediately. "We were a community made up of aunts, uncles, grandparents, cousins, parents, orphans, children, and strangers who travelled the countryside as nomads. We spent our days singing, laughing, and entertaining an audience that mistrusted and judged us as thieves and con artists."

Lola chuckled in a pitch that didn't match Nadya's tenor at all. "I suppose there were those among us who were less than honest, but we were mostly sought after for our mysterious abilities to foretell the future."

Nadya took in a gigantic breath and exhaled with an enormous snore. Ruth and I looked at each other, wondering what we should do if our intermediary had truly fallen asleep, but eventually she began to speak once more.

"Every female within our band was raised to know the Goddess which exists within each of us. We grew up knowing our true nature, and the innate gifts that belong to our gender alone. We studied the occult to sharpen those talents, which enabled us to make a good living. Fortune telling was lucrative"—Lola guffawed—"but those abilities were trivial compared to the power of the Goddess, which awakens when women cultivate a collective consciousness to bridge the inner and outer worlds.

"My own powers surfaced at a very young age. By the age of twelve, I was no longer a novice, and I was made a full member of the circle. That was the night I was given the box that now belongs to you. The relic traveled with our earliest ancestors from Egypt, through India, and eventually into Europe, a trip which took our people a thousand years."

Lola's spirit filled every corner of the room with her energy. The air crackled as the candlelight intensified, and an unusual scent of musky spice floated on the air. The smell was coming from Ruth's box. The ward seemed to come alive with the conjuring of its past.

"The ancient ward has always held within it the powers of every women who has ever possessed it. I can remember the night my mother passed it to me with words of both praise and warning. I sat at the center of the circle, surrounded by the formidable women who had been my inspiration. It was explained to me that the power of the ward contains both the light and the dark—the nurturer and the destroyer—and that it was now up to me to decide whether I would bring forth the shadow or the light. I took my responsibilities seriously … until puberty overpowered my better judgment."

Nadya tittered in an octave that belonged to a much smaller person. Lola's laughter was infectious, and I watched Ruth struggle to hold back her own laughter.

"I was a very pretty girl at the age of fourteen, and when I applied makeup and wore my older sister's clothes, I could pass for someone much older. My mother taught me to read people's faces and mannerisms, and by doing so, I could guess quite accurately what life held in store for them. They were more than willing to fill in all the blanks with names and places, and I began to perceive it as a game. My mother saw it as a career. You see, I not only had the *power* of observation, but I also had the *sight* if I wished to tap my inner knowing. But most were not worth it.

"I was only playacting the evening I met my future husband, your great grandfather. There was no need to access any of my inner powers, because what he wanted was written plainly on his face." Her lightheartedness carried a hint of sorrow. "He loved me with purity, and with such conviction that I convinced myself that if I tried hard enough, I could change myself to fit into his world. I was very young and foolish, but I never looked back with regret.

"I set aside everything I knew, including my family, when we moved to America. It broke my heart to know I would never see my mama again, so I etched her face into my memory and followed my husband toward *the new world*. But dear Ruth, in the end we are who we are. I could change the outside, but I found changing my beliefs far more difficult than I could ever have imagined."

Ruth's hand began to warm, and I heard her whimper as she felt Lola's pain.

"Fred taught me about Jesus, so I wove him into my tapestry along with everything I had come to believe throughout my long and varied life. All of my childhood beliefs still existed inside me, and my new ones only strengthened my belief that we are all on the same path toward self-realization, but are using different words."

Nadya thrust her head forward to look directly into Ruth eyes. "He never knew that I had the ward tucked away. Or maybe he did, but didn't have the heart to confront me. I could not let go of what had been passed down through generations, so I kept it hidden until I felt my death was growing near. I knew then that I must pass it on, even though there was no one who would feel the ancestral power it carried. I left it, with a final prayer that it would find its way. I never became a great mystic. That career was cut short by the life I decided to live, but I dreamed of the possibilities, and I see all of them in you."

I could feel Ruth wanting to sputter and deny that she had any abilities at all, and I was proud when she just sat still. In the now dimming sky that made the shadows grow long in our small room, I had a feeling that Ruth was finally going to accept that she had always been destined to be remarkable.

CHAPTER TWENTY-EIGHT

September 22, 2012, night of the equinox

Will was in our room when we arrived back at the hotel. I unlocked the door and saw his clothes lying on the floor like a path of breadcrumbs left for me to find my way home. I dropped my clothes on top of his, and without turning on a light, snuggled in next to him.

"Oh, I am so tired of being with the guys," he signed. "They aren't as soft as you."

He turned to face me and gathered me in his arms. "Do you remember our wedding?" he asked.

"I do," I replied. Images began floating through my mind, and a feeling of absolute peace settled into my bones.

"Do you ever wish we'd had a larger wedding?" he asked.

"Heavens, no! I understand why you might ask, after days of being bombarded by the details of the Ruth and George extravaganza, but seriously, I would never have wanted any of it for myself."

"Me neither," he said, and I felt all the tension release from his shoulders. My eyes began to adjust to the small amount of light that shone through the curtains from the city lights. It caught Will's eyes in such a way as to make them twinkle, and my heart overflowed with love for this fine man. "What about the huge diamond that George is going to put on Ruth's finger tomorrow?" he asked, as he brushed my hair away from my face. I felt the warmth of his hands and melted into them.

"No, that's not my style either. I'm not attracted to large, shiny things. My gold band is perfect."

"What about—" Will began to ask. I muffled his voice with a kiss before answering.

"There is nothing else I want, Will. All my dreams came true the minute I became your wife."

Will brushed my hair back and kissed my forehead before tipping my face into a beam of light so he could see my expression. "My heart has never wanted anything but you, Hillary, but that wasn't what I was going to ask you." His mood turned a bit somber, and his touch was tender. I must have looked concerned, because he gently ran his thumb over my forehead to erase the crease between my brows. "I was going to ask if you'd like to meet my family someday?"

I think he was encouraged by the spontaneous smile that lit my face. "Really?"

"Well, George has been talking about his family lately," he said, lying back on his pillow with me cuddled tight against him. "The idea scared me at first. I wondered if they had forgotten about me, but I know they must still love me, and they would absolutely adore you, so I think it may be time."

We made love at that magical moment when the Earth was balanced perfectly on its axis, making the day and night exactly the same length. I felt the same pull on my soul that I had at the last equinox, but tonight I didn't go to a life I had lived before. This time, I stayed in this life.

September 30, 2012

Will was up at dawn. As best man, he had duties to perform, and even though I couldn't fathom George having cold feet, it was Will's job to be at his side.

I, too, had duties, and I knew that with a mere five hours until showtime I needed to find Ruth, because my dearest friend, *the drama queen*, was sure to be going through something earth-shattering.

I knocked on Ruth's door. "Ready for breakfast?" I heard nothing. "Ruth!"

The door opened and I saw Ruth; she appeared to be in shock. "I want a wedding like yours, Hillary. I want a quiet ceremony with a few dear friends. What was I thinking?"

I led Ruth to a chair and sat her down as she mumbled in despair, "George is going to have to stand up in front of hundreds of people he doesn't even know—has never even seen before—and declare his love for me. How could I do this to him? My ego, Hillary—"

"Shhhhh, Ruth." I took her hand and made her look at me. "George will love every minute of this celebration because he loves you. You'll be the most beautiful woman in the room, and you will be declaring your love for him in front of everyone who has ever been a part of your life. That is monumental, and George will be thrilled just to see you in all your splendor."

"You really think so?"

"Darn tootin'."

Ruth's face broke into a smile, and I knew she was ready to buck up and begin her big day.

"Get dressed and we'll have breakfast. Just you and me, one last time before you're joined in holy matrimony."

We snuck out the back door of the hotel and down the street to a little coffee house. We found two seats on the deck and settled in for some quiet time together.

"Black and strong, please," Ruth said to the waiter. "I'm getting married in … four and a half hours." Her face beamed as she added, "With a side of cream."

We turned our chairs and tilted our faces toward the warm sun. "Okay?" I asked, taking her hand in mine.

"Okay," she replied, and we knew today would be exceptional.

We met the bridal party in a special room that had been set aside for us at the event center. Mrs. Witherspoon had picked up all our dresses from the seamstress, and a special team of make-up and hair stylists were preparing to make us the most astonishingly breathtaking wedding party ever to grace Kansas City. We were washed, polished, brushed, and gussied up until there was nothing else that could be done. We sat in our undergarments, sipping cucumber water, until it was time to get dressed. Indira and I were sensitive to the necessity of keeping our conversation light. No need for Ruth's mom to discover that Ruth and George were already married, that this was just a flaunting of her husband to her high society friends. The word *friends*, I use loosely.

The groom and groomsmen dazzled the guests as they stood waiting for our entrance. The combined Shakti of George, Will, Gilbert, and Dr. Edwards was enough to make the first few rows feel an extra jolt of merriment. When we heard the music change and the monks begin to chant their interpretation of the bridal march, the double doors in front of us opened, and I too was spellbound by the splendor of the men. They stood bathed in the elegances of lives well lived, and the jet-black tailored tuxedos didn't hinder the vision in the least.

Sissy, Ruth's sister, was the first down the aisle, and the gasp that accompanied her entrance didn't diminish when Indira and then I walked toward the alter. But it was Ruth who took everyone's breath away. The room was spellbound, but I kept my eyes on George. He was every bit the Druid warrior who had fought to the death for Ruth. He was also a man very much in love, and I choked when I saw a tear escape one of his masculine eyes.

This ceremony was Catholic, so there was a lot I didn't understand, but the meaning of the looks between Ruth and George where unmistakable as they faced each other, heart chakra to heart chakra. I knew in those silent moments that they were making silent declarations of love that meant more than any words being spoken.

I remember hearing "you may kiss the bride," followed by a deafening roar. I looked at the guests, and everyone was on their feet. Clint was standing on his chair whistling, towering above everyone, and I was momentarily surprised that his date seemed to be Bennett Taylor.

The wedding party was ushered out onto the grounds for the mandatory photographs. The flower gardens were still in bloom, and their brilliant colors were a perfect accent to our black-and-white clothing. Ruth had the photographer take a picture of just Will and me in front of the rose garden, and I was pleased to think that I would finally have a nice picture of my handsome husband. I brushed his hair away from his beautiful blue eyes and remembered the first time I had seen him. Looking back on that first evening, it was hard to believe that Will and George had had the nerve to go behind McCollum's back to invite us to their private Spring Fling party. Will seemed to know exactly what I was thinking as he grinned back at me.

"I knew I loved you from the very first moment I saw you, Chelsea," he teased, using the name I had given him that night.

Ruth followed every bridal tradition imaginable. She had something old, new, borrowed, and blue. Her receiving line gave Ruth a chance to show George off to everyone from childhood friends to the country club girls, and because it made Ruth so happy, George managed to smile the entire time. She chatted and teased, introduced and told stories. But when the band began to play, George led her away to the dance floor.

I'd watched him practice for weeks with Mom, moving in a box step, then spinning, counting one, two, three, four, over and over. For a muscular guy, he moved pretty gracefully, and luckily for him, self doubt and nerves weren't a part of his personal make-up. He had set a goal and was determined to make Ruth proud.

Everyone's eyes were on them as he walked her to the center of the dance floor. Ruth reached up to straighten George's tie and gave him a wink. George gently kissed her hand before placing it on his shoulder, and when the music began, we were all blown away.

They circled the room as if they were suspended, the black of his tux enveloped by the flowing white fabric of her gown. And never once did his eyes look away from hers. I saw Ruth's eyes begin to water, and held my breath to keep from crying myself. I knew George had picked the right song as I listened to Bob Dylan's beautiful lyrics.

When the evening shadows and the stars appear,
And there is no one there to dry your tears,
I could hold you for a million years
To make you feel my love.
I could make you happy, make your dreams come true
Nothing that I wouldn't do.
Go to the ends of the Earth for you
To make you feel my love.

She had definitely found her Prince Charming.

I saw McCollum's face light up and the boys' eyes open wide in amazement at the grace of the powerful Druid warrior. Then I scanned the crowd for Mom, who had her hands to her face, caught somewhere between bliss and tears.

Ruth had asked the boys if they would preform one chant during the reception, so once the dancing was done and they had their fill of an absolutely decadent cake, they lined up by height on the staircase. They had picked a particularly upbeat piece that they sang partially in Sanskrit and partially in English. Each one of them was decked out in new white robes, courtesy of Ruth and each looked more angelic than the next.

I watched Will and McCollum make their way over to George and his overjoyed parents, and I found a place at the back of the room to relax and take in the boys' beautiful voices.

No one had to quiet the room when the chant began. It happened spontaneously. I suppose most thought they were a chorus. But when the first baritones began and the higher voices joined in, the crowd was entranced.

I felt someone move to stand beside me and knew it was Bennett Taylor. I couldn't help but smile.

"Your husband seems like a really great guy," he whispered into my ear as he moved closer. "I am sincerely happy for you, Hillary, but it should have been us," he teased.

"Always the flirt," I reminded him, but not harshly. I knew better than to think he was serious. "Isn't Ruth beautiful?"

"She really snagged a good one when she reeled in George. Convenient for you two that George and Will are such good friends."

"I see you brought a good looking date yourself." Our eyes went to Clint, who was looking pretty lonely in the corner.

"He's thrilled that Ruth found someone special," Bennett said.

"But he's going to miss her. She just won't be around like she used to be. Maybe you two will have to sneak away to Kansas City every so often."

That was when Bennett spotted a more likely candidate for his attentions and politely excused himself. I smiled and said goodbye as he gave my hand a gentle squeeze.

"It was nice seeing you again, Bennett," I said as I turned to see Will's beautiful blue eyes gazing at me. I tilted my head, just smiling back at my husband and taking in every beautiful detail. He was so handsome in his tux, tall and straight with that *inner knowing* that made him irresistible. My heart fluttered with desire, and the knowledge that we would be together forever, for part of my soul also existed within him.

CHAPTER TWENTY-NINE

October 1, 2012

The morning after the wedding George and Ruth left on the honeymoon of a lifetime—any of them. Ruth's folks were also headed out of town for some well deserved relaxation, and had generously offered Will and me a wing of their magnificent home for the weekend, giving us the honeymoon we'd always dreamed of.

We tucked ourselves into the furthermost bedroom on the second floor of the east wing, where we'd be able to enjoy the sunrise through an expanse of trees outside the window. I marveled at the lovely bedding. I'd never seen so many pillows artfully piled atop such a thick, luxurious comforter. I turned around and freefell into the softness that would be our bed for the entire weekend.

I laughed when I saw the look in Will's eyes as he launched himself onto the bed beside me. This was going to be fun.

It was then that we heard the soft tap on our door. It was the final resident looking for her ride to the airport.

Will reluctantly rolled out of bed and opened the door. Ruth's little sister had her stylish leather luggage all packed, and Will grabbed the largest bag by the handle and cheerfully rolled it down the hall.

"Don't move, Hillary. I'll be right back," Will shouted as he descended the stairs causing my mind to fill with romantic daydreams about his return.

I caught a glimpse out of the window of them pulling away from the house. I smiled when I saw Will behind the wheel of the Witherspoons' hot new BMW convertible because I knew it was a couple of hours to the airport and back. He'd have plenty of time to relish the experience of driving it.

I took my time unpacking and actually hung up our clothes and put away the luggage. Everything in my life was going so perfectly that I felt a little like dancing … until I experienced an odd jolt of déjà vu.

I walked to the bedrooms east most window and parted the curtains. To my relief, I saw that it was only Bennett walking across the patio. But my relief quickly turned to dread when I saw Jackson Black behind him.

The End

SOUL CHOICE
BOOK THREE

CHAPTER
ONE

October 1, 2012

"Not expecting me, Hilsbeth? Seriously," he said, raising his hands in amusement. "Of course I'd come for you. "You're the last of the Druids, my crown jewel ... the gem that will ensure my place in antiquity!" Jackson Black shouted up to where I stood in the window. "I have your friend, the great Roman general, Marcus Flavius, but this time he's in no position to save you."

Bennett's hands were zip-tied behind his back. Black brandished a knife, and as he yanked Bennett's head back and laid the blade across his throat, I realized that Black was utterly insane.

Swept up in a rush of panic, I shoved the window open and begged, "You can have me. Let him go!"

"This Roman filth?" he said, pushing the knife just deep enough into to Bennett's flesh to draw blood. "Flavius ruined my military career and should die for that alone. He stole my glory!" he screamed with such vehemence that I feared his knife might slip deeper. "It was me who tracked each repulsive Druid down! I was the one covered in blood after hacking off each head, while the General sat drinking wine at court in his spotless tunic. His hands remained clean, while the bloody guts of your friends covered mine.

The memories of my Druid lifetime came flooding back and I saw the horror he spoke of vividly. And yes, I knew that my friend Bennett had been the Roman general sent to kill us, but that was then and this was now.

"Don't hurt him!" I yelled. "I'm coming down!" I turned from the window and ran down the hall. My hands began to heat and whether from chi or fright, it was what I had to work with. I squared my shoulders as I opened the patio doors. "Now let him go."

I saw the knife slice the plastic on Bennett's wrist a moment before Black drove the butt of it into Bennett's temple. I winced when I heard my friend's head crack against the flagstones. My chest exploded and heat raced down my arms. My eyes locked onto Black's and I knew he was toast … right before I saw his smile and the Taser in his hand.

He was faster.

My chest hurt like hell when I began coming around from the brain numbing shock I'd taken. Black's face was inches from mine, and in a rush to get away I felt the bite of restraints around my wrists. The creep had me tied to a chair.

I saw Bennett's eyes flutter open and wanted to tell him to run, but the Taser had blasted everything out of me but the most basic ability to breathe.

I knew Black was every bit the killer he had been in the lifetime we shared two thousand years ago, so when I watched Bennett climb to his knees, I prayed there was still a remnant of the great Roman General existing inside of him.

Jackson Black whirled around to face him, evidently deciding that I was no threat. Bennett held his hands out in submission and began to talk, averting his eyes as you would with a wild animal. "Explain to me what's going on here?"

"I've come for the last Druid, General," Black said, as he drew a long blade from the duffle bag by his feet. "And to force Marcus Flavius to his knees!"

"Don't worry, Hilsbeth. This one isn't for you," he whispered, as he swung the blade above his head in a pattern that made it howl with a shrill pitch. "I've brought something very special for you."

I knew Black—or whatever he called himself two thousand years ago—no longer existed in this reality. He was completely immersed in the past.

"Look into my face Flavius," Black said, as he placed the point of his sword at the soft spot in Bennett's throat. "Always the one with the fancy ribbons and polished armor, mingling with the elite. Well, no more. I killed the governor, and you'll soon meet him in hell.

I closed my eyes, desperate to locate Hilsbeth, the leader of Druid armies. She had to be inside of me somewhere.

Vicki Renfro